MW00613823

FRAMILY

FRAMILY

BY
ALESHA NICHOLE

Published by Alesha Nichole Publishing

Copyright © 2019 by Alesha Nichole

All rights reserved.
No part of this book may be reproduced in any form or by any
means including electronic reproduction and photocopying
without written permission of the author.

ISBN: 978-1-7332364-1-6

Interior design by booknook.biz

DEDICATION

This is dedicated to all the gay girls and women out there. In a world occupied by billions of people, millions of friends on social media, and thousands of followers, we still find ourselves lonely. This is dedicated to all the past LGBTQ+ people and supporters. Whether you played a big or small role in changing history, I wouldn't be able to write this book today if it weren't for you. To everyone. Young and old, in small towns and big cities, who may still be in the closet due to fear of how people will react. I hope you know that you are loved and there is support out there. This one is for all of you. May love flourish and hate die.

ACKNOWLEDGEMENTS

First and foremost, I want to thank God. I know I'm not perfect, but He still loves me. He has blessed me with the ability to put my thoughts into words, and I am grateful. Next up, is my beautiful mother. Thank you, Mom, for raising me to be the bold, confident woman I am today. You have always allowed me to be myself and supported me every step of the way. Thank you to my father. Although distance has kept us apart, you still find a way to encourage me. To all the amazing strong women in my life who played a role in my upbringing. Each of you, at different times in my life, has taught me what it means to be a strong woman in your own ways. I thank you. To my brothers and sisters, we may not be blood, but you guys have stuck by my side since childhood and are still with me to this day. I couldn't ask for better people in my life. Thank you to all my brothers and sisters in arms. It was a pleasure to serve with you all and I don't know how I would've made it through without you. I would also like to thank all my friends who have inspired me to write this book and given me feedback and ideas. I want to thank everyone who has helped me proofread, edit, and had a hand in turning this dream into a reality. I couldn't have accomplished this without you. Last but certainly not least, thank you to everyone who has chosen to read this book. I appreciate that with all my heart and I hope you enjoy. I am forever grateful to each and every one of you. Much love.

CONTENTS

PART III: FOUR MONTHS LATER

PART I

ONE

Nevaeh opened her eyes. WITH a heavy head, weak body, slightly blurred vision, she silently questioned her surroundings. *This is not my ceiling. Where am I? What am I doing here? How did I even get here? Most importantly, why am I naked?* She sat up and wiped her face. As she looked around, she recognized nothing in the decently-sized, colorfully decorated bedroom. She spotted a trail of clothes leading to the bed. There were half-drunk beer bottles on the nightstand.

She softly whispered, "Fuck, I did it again."

At that moment, she felt a shuffle in the bed next to her. There was a naked woman, of whose name she had no clue. She lifted the cover to see what her late-night friend looked like. She nodded her head in approval and gave herself a celebratory high five.

"Go me," she whispered.

As she crept out of bed, she tried her hardest not to disturb the passed-out woman. She put on her underwear and frantically searched for her bra. Nevaeh admitted defeat for the bra search. She threw on her shirt, jeans, and shoes. She grabbed her cell phone along with her other belongings and quietly walked toward the door. Before leaving, she looked back at the no-name woman sleeping so innocently. Nevaeh thought to herself, *Should I leave a note saying that I will call her? Should I kiss her on the forehead implying that I would be back? Maybe I should just get back into bed until she wakes up, only so we can experience that awkward, drunken one-night stand morning conversation.* None of those sounded appealing, knowing that she had no intention of purposely seeing this woman again. She then quietly walked out, leaving her late-night mystery woman to her sleep.

Nevaeh was a work hard, play hard kind of girl. She wasn't the most feminine woman but wasn't extremely masculine either. She was 5'9, dark caramel complexion, athletic frame, and rocked various natural hairstyles. Her style was androgynous, and she beamed confidence. After college, she became an event planner, and she was well known in her area.

For her, waking up to a random girl wasn't anything out of the ordinary. After her first heartbreak from her girlfriend in college, she vowed that she wouldn't allow another woman to hurt her again. It was best to hurt them before they hurt her. Not the best motto, but it worked for her. It was her thing.

She stepped outside the apartment. She still had the hint of cigarettes and alcohol on her breath as the sun instantly blinded her. "Ugh," she groaned. "Why must you hate me, sun?" Her sunglasses were M.I.A, so she squinted and kept walking. It was what most would consider a beautiful day in Geibourne. A gay-friendly city on the coast of Virginia. The faint sound of dogs barked in the background, and there was a smell of freshly mowed grass.

"Today is going to be a good day," she said aloud. Still slightly intoxicated, Nevaeh was unaware of the three little steps ahead of her. She lost her balance and tumbled to the ground. Drowning in embarrassment, she quickly jumped up, brushed herself off, and tried to smoothly walk off as if nothing had happened.

"Karma," she admitted. Suddenly, she heard laughter. She turned around to spot two women, roughly in their early twenties, laughing at her.

"Shit." She waved to them. "Hi, ladies," she said in a sarcastic tone along with a fuck-you smile on her face, and walked off. Her pocket began to vibrate. The name Imani flashed across her screen.

"Hey Imani."

"Uh! Don't hey Imani me like you didn't disappear last night. One second you were in the bar, the next you weren't."

"Yeah, I kind of got…" she cleared her throat. "I did some networking last night."

"And by networking you mean you got some butt last night? You know you don't have to lie to me," Imani teased.

"When you put it that way it sounds so vulgar," she said in a playfully disgusted voice.

"Girl, please. I would ask you who it was, but I know you don't remember the chick's name."

"See, this is why we're best friends, you know me so well," Nevaeh chuckled.

"Yeah, yeah. Where are you?"

"Well, from the looks of it, I'm in walking distance from No Man's Land. I think I'm going to head over for a beer or two. Figure out how to get my life together, then come home and actually try to get my life together. Only to repeat the entire process again tonight." She laughed to herself. "You want to join?"

"Let's see, it's noon on a beautiful Saturday afternoon. Uh, I don't know." She paused. "Just kidding. This is perfect drinking weather. I can hit up Tiara, and we can meet you there?"

"Sounds like a plan."

"Cool, later."

"Hey!" Nevaeh shouted before Imani disconnected. "Can you bring me a pair of sunglasses?"

"Yeah, I got you."

"Also, can you go in my room, look in the top drawer of the dresser next to the bathroom and grab me a bra?"

"A bra? Seriously, Nevaeh? You need to get it together, girl," she joked. "Yeah, I got you."

They hung up the phone.

Imani was 5'8 with a dark chocolate complexion, masculine style, and rocked well-maintained dreadlocks that fell just below her shoulders. Since she had a passion for cooking, she started her own catering company after graduating from college. She, too, was awful with holding onto relationships. There was no particular heartbreak that made her this way. In Imani's mind, there were too many beautiful women out there to settle down with just one. Which is probably one of the main reasons she and Nevaeh became friends so quickly. They both had that unsettled restlessness about them. They decided to become roommates after college.

Nevaeh arrived at No Man's Land and opened the door. No Man's Land was a popular lesbian bar and despite the name, men were welcomed. The smell of beer, liquor, and air freshener rushed to her nostrils. There were sounds of glasses clinking, laughter, pool balls smacking together, and Janelle Monáe's "Pynk" playing on a jukebox filled the air. She looked around and saw there were roughly twenty people. Some played darts, a couple of people were shooting pool, and others simply sat around enjoying the good booze and great company. Everyone was there to enjoy their favorite pastime of day drinking. She looked over to the bar where Marie was waiting on a customer. They met eyes, and Marie waved at her. Butterflies instantaneously fluttered around in Nevaeh's stomach as she waved back at her. She walked over to the bar and sat down.

"Long night, Nevaeh?" Marie asked.

Nevaeh let out a light chuckle. "I guess you can say that. But hey, you know what they always say; long nights make for a short day."

"No." Marie shook her head. "Never heard it. I don't think anyone says that but you. Logically, if someone were to stay up all night, it makes their day suck because they're probably hungover or tired as fuck all day. Which would essentially make the day seem really long."

"Hm. Well, you see life your way, and I'll see it my way," Nevaeh smiled. "And I just so happen to like my way better."

Marie smiled back. Their gaze lingered. Nevaeh always had the feeling that Marie might like her in more than just the normal bartender and regular customer relationship. Marie broke the stare and cleared her throat. "So are you going to start off strong and dive right into the rum and cokes?"

"Oye. I think I'm going to get a pitcher of Bud Light and two glasses. Imani and Tiara should be here any minute."

"Bud Light? That's different from your normal."

"Yeah, I need to hydrate."

Marie smiled, "And two glasses? Don't you mean three?"

"No. I'm drinking out of the pitcher. I need it. The glasses are for them."

She smiled at Nevaeh and shook her head playfully. "All right, a pitcher of Bud Light and three glasses coming right up."

As she walked off to go get the beer, Tiara and Imani walked up and sat down on each side of Nevaeh. She gave them both a hug.

Tiara was 5'6 with a mocha complexion and long, wavy black hair. When she wasn't in gym clothes, she loved to wear dresses. She would often get those advances from ignorant men telling her that she was "too pretty to be gay," which aggravated her to no end. Tiara's parents had money, but it wasn't always that way. Her parents struggled financially while raising her and her younger sister. Growing up in a rough neighborhood caused Tiara to have a temper at times. Her parents strived to provide a better life for their children. Her father was a bit of a computer nerd. One day after the family watched *Dope* in the theater, he decided to look more into Bitcoin. He had managed to save about $1,000 without his wife knowing. He had a hunch and took it upon himself to buy some Bitcoin with that money. Years later he was a multi-millionaire.

Tiara was very headstrong and knew what she wanted in life and wasn't afraid to go get it. She loved dealing with athletics and nutrition, so naturally, after college (with a little help from her parents) she started her own personal training business. It became popular in the local area. Tiara was a people person. She had excellent customer service, which allowed people to feel comfortable telling her what they wanted to change physically about themselves. She used that information to compose a meal plan and workout regimen for her clients. She would push and motivate them to their body goals. She was very good at what she did, and her clients loved her for it.

"Damn, girl, you look like shit." Imani wasted no time.

"On some real shit, it's gross," Tiara chimed in. The three of them laughed in unison.

"All right, guys, I get it, damn," Nevaeh said with a laugh.

Marie walked up with the pitcher and three glasses. "I don't think you look like shit." She gave Nevaeh a side smile.

"Thanks."

Imani rolled her eyes, "Um, I don't know what you're looking at, Marie, but as her best friend I'm going to keep it real and say she looks like shit."

Tiara shouted, "Ayooo!"

Marie chuckled and walked off to tend to another customer.

"Here, Nevaeh." Imani pulled out a bra and a pair of sunglasses from her pocket and handed them over. "Go strap those bad boys down."

"Thanks. You're a lifesaver." Nevaeh went into the bathroom, put it on, then came back out and sat down.

She grabbed the pitcher and started pouring the beer. "Anywho. Now that we all know what I did last night, how did the rest of y'all's night go?"

Tiara attempted her best to sound unimpressed. "I didn't get any action, if that's what you mean. I went home, watched some Netflix, and passed out on my couch."

"Imani?" Nevaeh pried.

"Oh, I have no shame. I hooked up last night too, and no we're not going to call one another. End of story."

"You two are a mess." Tiara shook her head.

Nevaeh playfully gasped, "Tiara Morris, are you slut-shaming us?"

"No. I'm shaming y'all for being fuckboys, there's a difference."

"Ouch," Nevaeh responded. Imani shrugged her shoulders.

"The truth hurts, but we all need to hear it from time to time. Keeps us humble," Tiara stated.

Nevaeh held up her glass to make a toast. "Cheers. Here's to participating in my favorite daytime activity with great friends." Marie looked over and sent a smile Nevaeh's way. She caught her and as soon as they made eye contact Marie looked away.

"Jesus, Nevaeh," Imani said. "Ask that girl out already. You know that girl likes you and you like her too. Shit, according to my lesbian calculations you should be looking at U-hauls and arguing over whether you guys want to adopt a cat or a dog as we speak."

"Let's make one thing clear right now. If she doesn't want a dog, then it's not the relationship for me," she joked. "But in all seriousness, no, she doesn't. There's no way an amazing woman like Marie would have a thing for me. She's 29 and she already owns one of the most popular bars in town. She's gorgeous, obviously smart, and doesn't mind bartending at her own establishment. She's just a friendly bartender and I'm a regular customer. No more. No less."

"I'm going to have to agree with Imani on this one. That girl is feeling you. And you? Psh, you shook," Tiara stated.

"No. No, you guys got it all wrong. You both know that I am very content with playing the field at this point in my life." Nevaeh was lying to herself. She knew she wanted to get to know Marie on a deeper level. She was just afraid to put herself out there in that way again. "Besides, if we did end up going down that road I'd ruin her."

Imani placed her lips to her glass, "Or she'd ruin you."

"Mmmmmmm," Tiara instigated.

A little irritated, Nevaeh asked, "What the fuck is that supposed to mean?"

Imani said, "All I'm saying is I've known you for like fifteen years now. I know you. Ever since Saria broke your heart you've been content with playing the field. Maybe she'd ruin that *I'm a smooth-talking badass who can have any girl I want* persona you hold on to ever so tightly. Maybe she'd make you consider renting that U-Haul. Something only one girl has been able to do, and that scares the shit out of you because last time that happened your heart was shattered into a million pieces."

Tiara took a sip from her beer and teased, "Not the U-Haul."

Nevaeh made a disapproving sound but had no response. She knew Imani was right. They sat at the bar for a while, finished the first pitcher, and ordered another one. They grabbed their second pitcher and headed over to the dart board. None of them were particularly good at darts but they played anyway. They laughed, cracked jokes, and were having a great time. They finished the second pitcher, and Nevaeh's buzz started to come back from the night before. "I feel like I need to go shower before this turns into an all day and night marathon."

Tiara responded, "Yeah, you're right, because you can't go out with us tonight looking like," she paused and ran her finger up and down in the air, "last night." They all laughed and took their glasses and pitcher back up to the bar. Nevaeh paid the tab while Tiara and Imani walked out to the parking lot to wait for the Lyft.

"Are you guys heading out?" Marie asked with a sad tone in her voice.

"Yeah, I need to go get my life together for a little bit. Only to lose control of it again tonight," Nevaeh chuckled.

"You guys are going out tonight? What? No invite?" Marie asked.

"I would invite you, but I don't have your number. Also, it's a Saturday, I just figured you had to work," Nevaeh stated.

"Well, it's my bar. I can take off when I please. I haven't taken a Saturday night off in a while. It would be a nice break." Marie took a napkin and a pen, wrote down her number, and slid it to Nevaeh. "Now you have no excuse."

"Ah. The classic number on a napkin. Old school, I like it." They smiled at each other for a few seconds as they locked eyes. "Well then, I guess I have no excuse." Nevaeh put the napkin in her pocket and headed out to meet her friends in the car. Since Imani and Nevaeh lived together, Tiara went back to their place to hang out until they decided on what to do for the evening. Nevaeh showered, then put on some clothes to lounge around in. She walked downstairs to the living room and saw Tiara and Imani on the couch watching a movie.

"Are you guys seriously watching *But I'm A Cheerleader* right now?" Nevaeh asked as she flopped down on the couch.

Imani looked at her with a serious expression on her face. "Yes, in fact we are."

"Why?" Nevaeh asked.

"I love all things Ru," Tiara explained.

"And we need our happy ending lesbian movie intake before we indulge in a night of noncommittal lust and empty promises."

Nevaeh paused before she asked, "How are you so gay?"

Imani shrugged, "I don't know. Birth?" she responded nonchalantly.

"Fair enough."

Imani continued, "Plus I like to watch these kinds of movies because we don't have to watch all the boring, U-hauly, bed death shit after it ends." She shuddered.

"Yeah, I guess there's nothing wrong with that." Nevaeh paused for a minute before she hesitantly said, "So…" she cleared her throat. "So, I don't want you guys to make a big deal out of this or anything, but Marie gave me her number before I left the bar today. She told me that since I had her number, I have no excuses not to call her and invite her out with us tonight."

Imani paused the movie. "Wait, what?! She gave you her number?! Bitch! This is huge!"

"Why'd you pause the movie like you haven't seen it a million times?" Nevaeh attempted to change the subject and failed.

Tiara jumped in. "Oh my goodness, if you don't call that girl, I'm going to donkey kick you in the vagina bone."

"Damn!" Nevaeh shouted quickly.

"She's beautiful and a good person. What she sees in you, I have no clue, but just go with it."

Nevaeh stuck her tongue out. Tiara smiled and blew her a playful kiss.

"You know what we should do this lovely Saturday evening," Imani spoke before Nevaeh could even get a word in, "is throw a house party instead of going out! We can invite the crew over, the rest of our fellow partiers, and get Marie to come over."

"Oh! Yes! Great idea, I'm smelling a love connection!" Tiara agreed with a shimmy.

"Me too!" Imani said excitedly.

Tiara gasped as if she had an epiphany. "Imani. What if Marie has some bad friends for me, you, and Cassidy? That would be the icing on the cake!"

"Girl. Now you are speaking my language." Imani nodded in agreement. "I'll send out a mass text to the crew and Tiara, do you mind making an event on Facebook? Then let's go to the store and get some supplies." Imani and Tiara turned off the movie, jumped off the couch, and gathered their belongings to go to the store.

Nevaeh sat there dumbfounded at how fast everything happened. "Guys, this is the exact opposite of not making a big deal out of it. Do I get a say in anything?"

"No," they responded in unison. They started to walk out the door. They turned back and noticed that Nevaeh was not behind them. Imani looked back and said, "C'mon, Nevaeh! Let's go! We gotta make this happen! You haven't had a girlfriend, let alone a crush on a girl, in like a billion years. You're almost thirty. You're not getting any younger. We, I mean you, need this."

"Guys," Nevaeh said self-consciously. Tiara and Imani realized the worry on her face. "I'm not even going to begin to lie to you guys. I'm fucking nervous." Imani and Tiara sat down on the couch on each side of her. "Like I know that I can get a lot of girls, and I do, but I never actually have true feelings like that for them. I like Marie, and what you said, Imani, about her ruining me hit home. Because what if she does, like Saria did? I don't know if I can handle that again."

Imani responded with concern in her voice, "Nevaeh. Me and T know you better than the masses, and I know that I can speak for the both of us when I say if this works out, I really think you guys would be good for one another. From the interactions I've had with Marie, she's a great match for you, and if she did end up hurting you like dumb bitch, we will end her," Imani said as she referred to Saria. Ultimately Imani and Tiara wanted to see Nevaeh happy. They could read right through Nevaeh's façade and knew how much she liked Marie.

"She's not a dumb bitch." Nevaeh's voice softened.

"But for real though she'd be done," Tiara chimed in. "And this really will be the first outside of the bar interaction. If you guys don't click, just look at it as another party where you can free-roam and do whatever your heart desires."

Nevaeh smiled, "Well, when you put it that way, you guys know I'm always ready to party!" They all jumped off the couch. "Hey thanks, guys. I needed that."

"Of course," Tiara said.

"Group hug?" Nevaeh asked with her arms wide open.

"Aw, group hug!" Imani shouted as the three of them hugged it out.

"All right, you lesbos, let's go. We have shit to do!" Tiara commanded.

They went to the store and bought a mixture of hard liquor, beer, mixers, snacks, cups, plastic shot glasses, and party supplies that totaled a little over $600. When they packed everything in the car and finally got situated, Tiara pulled out her phone, typed, and sent out the Facebook event invitation:

We are throwing yet another party to put down in the books! If you have come to any of our other parties, you know how wild they can get! I know this is last minute, but aren't all the best parties that way? For this particular party, I think we are going to gay it up a bit and make it a ROYGBIV kind of event, which means come dressed as colorful as you like, or you can wear nothing but body paint! Get creative! We have booze, but please feel free to bring more; we don't want the party to end because we ran out of alcohol. DON'T BE CHEAP! WE KNOW ALL OF YOU HAVE JOBS! There will be drinking games, cards, good music, and great times! So, my fellow gay girls, boys, gender fluid, transgenders, and our lovely hetero supporters, come on out and let's party like there's no tomorrow!

"I put the start time at nine o'clock but I told our girls to be there around 8:30. I invited about thirty people, which means either about fifteen people or sixty people will show up. Either way, it's a win because if fifteen people show up that's more alcohol, but if sixty people show up then we have ourselves a wild night!" Tiara shimmied. She loved to shimmy.

Imani got excited, "We haven't had a party in our house in a while and I am so ready for this. I love gay parties!"

"Haaaaaay!" they all screamed in unison. Imani cranked up the music, and they sang along as they drove off.

Once the girls returned to the house, they unloaded all the groceries.

"All right y'all," Tiara said. "It's three. I'm going to head back to my house to shit, shower, shave. I'll be back around eight o'clock to help you guys set up. I'm going to bring some clothes to sleep over if that's cool with you guys."

"Bet," Imani said.

"Of course, see you in a few," Nevaeh chimed in.

"All right, later," Tiara said as she walked out the door.

"Okay, Nevaeh." Imani looked at her. "It's your time to shine. You need to hit up Marie and invite her over tonight."

"Fuck," Nevaeh thought to herself. "All right, should I call or text?" she asked Imani.

Imani teased, "Are you kidding me? Miss Smooth Talker over here doesn't know what to say to a girl?" Nevaeh looked at her with the "just tell me what to do" look on her face. Imani sighed, "Look, Nevaeh, if you actually like this girl, which I know you do, call her.

Flirt a little on the phone to build up some tension, hype up the party a bit, and let her know if she gets too drunk to drive home, she can crash here. Which means make sure she crashes here. Don't act brand new."

"I feel like I'm brand new again. It feels like it's been ages since I've felt like this."

"I have all the faith in you. I'm going to go shower and get a nap in." She grabbed Nevaeh by the shoulders and looked her in the eyes. "You got this, just breathe and be the smooth-talking, fun-loving girl that I know you are."

"All right, all right. I can do this."

Imani went to her room. Nevaeh headed upstairs to hers. Imani hated upstairs bedrooms for some reason. Luckily for Nevaeh, the master bedroom was upstairs, so she got it by default.

Nevaeh closed the door behind her. She rummaged through the pockets of the clothes she had on earlier and found the napkin with Marie's number on it. She stood there holding the napkin for a few minutes. She stared at it with thoughts of where this could lead her. Eventually, she snapped out of her daze, walked over to her bed, and belly-flopped down onto it. She pulled out her phone and took a deep breath, "Here goes nothing," as she dialed the number.

"Hello?"

"Hey Marie, it's Nevaeh."

"Who?"

"Nevaeh, the girl from—"

Marie interrupted "I'm kidding, I know who you are." She giggled. "A call instead of a text? Old school. I like it."

A big smile came across Nevaeh's face. *Good call, Imani,* she thought to herself. "Well, I'm glad to hear that." Nevaeh was caught up in the moment and forgot what she was going to say, so there was an awkward pause.

Marie realized the pause was a little too long and decided to break it. "So are you guys going out tonight or did you just call me to listen to me breathe?"

"Ha. Yeah, well, lucky for you, I actually just called to listen to your voice." Nevaeh could feel Marie blushing through the phone. "But really I'm calling because we're actually not going out tonight."

"Oh," Marie said disappointedly.

"Instead we are throwing a house party and I was hoping that you would want to come. There are going to be drinking games, shots from a body or from a glass, glow sticks, the works."

"Oh, wow, that definitely sounds better than going out!"

"Yeah, it's going to get pretty crazy. If Imani, Tiara, and I learned anything from college it's how to throw a party. So, do you want to come?" Nevaeh cleared her throat. "Over. Uh, do you want to come over? Tonight. For the party." Nevaeh slammed her eyes shut in embarrassment. She couldn't believe that she just stumbled over her words. *Rookie move,* she thought to herself. She couldn't believe how nervous she was.

Marie laughed, "Yeah, I would love to. What time does this party start and do I need to bring anything?"

"It starts around nine, it's a ROYGBIV party so wear as many rainbow colors as you would like, and you don't have to bring anything, except that beautiful smile of yours." Nevaeh smacked herself in the forehead for the cheesy line she just spit out.

"That's cool. Never heard of an LGBTQ+ party nicknamed ROYGBIV. I like it. Maybe I might steal that for a themed night in one of my bars."

"Oh, that's going to be pretty expensive," Nevaeh joked.

"I'm sure I can think of a way to repay you," Marie flirted.

Nevaeh cleared her throat.

"Alrighty," Marie broke the pause, "nine o'clock sounds like a deal. I will be there. Is it cool if I bring a few friends?"

"Of course, well, as long as they're sexy female friends who enjoy the company of other females that I can shamelessly flirt with."

"Yeah, they are, and you can. They have a great sense of humor, but I don't know. I might get a little jealous if I see you hit on them. I was hoping you were going to save that for me."

Nevaeh smiled.

They spoke on the phone for about twenty minutes, laughing and flirting.

After they hung up Nevaeh felt as if the conversation went well and she was looking forward to the night. She got up and walked over to turn on her Bluetooth speaker, with a little pep in her step, and put on some music to get ready with. After she got out of the shower she danced around singing as she looked for an outfit. She laid her outfit out on her chair. She lay down in bed with her laptop to aimlessly search the web. She was too excited for a nap, but didn't want to keep drinking just yet. She couldn't wait for the party.

TWO

"**H**ey babe, did you read the Facebook invitation Tiara sent out?" Jasmine shouted as she lay in bed in her boxers and tank top, scrolling through her phone.

Anita was in the bathroom drying off from the shower, and shouted back, "No, I didn't get a chance to read it yet. What's it saying?"

"They're going to throw a house party. Looks pretty fun, and you know our girls know how to throw a party."

Anita came into the room dressed in boxer briefs and a tee shirt. She flopped down next to Jasmine. She picked up her phone and found the event on Facebook. "Yeah, this sounds awesome. They haven't had a party in a while. I love last minute parties." She kissed Jasmine on the lips.

"What do you think we should wear? The invite says it's rainbow themed," Jasmine wondered. "I don't think I own a terrible amount of rainbow stuff anymore. People spot me and know I'm gay. No need to rock the rainbow. I sprinted out of that closet," she chuckled to herself. She started to go off on a tangent. "Oh, wait, I think I have a rainbow tie-dye shirt, but who the fuck wears tie-dye anymore?"

Anita gasped a little bit, "Jas."

"What's wrong with you?"

"I see Marie said she's going."

"So?"

"So? Do you think they might try and set up her and Nevaeh?"

"I hope so! There is clear chemistry between the two of them. Nevaeh deserves somebody great."

"Well, I guess we'll see!"

Jasmine jumped up, "You want me to make lunch?"

"What kind of question is that? Of course I do," Anita smiled. "You cook, I clean?"

Jasmine smiled back, "You already know." Jasmine leaned over and kissed Anita on the lips before she walked out of the room.

Jasmine was in the kitchen preparing the food when Anita came up from behind and hugged her. She started kissing on Jasmine's neck and rubbing on her body.

Jasmine moaned, "Babe, I'm trying to cook."

"Shhh," Anita demanded as she ran her hand down Jasmine's body and slipped into her boxers. She began to massage Jasmine's clit with her fingers. Jasmine's moans grew louder, and her breath was choppy. Anita licked the fingers of her free hand and started playing with Jasmine's nipples with her wet fingers.

Jasmine leaned back into her girlfriend. "Fuck," she whispered and started moving her hips against Anita's fingers. Jasmine spun around to face Anita. She didn't go in for the kiss immediately. Instead, she grabbed her face and stared at her for a couple of seconds. She stared at her as if she was saying, *how did I get so lucky?* She began to kiss her deeply and passionately. Jasmine's hands glided up and down Anita's muscular back. Anita picked Jasmine up and sat her on the counter. Anita ripped off Jasmine's boxers and dove into her pussy face first. Jasmine let out a loud moan. Jasmine attempted to play with her nipples, balance herself, and rub Anita's head all at the same time without falling over. It was an impossible task for her, so she caved and allowed the sensations to overtake her.

After a few minutes, her chest began to rise and fall rapidly, stomach sucked in, toes curled. She used one hand to lean back to balance herself and pulled Anita's head in deeper with the other. She bucked against her face. Anita gripped on to Jasmine's thighs.

"I'm cumming! I'm cumming!" Jasmine shouted as she climaxed. After Jasmine finished trembling, Anita stood up and wiped her face.

Jasmine looked her in the eyes and asked breathlessly, "So you want your sandwich toasted or not?"

Anita smiled, "Toasted."

They both laughed and Anita went in for a quick kiss on the lips.

Anita had a rough childhood, to say the least. Her father was abusive to her and her two younger brothers, and her absentee mother was always in and out of jail for drugs. Because of her childhood chaos, she liked a life of structure and rules as an adult. She enjoyed the idea of being able to help people, and with the hope of helping clean up the streets, she became a police officer after high school. She was a six-foot stud with a very athletic body and a buzz cut that rendered a tough persona about her, but she was a true sweetheart.

Jasmine was the opposite of Anita. She grew up with two very loving parents, an African American father and a Japanese mother. Her mother grew up in a strict household, and didn't want that for her children. Jasmine's parents were both supportive of her and her older sister. They loved that their children could be who they wanted to be. As Jasmine grew older, she developed a love for dogs, so she became a dog groomer. She was also a stud. She was 5'11, with her sides faded and medium-length hair on top that she kept neat. She was more of a free spirit, which made her a good balance in Anita's structured lifestyle.

One morning, Anita went to her favorite coffee shop to pick up her dose of caffeine before shift, and someone had already purchased it for her. The cup read "I would like to thank you for your service," with the name Jasmine signed and her phone number. Anita was very grateful but thought nothing else of it. Throughout that day something kept tugging at her to call the number. So the next day she called and scheduled a meet-up with this mystery woman. Anita never really pictured herself with another masculine woman, but she fell for Jasmine rather quickly. Their friendship developed into a happy, healthy, loving relationship.

After they finished fixing their plates, they wandered into the living room. Anita always sat on the couch and Jasmine sat in the recliner. Those were their unspoken spots they had claimed. Jasmine turned on the TV so they could binge-watch Netflix as they ate. They both had a thing for crime shows. They loved to hang out with their girls, but they cherished the time they had to themselves. Neither one of them had the need or desire to go out all the time. They were happy with staying home and vegging out, cuddled up on the couch. The girls would always tease them about being like an old married couple, but really they wanted what Anita and Jasmine had. A deep, genuine love for one another. They accepted each other for who they were as individuals. They had the rare kind of love that most people dream about.

"So baby, there's something I want to tell you." Anita broke the silence.

"What's going on?" Jasmine asked with a mouth full of food, not breaking eye contact from the television.

"Well, my sergeant told me the other day that he thinks I would make a great detective."

"What?" Jasmine exclaimed as she paused the TV. "Baby, that's great!"

"You think so?" Anita asked, unsure.

"Of course! You're great at whatever you put your mind to."

"But I have to take an exam. What if I get rejected? It scares the shit out of me. I'm comfortable where I'm at," Anita stated self-consciously.

"Oh, Anita." Jasmine sat next to her on the couch and put her arm around Anita. "That's why you should do it. You can't figure out where life is going to take you unless you step outside of your comfort zone. You know I have your back no matter what, and I will always be on the sidelines cheering you on. If you happen to fail, which I doubt you will, I will be there to pick you back up. Look where you came from, your past. You a bad bitch."

"Yeah?" Anita questioned self-consciously. "You think so?"

"I know so! You pretty much raised your younger brothers. You pulled yourself out of a tough situation and brought your brothers up with you. I mean look at the life you've made for yourself. Your brothers are thriving, you have a home, a framily, an amazing girlfriend, toot toot." Jasmine mimicked as if she were tooting her own horn. Anita chuckled with tears in her eyes. "You have a great job, and you're now facing a promotion. You're such a strong, amazing woman and I need you to never forget that."

Anita hugged Jasmine. It was a tight hug. "Thank you, baby." She sniffled and wiped away a few tears that managed to roll down her cheek. "Can we keep this between us for now? I don't want to tell the girls yet."

"No doubt."

Anita pondered, "I do want to ask you something, though."

"Anything."

"What the hell is a framily?"

"You know our girls. They're our friends, but they're our family. They're our friend family. Our framily."

Anita snickered, "I love you so much."

Jasmine smiled, "I love you too." She leaned in to give Anita a quick kiss on the lips. "Do you want to finish eating, watching TV, and being the old boring married couple that we are?"

"I would love nothing more," Anita smiled.

Jasmine sat back in the recliner and pressed Play. Anita smiled to herself as she watched her girlfriend devour her sandwich with her eyes glued to the TV. Anita was so grateful that she could be so vulnerable around Jasmine. She was able to let all the walls that she had built over time come down. Jasmine made Anita feel emotionally safe. Because of her past, Anita kept her emotions heavily guarded prior to Jasmine. Jasmine came into her life and effortlessly won over Anita's heart.

It was in that moment Anita knew Jasmine was the woman she wanted to spend the rest of her life with. The woman she wanted to marry. Anita took a bite of her sandwich and continued to watch TV.

THREE

It was Saturday afternoon. Eliana decided to take advantage of her girlfriend's day off and didn't schedule any photo shoots for that day. Trisha was a Fourth Grade school teacher at a local elementary school.

Eliana was a little tomboyish but leaned more on the feminine side. She was 5'7 with shoulder-length hair and a deep caramel complexion. She was a very driven photographer and loved what she did. Trisha was her on-again, off-again girlfriend of five years. Nobody cared for Trisha because of the way she treated Eliana, but they tolerated her for Eliana. They all attempted to warn Eliana that Trisha was bad news, but she didn't listen. Eliana knew her friends didn't like Trisha; half the time Eliana didn't even like Trisha, but frankly Eliana was afraid to be alone.

"Hey Trish." Eliana rolled over in bed to see her on-again, off-again girlfriend texting away on her phone.

Yeah?"

"Since we both have the day off do you want to do something?"

Trisha stared at her phone, "Like what?"

"It doesn't really matter; it would just be nice to spend some time with you outside of this apartment."

"Okay, baby, whatever you want."

"For fuck's sake, Trisha, can you get off your fucking phone for five minutes and have an actual conversation with me?" Eliana said as she angrily jumped out of bed.

Trisha exhaled as if she were annoyed, put her phone down, and sat up in bed, "I am not always on my phone."

"You know what kind of people say they're not always on their phone? The ones who are always on their phone!"

Trisha softened her voice. "Okay, baby, you're right. That is my bad. It's just sometimes I get so wrapped up in the stupid social media life that I forget to pay attention to what's going on in my reality. I truly am sorry. Come here." She opened her arms for Eliana to come back into bed with her. Deep down Eliana knew she was full of shit, but she fell for that big smile and dimples every single time. So Eliana climbed back into bed and into Trisha's arms. "All right. So, what shall we do today? Maybe lunch and then bowling?" Trisha suggested.

"Yeah, I could go for some beers and bowling. Also, I saw on Facebook that Tiara posted a party invitation for tonight. You want to go to that?"

"Hm, spending time with my favorite girl, day drinks, and then partying all night. I'm so down. Your friends always throw the best parties." Trisha leaned in and kissed Eliana. Their light kiss soon began to get deeper as their hands wandered. Trisha pulled away from Eliana, "Okay, okay. Let's not start because then we'll never leave this apartment. You know how we are once we get going."

"Yeah, I guess you're right," Eliana pouted. "Fine, I'll shower first."

"Yeah, good idea. One of us has to start getting ready if we ever want to leave."

Eliana got up from the bed and headed to the bathroom. Once the door shut, Trisha went back to texting and scrolling through social media sites. Eliana turned the water on and stepped inside. As she was washing her body, she felt a cool breeze that caused her to spin around. She turned to see a naked Trisha standing there with the shower curtain pulled back.

"Well, don't just stare. Are you going to invite me in or what?" Trisha asked with seduction in her voice.

Eliana didn't say anything. She smiled and motioned for Trisha to join her. Trisha stepped into the shower, shutting the curtain behind her. As soon as she stepped in they started making out. They kissed slowly, as their hands explored one another's bodies. Trisha pulled away from the kiss to grab the shower head. She set it to the pulsating setting and pointed the water on Eliana's right nipple. With the water pulsating on her right nipple, Trisha devoured her left nipple. She made sure she did not miss anything. As she sucked, nibbled, and caressed, Eliana began to moan in ecstasy.

"Mmm, I like that," Eliana managed to choke out between breaths. Eliana pulled Trisha's face back up to hers and their kiss grew even deeper than before. Eliana took the pulsating shower head from Trisha and moved it down between Trisha's legs. Trisha's body jerked a little from the pressure and she moaned into Eliana's mouth. Trisha slid her hand down between Eliana's legs and started massaging her clit. Their breaths began to quicken as the pace sped up. Eliana began to grind faster on Trisha's fingers as she knew her climax was approaching. Once she climaxed, she took the shower head and gave it to Trisha.

"Hold this on your nipples," she said in a deep, seductive tone. Trisha obeyed. She kept the water pulsating on her nipples, switching back and forth between the two. Eliana began to kiss her way down to Trisha's pussy. Once she was there, she teased her pussy until Trisha couldn't take any more.

"Please, baby, make me cum." Eliana loved when Trisha begged her, she couldn't help but smile. Eliana dove in. She used her fingers, tongue, and lips until Trisha's body couldn't do anything else but cave in. Trisha's knees buckled as she slowly went down to the shower floor and kissed Eliana. Trisha's body was still trembling. Eliana stood up and helped Trisha stand. She then started washing her body from head to toe.

"So much for not getting started, huh?" Eliana said with a smirk on her face.

"Yeah," Trisha chuckled. "I guess so. In my defense, I figured at least in the shower we have a certain amount of time before the water got cold, so eventually we would stop. In the bed, there's no telling when we would stop."

"Logic." After they finished washing one another they hopped out to get dressed. Eliana opened the Uber app on her phone. "Awesome. Says there's one three minutes away," she said to herself. "Hey Trish, let's go. The Uber is around the corner." Eliana opened her apartment door. As Trisha walked by, Eliana kissed her on the lips, "Love you, baby."

Trisha said with a smile, "Love you too, now let's go." Trisha continued out into the hallway and Eliana smacked her butt as she passed. Eliana locked up the apartment. They walked hand in hand downstairs. The car had pulled up as they walked out and hopped in.

"You ladies heading to the bowling alley?" The male driver asked in a chipper voice.

"Yes sir. That would be correct," Trisha responded.

"Alrighty." As he drove, Eliana made small talk with the driver. Trisha texted. Eliana glanced over a few times and noticed her grinning at her phone.

Eliana and Trisha were off again because their personalities clashed so much. They were on again because their sexual chemistry was out of this world. They got along for the most part, usually for a short period after sex. A lot of the time Eliana wondered if she truly loved Trisha, or if she was just settling.

"Hey Trish, who are you texting?" Eliana questioned.

"Oh, no one, babe." Trisha replied without looking up from her phone, "Just Jordan."

"Just Jordan? The guy that works at the bowling alley that you suggested to go to today? The guy that you think is so cute? That Jordan?"

"Yes. That Jordan," Trisha said with annoyance. "What? Is there a problem? Just because I'm bisexual doesn't mean I want to sleep with every guy, Eliana," she said with attitude.

Eliana cleared her throat and slightly glanced at the driver through the rearview, "I didn't say that, Trisha," she said calmly. "I'm just saying you've been giggling at your phone all morning. Then you tell me you've been texting Jordan. A guy that you told me to my face you're attracted to. How do you think that makes me feel? Do you think I'm just supposed to be cool with it? I would feel the same fucking way if you told me that about a female. It's not just a male thing."

The driver interrupted the conversation before Trisha could respond. "Here we are, ladies." Eliana looked out the window and noticed they had arrived at their destination.

"Thank you, sir. My apologies about the argument." Eliana exited the vehicle.

"Ellie, wait." Trisha grabbed her arm as she pulled her off to the side before she went into the front entrance. The Uber drove off. "Look, I want to apologize. Sometimes I don't realize what I'm doing until you call me out on it, and I am sorry for that. I'm sorry for hurting you. I know many of our arguments come from the crap that I'm doing or have done. You tell me how you feel, and then I catch an attitude about it."

"It's whatever, Trisha. Let's go inside." Eliana started to walk off. Trisha grabbed her arm again.

"It's not whatever, Eliana. I love you and I would never intentionally hurt you. I need you to know that. There isn't anything between Jordan and me. I love you. You are who I want to be with." Eliana scoffed. "I hit him up to let him know we were coming to the bowling alley today and he sent me back some funny memes and videos. We can go somewhere else if you would like."

"Yeah? That's all?" It was at that moment that Eliana knew the relationship was close to being over because she didn't believe a word that came out of Trisha's mouth. When Trisha said she loved her, Eliana felt nothing. She said it back, just because. Eliana knew she deserved better, but she was too afraid that if she didn't have someone she would be lonely. Ending up alone was her deepest fear. Eliana decided to try and fight through her thoughts. She thought she might've been overreacting. She disregarded her gut feeling. Ignored all the red flags. She decided to give Trisha one last chance to make things right. "You know what? It's okay. We don't have to go anywhere else. Let's go bowling, get some food, and day drink. No need to ruin our day together."

"Good." Trisha kissed Eliana on the cheek, and they walked inside, hand in hand, to begin their day drinking adventure.

FOUR

When Nevaeh walked into the living room, she saw Tiara and Imani playing a game of beer pong.

"So, how'd it go?" Imani asked, being nosey.

"How'd what go?" She gave Nevaeh a look. "Oh right, uh, it went well. She's coming and inviting some of her friends!"

"Fucking jackpot," Imani said. They continued their game of beer pong while Nevaeh went into the kitchen and took a shot. Around 8:30 the doorbell rang and rest of the gang showed up. The last of the group to show up was Cassidy.

Cassidy was a six-foot, fair-skinned, green-eyed brunette. She was the only bisexual woman in the group. Cassidy had what she considered a boring upbringing. She chose to join the Air Force after high school because she wanted to get out of her small town and experience what other places in the world had to offer.

They all gathered around the table, drinking, laughing, and enjoying each other's company until the party started. Nevaeh poured everyone a shot and stood up. "Hey ladies. I just want to say, well we," she motioned to Imani and Tiara, "would like to thank all of you for coming out tonight. We know it's not our normal Friends'

Friday, but glad you all could make it. You all are the best friends any lesbian could ever ask for! So let's get fucked up! Ch—"

"Wait!" Imani interrupted as she stood up. "Nevaeh left out the main reason this party is being thrown. Marie gave her her number and wants to hang out tonight!"

"Oooooouuuuu!" they all teased playfully.

"Y'all are childish," Nevaeh blushed.

"I called that shit," Anita proudly whispered to Jasmine.

"Good work, detective." Jasmine winked at her.

Anita smiled.

"So," Imani continued, "we have to make sure we keep her on the lookout and hope Nevaeh gets the girl and doesn't fuck it up!"

Jasmine stood up, "Here's to Nevaeh not fucking it up and to our framily!"

"Here's to what?" Tiara asked.

"To Nevaeh not fucking it up."

"Nah, I heard that. What'd you say after that?"

Jasmine looked down at Anita then looked back to the group. "To our framily."

"Da fuck is that?" Imani asked.

Jasmine sucked her teeth. "Man, y'all don't know what a framily is? It's a group of friends who become your family, a friend family. A framily." Jasmine spoke as if they should've already known what that meant.

"You stay making up shit," Tiara said.

"It's a thing—look it up," Jasmine responded in a matter-of-fact tone.

Cassidy stood up. "Cheers, ladies!"

"Cheers!" They tapped glasses.

After about an hour, the house was full. People walked around in ass-less chaps, nipple pasties, and various rainbow gear. It looked like a mini Pride in that house. Beer pong commenced, flip cup had people excited, body shots were happening on the counter, and people danced with each other while the bass vibrated the floor.

Nevaeh chatted with Carla, a woman who had been trying to hook up with her for a while. Unfortunately for Carla, Nevaeh had no interest in doing so and made that clear upfront. Nevaeh didn't want to be rude, so she chatted with her. Nevaeh spoke with Carla, but her eyes discreetly scanned the room for Marie. Marie was who she wanted to talk to at that moment. Suddenly, she felt a tap on her back. She turned around to Marie's smiling face, with three of her gorgeous friends. Nevaeh sighed with relief when she saw her face. When Marie smiled at Nevaeh, Nevaeh got that feeling that no one else was in the room but them. Her smile made her entire day better.

"Hey, Nevaeh. I hope I'm not interrupting anything," Marie stated. "Hey Carla." She peeked around Nevaeh and waved.

"Hey, Marie," Carla smiled.

"How do you guys know each other?" Nevaeh asked, slightly confused. *Please don't tell me they hooked up,* she worriedly thought to herself.

Marie noticed the worry on Nevaeh's face. "Well, I do own one of the most popular lesbian bars in town," she chuckled.

Nevaeh nodded her head. "Right."

Carla said, "I've been thinking about trying to get in on this flip cup game. It was great talking to you, Nevaeh; maybe we can finish our conversation some other time."

"Yeah. Sorry. Maybe," Nevaeh responded without breaking her gaze with Marie. Carla walked off and Marie introduced Nevaeh to her friends.

"Nevaeh, these are my girls Camilla, Deja, and Nia. Nia used to live out here but moved out of town for work. She's gracing us with her presence for the weekend."

"Yes, and I'm ready to let loose!" Nia enthused.

"All right, well we have plenty of things that will help you let loose. Welcome to our home, where beautiful women as yourselves are always welcome. Would you all like a shot or a drink?"

"Well, we didn't stand around to look at everyone else drink!" Deja said in an enthusiastic tone.

"All right then, do you guys like fireball shots?"

"Hell yeah!" they all said.

"Let's do it!" Nevaeh led the way to the kitchen.

She poured five fireball shots and raised her glass, "Here's to meeting you beautiful ladies, Marie finally being able to hang out with me on her off time, and many more house parties and good times. Enjoy yourselves, ladies. Cheers!"

"Cheers!" They all threw their shot back. The burn and taste of the shot caused all their faces to scrunch up. Nia slightly gagged.

Nevaeh coughed and made a single clap with her hands, "All right, ladies, you all enjoy yourselves, please help yourselves to anything, there are snacks and plenty of alcohol. Make out, make bad decisions, blackout, and sex. Always sex." They all laughed.

"You are all in a safe place. If anyone makes you feel uncomfortable, let me or any of my girls know and we will kick them the fuck out. Now if you all would excuse me, I will be right back. I am going to try and find my best friend, lesbro, roomie so I can let her know you all are here." Nevaeh scurried off to find Imani. She looked all over. Finally, she spotted Imani chatting it up with some girl. Nevaeh signaled that she needed to talk to her, but Imani wasn't paying attention. Eventually, Imani saw her but tried to ignore her. Nevaeh kept signaling. If Imani didn't respond, Nevaeh would embarrass her; Imani knew it too. So she excused herself from that conversation and walked over.

"Bitch what?! That girl was into me and wanted this sexy body." She bit her bottom lip and did a body roll as she ran her finger down her body.

"Gross," Nevaeh deplored. "Whatever. Look, Marie and her bad bitch friends are here, and I need your help."

"How bad?"

"Life in prison."

Imani took a quick sip of her drink and looked at Nevaeh with a serious gaze. "All right. I'm in."

"You're so silly. What about that girl you were talking to? I thought she wanted some of this." Nevaeh imitated her doing the body roll, as she ran her finger down her body.

"Fuck her. I'm over it."

Nevaeh shook her head and they both laughed and walked off to find the girls. Nevaeh spotted Marie and her friends watching two teams go at a game of survivor flip cup.

Imani grabbed her shoulder, "Are you talking about those three girls standing with Marie? Those are her friends?!"

"Yeah, that's them."

"Have mercy!"

"All right, Uncle Jesse, keep it in your fucking pants."

Imani rolled her eyes. "All right, homie. Let's get it." They both licked their pointer and pinky fingers and ran them across their eyebrows and walked toward the girls. Nevaeh introduced all of them to Imani. Imani always had a way with charming the ladies. Cassidy and Tiara walked up as they were talking. Nevaeh introduced the two to the group. Nia and Imani hit it off, so they decided to go take shots; Deja and Cassidy wandered off to play Kings Cup, and Tiara and Camilla decided to go play beer pong.

Marie pulled Nevaeh over to her and whispered in her ear, "You want to step outside?" Nevaeh looked back into her eyes and nodded. Marie grabbed her hand and pulled her to the back yard.

"So I overheard you bragging about how good you are at flip cup," Marie said.

"I am. It's all in the finesse of the finger," she replied while doing a flipping motion with her finger.

Marie smiled. "Is that right? Well, maybe you can show me that finesse some time."

"I'm sorry I can't reveal my secrets or else how will I be able to keep stringing you along?"

"Well, I know other ways you can keep stringing me along." She leaned in and kissed Nevaeh on the lips. Marie slightly pulled away. She scanned Nevaeh's face as if she were searching for confirmation. There was a pregnant pause before Nevaeh took her hand and pulled Marie's face into hers. An instant rush filled Nevaeh; it felt like her entire body was on fire. She wanted to fuck her right there in the back yard, but she kept her composure. Nevaeh began caressing Marie's body as they kissed. Nevaeh knew Marie wanted the same as she did because she pressed her body into her. She got so close that Nevaeh could feel the heat that escaped from her body. *Nevaeh, you have to gain control,* she thought to herself over and over. Nevaeh eventually gained control and pushed herself away from her.

"I'm sorry," Marie said bashfully. "I don't know what came over me."

"Trust me, there is no reason to apologize. I've wanted that longer than you can even imagine. Plus, it takes two to tango."

Marie responded with a smile.

Nevaeh said, "I guess the only thing you should apologize for is not letting me take you out on a date first."

She grinned from ear to ear. "All right. Well, I apologize for not letting you take me out on a date first, but if I waited for that to happen, I would be waiting forever."

"What? Why do you say that?"

"Oh, please, Nevaeh. I see you. I see the kind of games you run. You and Imani. You're both smooth talkers and you run through girls. I'm not blind."

"Ah yes. I suppose you do see a lot of episodes of my shit show. Well, fine then. If you are still okay with it, Marie... uh..." Nevaeh whispered, "what's your last name?"

She chuckled, "It's Diaz."

"Marie Diaz, would you do me the honor of going on a date with me?"

She nodded her head. "Well, let me check my schedule."

"Check your schedule? Ouch. Well, I don't do well with getting put on the back burner, so if you don't have time, I think I'm going to have to pass." Nevaeh started to playfully walk away.

Marie grabbed her arm. "No. Nothing like that. I mean I literally have to check my work schedule to see what's going on with my bar."

"Ah. Well, I guess that's okay with me." She grinned. "You want to go back inside? I can make you a drink or we can do some shots or something."

"I could go for a shot, as long as it's a body shot," Marie smirked. "You can take it off me." She leaned in and whispered in her ear, "I want to feel your tongue on my body."

Nevaeh licked her lips and tilted her head toward the door. Marie grabbed her hand and led her inside. As they walked through the crowd of people Imani spotted them. Nevaeh and she made eye contact and Imani flashed that goofy smile she always did when she got excited. Nevaeh mouthed, "I know!" in excitement.

When they got to the kitchen, Nevaeh grabbed the tequila, salt, and lime. Seductively she asked, "So where do you want it?" as she intensely stared into Marie's eyes.

"Hm. On my neck." So Nevaeh set up the shot. She licked the salt off her neck, took the shot, and took the lime out of Marie's mouth with hers.

"Aaaahhhh! Fucking tequila. Makes my clothes come off."

"Uh! Please, somebody, keep giving this girl tequila!" Marie shouted spiritedly. She used her thumb to wipe Nevaeh's lips. Nevaeh instantly felt that rush of fire through her body all over again.

A lot was happening at the party that night. People were dancing; Cassidy and Deja were playing Kings Cup with a few others; Imani, Tiara, Camilla, and Nia were playing twister; Jasmine and Anita found some other lesbian couple they were talking to, and it appeared as if Eliana and Trisha were arguing again. The gang was all there doing what they did best.

Around two a.m. people started to trickle out.

"Hey Nevaeh, my love, Jasmine and I are going to take off. Our Uber is waiting out front for us," Anita said. "When Imani arises from her sex coma, tell her we said bye," she joked.

Nevaeh laughed, "I got you. Love you guys. Let us know in the group chat when y'all get home." They hugged.

"We will love," Jasmine confirmed. The couple walked out. Nevaeh looked around and noticed Eliana and Trisha had left; she concluded that they were either fucking or fighting. There was no gray area with those two. Nevaeh walked through the house to check out the after-party damage. She noticed Cassidy and Deja were passed out cuddled on the couch, heard giggles coming from Imani's room, and Tiara was on the back porch talking to Camilla. She wandered into the kitchen to Marie trying to clean up. "Marie, you don't have to do that, we'll get it tomorrow."

"Eh, it's okay. I don't mind. So, did you have enough tequila tonight to make your clothes come off?" Marie asked jokingly.

Nevaeh chuckled, "I definitely did, but I think I want to keep them on tonight." Marie pouted. "Trust me, it isn't because of what I don't want to do, it's because of what I want to do."

"Well, what is it that you want to do that's so terrible?"

Nevaeh approached her, leaned in close to her ear, and whispered, "Clear that dining table off and do unspeakable things to that gorgeous body of yours right this second."

She smirked and whispered back, "So why don't you do it?"

Nevaeh took a step back, straightened up, and tried her best to put on a serious face. "Because I promised to take you on a date first. I want to keep my word."

Marie made a face that looked slightly disappointed, but nodded in agreement.

"Well, from the looks of it your friends plan on spending the night. So, does that mean you are?"

"Is that an invitation?"

"Yeah, actually it is."

"Then I would love to."

Nevaeh locked the front door and walked over to the hallway closet to grab a blanket. When she walked past Imani's room, she could hear sex taking place. Nevaeh chuckled to herself and said, "Oh, Imani." She laid the blanket over Cassidy and Deja.

"C'mon." She motioned to Marie. "Let's go out back."

Marie followed her out back.

"Hey, what up, Chatty Cathies?" Marie said to Camilla and Tiara, once they got to the back porch.

"Everyone has left. You all are more than welcome to crash," Nevaeh offered. "Deja and Cassidy are passed out on the couch, and Imani and Nia sound like they're in there attempting to make the world's bestselling lesbian porn. If Tiara doesn't mind sharing the room, you can crash in there, if not we can make some room for you."

"I don't mind," Tiara responded.

"Cool. Appreciate that, you guys," Camilla said.

Nevaeh turned to Marie. "C'mon." She took her by the hand, and they walked out into the medium-sized back yard. Tiara and Camilla smiled at the sight of Nevaeh and Marie.

"I hope they hit it off," Camilla whispered.

"You guys too?" Tiara whispered back.

"Yeah, Marie really likes Nevaeh, it'd be nice to see her with somebody deserving."

"Same with Nevaeh," Tiara continued. "Hey, let's go inside and give them some privacy. We can enjoy the weather on the front porch."

"Cool." The two headed to the front porch.

Imani and Nevaeh had purchased a hammock when they first moved into the house. They both agreed that it was very relaxing. Nevaeh used it more often than Imani did. She loved to lie in it at night and look up at the stars. It was her happy place.

She lay down in the hammock and motioned for Marie to lie next to her. Marie got herself in the hammock and snuggled into Nevaeh. It was warm out with a slight cool breeze. Crickets sang into the night. It was one of those perfect weather summer nights. Nevaeh kept a stick near the hammock that she used to rock herself. She grabbed her rocking stick and pushed them until there was a good rocking motion. They cuddled there looking up at the stars.

Marie broke the silence with a whisper, "This is nice. It's quiet. Peaceful, even. Do you come here often?"

"It's one of my favorite spots in the house."

"One of? What are your others?"

Nevaeh chuckled, "One day I'll show you." Marie turned her face to Nevaeh's and kissed her. This time the kiss was soft. Sensual. Nevaeh felt those butterflies fluttering around in her stomach. When they stopped, Marie traced Nevaeh's face with her finger.

"I like you," Marie stated nervously. "And that scares me."

"Why does that scare you?"

"Because. Like I've told you before, I've seen you in action. I've seen the number of girls you hook up with, and that's only at my bar, who knows what goes on at other places. It just makes me nervous. How do I know I'm not falling into some trap? How do I know that this isn't some game you play? The shitty thing is, that I know and wonder all these things, but I can't help it. I'm drawn to you. I feel like you're a drug." She paused. "Well, and at the risk of

43

sounding super cheesy, I don't know how to shake these feelings. It also makes me wonder who hurt you in the past to make you act this way. I can't imagine you were always like this. You truly seem like a kind person."

Nevaeh paused for a minute to wrap her mind around what Marie had said and to gather her words. "Those are all reasonable concerns." She paused. "And I like you too. I know for a fact that this isn't a game to me. I know those are just words, but it's true. If I didn't care about you, we would be in my room right now, and I would already be planning on how to get you out of my house once we woke up. I don't play games. I'm just blunt. I tell girls up front that I'm not looking for anything, so to me, that's not a game. If they proceed to go on, that's on them."

"I guess that's fair. Well, you haven't told me you're not looking for anything. So, what does that mean?"

"I don't know yet. I haven't thought that far ahead. I just know that I see you more than a one-night stand."

"Fair enough. And as far as who hurt you?" Marie genuinely asked.

Nevaeh stared into her eyes for a few seconds, then turned her head to look back up at the sky. She took a moment and contemplated whether to tell Marie or not, but she decided to. "Saria. She was my first love."

"Yeah?"

"Yeah. It just ended so abruptly, and I didn't know how to handle everything that I was feeling. So, I acted out. Turned out that I actually liked playing the field and I'm good at it." Nevaeh exhaled. "But now? It feels like it's getting a little old to me. I think I'm ready to chill for a while. Allow someone to get to know me on a deeper level."

Marie smiled. "I feel the same at times. I mean I haven't played the field so to speak, but I've had my fair share of girlfriends. I would eventually like to find that special person," Marie paused before she continued, "or persons."

Nevaeh looked at Marie, surprised. "Persons?" she questioned.

"Yes." Marie hesitated. "I'm polyamorous."

"Polyamorous? Like you date more than one person at a time?"

"Correct."

"Lesbians do that?" Nevaeh was confused.

Marie chuckled, "Some do. Everyone is different."

"Do the other people know you're dating other people?"

"Of course," Marie reassured. "If they didn't, that would be cheating, not polyamory."

"Are you dating someone else right now?"

"No. I would've told you upfront if I were."

"Wow." Nevaeh was shocked. She never expected that from Marie.

"Is that a deal breaker for you?" Marie felt uneasy as she anticipated the answer.

"Not necessarily. I've never been in a polyamorous relationship before. It's not that I'm opposed to it, it just never has presented itself."

Marie smiled. The two fell silent. Marie kissed Nevaeh on the cheek. They lay there in silence swinging peacefully in the hammock until they fell asleep.

The next morning, Nevaeh and Marie were woken abruptly by the sprinklers.

"Ah fuck!" Nevaeh shouted as they both scrambled to get out of the hammock. After fighting for what seemed like an eternity, they finally fell to the ground. Marie stood up and began laughing obnoxiously with a couple of snorts as she attempted to inhale. Nevaeh stood there looking at her still being sprayed by the sprinklers and began to laugh as well. They both stood in the line of fire for the duration of the cycle, laughing.

"Oh my goodness, that was great!" Marie shouted, holding her stomach and laughing.

"It was only funny because you made it funny. I didn't know you snorted when you laugh."

"Yeah. It only happens when I think something is ridiculously funny."

Nevaeh noticed Marie seemed kind of embarrassed and spoke up. "Well, I like it. It's cute." They exchanged smiles. "Geez," Nevaeh scoffed at her phone. "It's only seven in the morning. I feel like we just went to sleep like an hour ago."

"That's probably because we did."

"Well, come on, let's go in the house and get dried off. See if the others are awake yet."

"Doubtful, but let's do it."

As they walked toward the house, Nevaeh stopped and turned to Marie. She stared into her eyes, then grabbed her face and kissed her. "I might've been drunk, but I meant everything I said last night. I do like you. And I hope that in time you see that I am not playing any games with you." She turned and walked into the house. She opened and shut the door as quietly as she could.

"Shhhh. Looks like everyone is still sleeping," Marie commented.

"Come on, I have the master bedroom. We can go shower and change in there." Marie smirked. Nevaeh noticed the sly smirk and responded, "I said shower. Then maybe I can make everyone breakfast. If you would like that."

"I would love that."

Nevaeh led the way up the stairs to her bedroom. "I like this view," Marie said, referring to Nevaeh's butt in her face as they walked up the stairs.

Nevaeh giggled, "I like to cater to my guest." She opened the door to her bedroom. "Come on in."

"So, this is where the queen herself sleeps, huh?" Marie teased.

"Queen? Hm. Never been referred to as that before. It has a nice ring to it." Marie sat down on the armchair and Nevaeh turned on the TV. "You can go ahead and shower first if you would like."

"Wow. You're such a gentlelady. But no. I appreciate the sentiment. This is your house. You go first."

"Well, all right. Here is the remote so you can watch whatever it is you like."

"Thanks," Marie smiled.

About twenty minutes later Nevaeh came out of the bathroom all clean.

"All right, your turn. There are towels and washcloths in the linen closet in there, and I have spare toothbrushes as well. Everything you need should be in there for you. If you want, I can take your clothes and throw them in the wash along with mine so they'll be clean for whenever you want to leave." She walked over and pulled out some basketball shorts and a tee shirt. "And here are some clothes for you to throw on when you're done."

"All right." She grabbed the clothes. "I really do appreciate this, Nevaeh."

Nevaeh sent a soft smile. "You're very welcome."

Nevaeh lay down on the bed and began to flip through the channels. "Ugh. There's never anything on TV." About twenty-five minutes later she heard the bathroom door open, but her eyes stayed glued on the television.

"Nevaeh," Marie said softly as she stood on the threshold. "Nevaeh, I can't stand it anymore."

Nevaeh sat up and turned to see Marie standing in the door frame with nothing but a towel on.

She stood up and turned the TV off. "Can't stand what anymore?" she asked with concern in her voice.

Marie lustfully stared into Nevaeh's eyes as she walked toward her slowly, as if she were in a trance. Nevaeh said nothing as she watched her approach. Marie stood about an arm's reach away from Nevaeh without breaking eye contact.

"Come here," she said so seductively that it made Nevaeh instantly wet. Nevaeh took a step toward her and she knew what was coming. Nevaeh gently grabbed the back of Marie's neck and pulled her face into hers. They kissed deeply. It was hot and heavy. Nevaeh almost felt as if she was going to pass out. She pulled away. "Look, Marie I want you. I really, really want you, but I don't want to go too fast. You said you at least wanted me to take you on a date first, and I want to honor that."

"You said that," Marie said as she dropped her towel. "We'll get around to that." Finally, Nevaeh saw what Marie had been hiding under her clothes all this time. Her body was phenomenal. She had a smooth caramel complexion, C cup breasts, a toned stomach with the ass to match. Drops of water glistened off her body as her wet, dark brown hair fell over her shoulders. Nevaeh couldn't contain herself anymore and was lost in the moment.

There's no way I could turn her down. She's practically begging me to fuck her. Nevaeh thought to herself.

Nevaeh wrapped both arms around Marie's naked body and pulled her into her. She ran her hand down Marie's back, which made Marie's body shiver. Nevaeh gently slid her other hand between Marie's legs where she felt her warmth. She was dripping wet. That turned Nevaeh on even more. She put light pressure on her clit and began rubbing it in a slow circular motion. Marie moaned into Nevaeh's mouth as they kissed. Marie slid her hands under Nevaeh's shirt and pulled it off over her head. As she moaned from the touch of Nevaeh massaging her, she placed her mouth on Nevaeh's left breast and began to nibble, lick, and suck on her nipple. She took her left hand, put it in her mouth and then rubbed on her right nipple with it. Nevaeh moaned in ecstasy as she felt her vagina throb from excitement. Marie's body began to shake as she felt herself getting close to her first climax. She felt her knees begin to buckle and that's when Nevaeh picked up the pace.

"Oh fuck, Nevaeh, don't stop," Marie panted.

Nevaeh added more pressure, but kept a steady pace. Marie's breathing stopped, her body tensed up. She managed to let a moan escape from her opened mouth. Marie's orgasm was intense and that made her want more. Nevaeh pulled Marie's face into hers and they kissed again, this time heavier, with more passion. Marie slowly slid Nevaeh's shorts off. As Nevaeh picked Marie up, Marie wrapped her legs around Nevaeh's waist. Nevaeh fell onto Marie on the bed.

Marie slightly gasped when she felt Nevaeh's warmth on hers. Nevaeh's moan deepened. Nevaeh began to move back and forth. Neither of the two had control over their breathing anymore. They were lost in the moment.

"Fuck, Nevaeh, I'm going to cum," Marie panted.

"Me too." Nevaeh kept up the motion until they both came. Marie rolled on top of Nevaeh. She began to kiss a trail down her body all the way to her vagina. She stopped and allowed her warm breath to hover over Nevaeh's throbbing pussy. Nevaeh's body wiggled as if it were begging Marie to taste her. Marie traced her tongue along Nevaeh's walls and felt her melt. She then dove in and ate her out until she came twice. She then worked her way back up to Nevaeh's mouth so she could taste herself. They passionately kissed and caressed one another. Nevaeh got on top of Marie and began to work her way down. "No, Nevaeh. It's okay." Marie was breathless. "I'm sensitive. Let's just lie here."

"Are you sure?" Nevaeh asked, ready to dive in headfirst.

"Yeah, I'm sure." Nevaeh obliged, and they lay there, once again in silence. Marie laid her head on Nevaeh's chest and she listened to her heart beat rapidly. "My goodness, Nevaeh. I needed that. I've been craving you since the first time I saw you. I just didn't know how to approach you."

"I know the first time I saw you working behind the bar, I thought you were by far the sexiest woman I had ever seen. Seriously. Then I found out that it was, in fact, your bar and you weren't just bartending. That shot my attraction toward you through the roof. You could've just approached me and said some cheesy pickup line or a simple hi and I would've melted in the palm of your hand."

"Yeah, right," Marie said with a self-conscious tone in her voice as she ran her finger over Nevaeh's body. "I couldn't have approached you like that. Like I said before, you're a fucking player. I saw that from day one. I've been working in bars for quite some time. I know the type when I see it. I just figured I could admire you from afar. A distant crush. Little did I know you were going to be a regular customer and I was going to get to actually know you and ultimately fall for you."

"I'm not a player."

"Look, call it what you want. You don't play games? Fine, but you have girls eating out of the palm of your hand. You are an alpha. Just face it."

"Well, I've never looked at it that way," Nevaeh flatly responded.

"Yeah, well I have and I still do." Marie fell silent.

"Hey," Nevaeh said as she lifted Marie's face so their eyes could meet. "Where'd you go just then?"

"Nowhere."

"Oh, you went somewhere."

Marie sighed, "I'm just happy and terrified at the same time."

"You're not the only one." Marie kissed Nevaeh softly. "We'll take things slow for now. Go on a few dates. See where we go from here."

"Yeah, well, I kind of fucked up the taking things slow part," Marie grinned.

"Worth it!" Nevaeh laughed. She glanced over at her nightstand where an alarm clock sat. "So do you still want to help me make breakfast for these clowns? It's like ten o'clock."

"Yeah, let's do it." They got dressed and Nevaeh put their wet clothes in the washing machine. They walked downstairs only to see the same scene as they saw before they went upstairs. Cassidy and Deja still slept peacefully on the couch. They looked cute together. Deja, like Marie, was a total femme. She went well with Cassidy's tomboyish femme look. Both were very attractive. "Wouldn't they make a cute couple?" Marie whispered.

"For realsies! I just thought the same thing."

"For realsies?" Marie asked with a giggle. Nevaeh and Marie were in the kitchen for about thirty minutes before the house started to smell like bacon. Nevaeh did most of the cooking, while Marie gathered all the plates and utensils, rinsed strawberries, and prepared mimosas. While they were doing their thing in the kitchen, Imani and Nia wandered in.

"Something smells delicious," Nia complimented as she yawned and stretched. She walked over and kissed Marie on the cheek.

"Well, well, well. Look who has decided to grace us with their presence," Nevaeh said playfully with a smirk on her face. "How was your night?" That question made Marie snicker.

Imani knew what Nevaeh was referring to, so she retorted, "It was great. How was your morning?"

Nevaeh and Marie looked at one another, blushed, and then looked away. "Touché, my friend," Nevaeh responded. "Touché."

Next to enter the kitchen were Tiara and Camilla. "Hey, guys," Imani said. "You guys slept in the same bed?" she asked teasingly.

"Yeah," Tiara said. "And before your nosey ass asks, no we did not hook up. My head is pounding. I need a beer to cure this hangover." She went into the refrigerator. "Anyone else?"

"Nope," everyone responded.

"I'm making mimosas, Tiara, if you want I can fix you one really quick," Marie offered.

"Ah. Yes. That sounds even better. Thank you."

"Not a problem," Marie said as she made Tiara a drink.

"So, Nia," Camilla said, "how was your night?" Everyone giggled.

"Man, why is everyone so concerned how our night went?" Nia was on the defensive side. "Obviously, you guys heard it went great and I'm hoping the morning goes even better!"

Imani looked up and had that *yeah, I'm the shit* look on her face. "Well, there it is, folks!" Nevaeh shouted. They all laughed.

✶ ✶ ✶

"Cassidy," Deja said tiredly. "Cassidy." Cassidy made some grunting noises but refused to wake up. "Cassidy!" Deja demanded.

"What?" Cassidy perked up. "Oooouuu, do I smell bacon?"

Deja laughed, "That's why I was trying to wake you up. Somebody is cooking."

"Maybe we should get up then." Deja looked at her as if she were saying no shit. They got up and wandered into the kitchen. "What is that delicious smell?" Cassidy asked.

"Ayyyyeee!" everyone shouted in unison.

"Our snuggle bugs are awake," joked Imani. "Be happy you guys woke up when you did because I was about to come jump on you to wake you up."

Nevaeh pulled Imani to the side. "Hey, what's up with Nia?"

"What do you mean?"

"I mean she's Marie's homegirl, and I don't want it to end up a nasty drama-filled hot mess. I know how you can be."

Imani chuckled, "Chill out, man, Nia and I have discussed it. She heads back home on Tuesday and is just looking to have a little fun this weekend. She's not expecting anything, and neither am I."

"That better be all."

"I wouldn't do that to you, Nevaeh."

"Yeah, I know. I just like Marie a lot and I don't want anything to fuck that up."

"Oh, I know you do. I got homie."

Nevaeh smiled, "Appreciate you."

"All right, guys!" Nevaeh made a single clap with her hands. "Let's eat, drink, and be merry." She spoke cheerfully. As everyone was fixing their plates, Marie was handing out mimosas. "Everyone eat and drink as much as you want. There is plenty."

FIVE

"Man, breakfast was delicious, guys. Thank you very much." Cassidy thanked Marie and Nevaeh with a hug.

"Oh, girl, you know you're welcome," Nevaeh cheerfully responded.

"I think I'm going to get going, though. I need to go be hungover in my own bed," Cassidy said with a smile on her face. "I'm excited to see what's on the agenda for next weekend. Maybe we could go out to eat and then party or something."

"Hell, yeah," Imani chimed in.

"All right, guys, as always keep me in the loop. Love you guys." Cassidy walked around and gave everyone a cheek kiss and hug.

When she got to Deja, Deja whispered into her ear, "I need to talk to you for a second."

"All right."

Deja walked out to the front porch with Cassidy and closed the door behind them. "What's going on?" Cassidy asked.

"So what's your deal?" Deja vaguely asked.

"What's my deal? What does that even mean?"

"I mean, like. Ya know."

"No," Cassidy said with a smirk on her face. "I don't know."

"Well, shit," Deja responded bashfully. "I mean I really enjoyed spending time with you last night. Do you want to, like, get to know each other better or no?" Deja said shyly, "Ya know. What's your deal?"

"Ah, that deal. Well, I know that I am attracted to you. Strike that. I am very attracted to you, and I would like to get to know you more."

"For real?" Deja said with some pep in her voice.

"For real. Well, I'm not doing anything today but lounging around, if you want to come back to my apartment with me." She pulled out her phone. "My Lyft says it'll be here in about five minutes, so you don't really have much time to decide, but—"

"I'm in," Deja interrupted.

Cassidy smiled. "Okay, well, go get your stuff and I'll wait for you."

Deja went back into the house to gather her stuff. While she was in the house, the Lyft pulled up and Cassidy hopped into the back seat. A woman who appeared to be in her mid-thirties was driving. "How's it going?" Cassidy asked once she got into the car.

"Great! It says I'm taking you to Northwood Apartments?"

"Yes ma'am, but I'm waiting on a friend to come out of the house."

"Alrighty, not a problem." They chatted casually until Deja finally walked out of the house and hopped into the back seat.

"Deja?" the lady asked, looking in the rearview mirror.

"Oh shit," Deja said under her breath. Cassidy looked confused. "Margaret. Hey." Deja forced a smile.

"Yeah. You never called me back." Margaret wasted no time. "I have been waiting to hear from you."

"Margaret, I don't think this is the appropriate time to have this conversation." Deja was annoyed.

"Really, Deja? Not the appropriate time?" Margaret put the car into drive, and they took off. "Then when is the appropriate time? I thought the times that I called you to meet up would've been the appropriate time, but you didn't seem to agree."

Cassidy sat in the car silently but listened. "Margaret," Deja said with more annoyance.

"Don't Margaret me. I hate when you do that. Who is she? Is this your girlfriend or something? Why can't we have this conversation?"

"Margaret, I don't have to explain anything to you. We're not together anymore. This isn't the appropriate time because you're working and on the verge of catching this one star if you keep fuckin' around with me." Deja closed her eyes and rested her head back on the seat. They all rode in silence back to Cassidy's apartment complex. Once they arrived, Cassidy and Deja hopped out.

"Cassidy, wait up." Margaret let out a sigh. "I would like to apologize for the mess I said in the car. Deja was right, that was highly inappropriate and unprofessional. I was just caught off guard."

Cassidy was a very understanding person and didn't allow it to show that the situation bothered her. "No problem, Margaret. I hope things get better for you."

"Thanks. Just watch out. If you're not careful, you'll fall for her too." With that, Margaret pulled off.

As they walked up to Cassidy's apartment Deja asked, "What did Margaret say to you?"

"Uh, nothing. Just apologized for acting the way that she did."

Deja scoffed, "I'm sorry that happened. It was completely unexpected, and it must have been awkward for you."

Cassidy put her key into the door and opened it. "Yeah, it was a little weird, but not much we can do about it now. It happened." She left it at that.

Cassidy opened the door to her apartment. It was a decent-sized two-bedroom place. She didn't really have an eye for decorating, so it was bare.

Deja noticed how bare it was. "You know, I'm pretty good at decorating if you want some help."

Cassidy chuckled, "Yeah, I guess I could use some help. I'm not good with that kind of stuff." Deja stood there awkwardly. "Here, let me take your jacket," Cassidy offered. "Take your shoes off, sit down, make yourself at home."

"Okay, cool. Thanks."

"I'm going to grab myself a beer, you want one?" Cassidy asked as she walked to the kitchen.

"Uh yeah, thanks. That would be great."

Cassidy came back into the living room, handed Deja a beer, and they both sat down on the couch. Deja noticed that Cassidy seemed a little distant. "Are you still thinking about that conversation with Margaret in the Lyft?"

"Kind of."

"She's old news. You don't have to worry about her."

"She didn't seem like old news. Seemed like she has current-event type feelings."

"She's old news to me. I don't have feelings for her anymore. It's over, for me at least. She just doesn't understand that."

"I just don't like drama, Deja. I've managed to keep myself out of that kind of life, and I would like to keep it that way."

"Cassidy," Deja said as she took in a deep breath, "there is no drama. I will make sure of that."

"The way she said what she said before she pulled off just has me feeling kind of weird."

"I thought you said she just apologized?" Cassidy just stared straight ahead. Deja sighed. "What'd she say to you?"

"She told me to watch out and if I'm not careful I'll fall for you too. What does that mean? Are you going around town breaking hearts? Like should I be nervous?"

"Ugh, that woman. No, I'm not going around town breaking hearts. It's a long story."

Cassidy took a sip of her beer. "Well, we have plenty of beer and sunlight. I also think I have some vodka left if you prefer liquor."

"Are you trying to get me drunk, Cassidy?" Deja asked flirtatiously.

"Maybe," Cassidy responded with a smirk. "But come on. We're supposed to be getting to know one another better, right? So, let's start with you and Margaret. Sounds like a legitimate place to start."

"How about a few beers in and we'll get there? Can we just start on a lighter note?"

"Okay, fine. Well, where would you like to start?"

"I would like to start with making out. I didn't get a chance to kiss you like I wanted to last night."

Cassidy turned and looked into Deja's eyes. She took another swig of her beer and put it down on the coffee table. "Well, show me how you wanted to kiss me."

Deja set her beer down on the coffee table and slowly straddled Cassidy. Deja brushed Cassidy's brunette hair behind her ear before she went in for a kiss. She kissed her softly on the lips, then pulled away to stare into Cassidy's big, emerald green eyes. She could tell she wanted more. This time Cassidy brought her face to Deja's. The kiss began slowly, and Cassidy finally got the confirmation to slip her tongue into Deja's mouth. The feeling of electricity that flowed through Cassidy was something she had never felt from the couple of other women she had been with. The way Deja's warm tongue felt against hers had her filled with ecstasy. As the kiss got heavier and hotter, Deja began to moan. Cassidy felt Deja's hips begin to grind on her as the kiss progressed. Cassidy put her hands on Deja's hips and followed her rhythm. Deja slowly pulled her face away from Cassidy, with her eyes still closed and said, "That's how I wanted to kiss you."

"Yeah?" Cassidy asked, slightly out of breath. "Well, I tell you what. If that was a distraction to keep me from asking about Margaret, you nailed it."

Deja smiled and kissed Cassidy on the lips again. "Looks like you've figured out my tactics. At such an early stage. Good for you." She climbed off her lap and sat next to her. "I really wanted to do that."

"I'm glad you did because I did too." There was a pause. "Now what?" Cassidy asked.

"Lie down," Deja instructed. Cassidy obliged, lay back placing the back of her head on the couch armrest. Deja lay on top of her and placed her head on Cassidy's chest. Cassidy exhaled from happiness and began to lightly run her fingers up and down Deja's back. "Mm, that feels so good. I love having my back rubbed."

"Noted," Cassidy responded.

"So, I'll start off on this getting to know one another thing. Didn't you say you were stationed here like three years ago? You and your friends seem tight knit. I'm curious to find out how all of you and your friends know one another."

"Well, Nevaeh and Imani met in high school and have been best friends ever since they discovered they shared a love for women. They both met Tiara in an LGBTQ+ group when they were in their freshman year of college. Um, Anita and Jasmine met because Jasmine bought Anita a coffee at Starbucks. Jasmine had the barista put her name and number on Anita's cup. Anita called to thank her, and they've been together for about nine years."

"Aw, that's really sweet. I thought that kind of stuff only happened in movies," Deja commented. "And nine years? Wow. That is amazing."

"Yeah, I love them. Anyway, Nevaeh is a successful event planner. Well, Anita and Jasmine wanted to host a Third Anniversary event, and they decided to go with Nevaeh to plan it."

"I've been to a few of Nevaeh's events."

"You have?" Cassidy wondered.

"Yeah. She's good. Marie has been low-key stalking her and pulling us to them."

"Really?" Cassidy was shocked.

"Yeah, but Marie has been wanting to talk to Nevaeh on that level for a while now but didn't want to seem like she was throwing herself at Nevaeh." Deja chuckled. "I'm glad Marie and Nevaeh finally linked up beyond social interactions."

"Wow. Learn something new every day."

"Yeah, anyway, continue with your story."

"Right." Cassidy continued, "So, Nevaeh needed a photographer. She had seen some of Eliana's work and loved it. She's pretty brilliant when it comes to photography. Nevaeh hired her to photograph Anita and Jasmine's event. They all became friends through the process. So, Nevaeh invited the three of them to go out with her, Imani, and Tiara one night, and they all clicked. I believe Eliana met Trisha shortly after they all started partying together."

"Trisha was the chick that Eliana was arguing with at the party last night?"

Cassidy made a sound of disgust. "Yeah. They've been on-again off-again for like the past five or six years. None of us really claim Trish, but we put up with her because we love Ellie. Trisha is the worst. I'm not too sure why Eliana continues to put herself through that relationship. She deserves better."

"Yeah, Trisha seemed awful. I overheard them fussing. Trisha pretty much ignored Eliana and was flirting with other women?"

"Honestly, that's nothing new with Trisha." Cassidy carried on with her story. "Anyway, they all made it a tradition where they all would get together at least once a week, typically Fridays, for drinks in or out or better known as Friends' Friday. That's where they vent about the week and blow off steam. I came into the picture a couple of months after I got stationed here. I finally decided it was time for me to go out and try to meet people. I ended up at the bar where they were hanging out because it was the first lesbian bar that popped up on Google. I was awkwardly sitting by myself because I didn't know anyone yet. Of course, Nevaeh tried to hit on me but I guess I was too shy." Cassidy slightly chuckled. "So, she decided to introduce me to the crew. I can't even lie, I was a little skeptical at first because I was the only white and bisexual girl, but they didn't care about any of that. They welcomed me with open arms. It was refreshing to find a group of women who I could relate to and be myself around. I guess I was the piece they were missing. It was as if I had known them for years."

"That's great you were able to find your crew. Seems like it was fate how everything lined up for you ladies. I can definitely see you being too shy though," Deja teased.

Cassidy giggled. "Yeah, I can't help it. I've always been that way. I get even more shy around lesbians because they can be very judgmental when it comes to bisexuals. I approach them with caution. I've actually opened up quite a bit since I've been hanging around them. They make me feel comfortable. They're like my family away from my family."

"Oh, so you're bisexual?" Deja asked.

"Yes. Is that an issue?"

"Honestly it used to be, but I'm trying to get out of that mindset. It's not fair to the bisexual women out there to be judged because of who they love. Kind of back-stepping to do so, if you ask me."

Cassidy smiled, "I couldn't agree more. Anyway, enough about that, what about you and your friends? How'd you all meet?"

Deja responded, "Oh, man, our story really isn't all that interesting. Camilla, Nia, Marie, and I are all childhood friends. When we graduated from high school, Camilla and Nia went to the same college. Marie knew she wanted to own her own bar, so she started aggressively working on that, and I started doing small gigs to get some extra cash as I worked. Nia moved out of town for a job opportunity but comes home every chance she gets. Throughout everything, we have stayed in contact because they are my sisters. We've been through a lot together, and I am so happy that we are still in each other's lives. Like you and your friends, they're my family."

"That's really sweet," Cassidy encouraged. "What do you mean by gigs, though? You're in a band?"

"Actually," Deja corrected, "I do standup comedy."

"What?!" Cassidy was shocked. "I mean, don't get me wrong, I think you're funny, but I never pegged you as a standup comedian. That's kind of hot."

Deja giggled, "Thanks. Maybe you can come to a show one of these days."

"I would love that," Cassidy smiled.

SIX

Eliana woke up by herself in her bed. She and Trisha had gotten into a fight at the party. Early that day, while they were enjoying their day drinking and bowling, Jordan flirted with Trisha as if Eliana wasn't there. For understandable reasons, Eliana got upset. When they got back to the apartment, they had makeup sex and went to the party. Unfortunately, alcohol brings out some deep-seated emotions. They were having a good time until Trisha started flirting with other women, which set Eliana off. Anita's law enforcement went into motion and she kicked Trisha out. Eliana was of course welcome to stay if she wanted to, but she opposed. She decided that she was no longer in the mood to party. She called a cab and went home.

When she awoke, she didn't have any missed calls or texts from Trisha, which made her feel annoyed. She decided to shrug it off and lay back down. When she threw the covers over her head, her phone buzzed. She saw that it was a text from Nevaeh.

Hey, Ellie you good? I saw you and Trishasorus Rex had a fight at the party. Just wanted to check in.

Hey Nevaeh, thanks for checking in. Woke up alone in my bed, no texts or calls from Trish. Not really surprising though. And stop calling her that lol. You know I love that girl.

Yeah well, I love you. I just want to make sure you're good. You already know I don't think she's good for you. None of us do.

Trust me I know. You guys tell me enough. I'm going to try and find her though. I'll hit you up later.

Yeah man. I'll ttyl.

She stared at her phone wondering where Trisha could possibly be, and why she didn't even attempt to get in contact with her after she assured her love for her yesterday before they went bowling. Eliana didn't want to, but she decided to be the bigger person and texted Trisha.

Hey, Trisha. Just wanted to check in to make sure you were ok. I want to talk about last night. Hopefully, we can put it behind us. About five minutes later her phone buzzed.

Hey, baby. I would love nothing more than to put this nonsense behind us. I know we have our differences which cause us to fight, but I love you and I want us to work.

All right. Do you want me to come to your apartment?

No it's ok. Last night was my fault. I'll come to you. I'll see you in a bit. I love you, Eliana.

See you in a bit.

About an hour later Eliana heard keys at the door and Trisha stepped through the threshold.

"Baby, I am so sorry," Trisha said as she closed the door behind her. "You know how I get when I get alcohol in my system, I flirt."

"Look, Trish. I want us to work," Eliana stated as Trisha walked across her studio apartment and sat next to her on the bed. "I really do, but I don't know how much more of this I can take."

"Ellie, don't say that."

"It's true. Our sexual chemistry is off the charts, but the other stuff." She paused. "We are broken and at this point, I'm not sure how to fix it. Sexual chemistry isn't enough. I need more out of a relationship than just great sex."

"I know that, and you deserve more. I want to be that person to give you more. I really do. If you would just give me another chance."

"I've been giving you five years of chances, Trisha! That's the problem!" Eliana shouted as she looked away, trying to hold back tears. "Every single time I give you a chance you fail. Miserably, might I add. Before we went bowling yesterday, you assured me that you loved me, and I believed you. Then you allow Jordan to flirt with you right in front of my face. Like I was some irrelevant side chick. Not to mention that you blatantly flirted with other women at the party. You acted as if you didn't even have a girlfriend. And then God only knows where you disappeared to last night. I didn't even get a fucking text."

"I know," Trisha defeatedly agreed.

"You say you know, but I don't think you really do because you keep doing this shit. You are constantly making me look weak in front of my friends, causing me to contemplate my self-worth. I hate that I allow you to make me feel this way."

"Ellie. I'm a mess, and I know this. I can't do this without you. You are my rock and I'm sorry that I keep putting you through this nonsense. If you give me one more chance, I promise this time I will make it right."

Eliana scoffed, "I've heard that way too many times to count."

"This time I mean it."

Eliana glared into Trisha's eyes. "You get one more chance, Trisha." She held up her pointer finger. "One more."

PART II
(THREE MONTHS LATER)

SEVEN

It was a Wednesday afternoon. Nevaeh, Tiara, and Imani decided to end their workday early and meet up at a popular restaurant to have lunch together.

"Damn, Nevaeh. You and Marie have been talking for what? Like three or four months now? When are you going to ask that girl to be your girlfriend?" Tiara teased as she took a bite of her pasta.

"Man, I don't know."

"Don't tell us you're getting bored, Nevaeh," Imani pleaded.

"I'm not. That's the crazy thing. I would've moved onto the next by now, you guys know that, but I can't shake this one."

"Maybe it's because you're not supposed to shake this one," Tiara stated. "Go for it with her. Let your little lesbian heart free from that prison cell, girl. I know she's ready for it."

"Yeah, I've actually been thinking about asking her to be my girlfriend, but just haven't found the right time."

"What is even the right time?" Imani asked. "Just fucking do it."

"Well, we have a date tonight. I might go for it then."

"That's what I'm talking about," Tiara encouraged. "Go get your girl!"

"T, you watch way too many romantic chick flicks," Nevaeh said playfully.

They all laughed.

Nevaeh wasn't surprised how hard she had fallen for Marie. Marie was everything she ever wanted in a woman. Their personalities meshed very well with one another. They made each other laugh, could have a deep intellectual discussion, had similar interests, and the sex was incredible. Nevaeh knew she could see herself falling in love with her and that's what terrified her the most.

Her ex-girlfriend, Saria, had done a number on her. Nevaeh met Saria sophomore year in college while working with the LGBTQ+ focus group. She was Nevaeh's first love. Saria was studying to become a journalist. Nevaeh fell for her like she was falling for Marie, except a lot faster. Saria was Moroccan. She and her parents moved to the United States when Saria was a baby, with her older brother, Noah. She was stunning, so Nevaeh immediately was mesmerized by her looks. When they got to know one another, she realized how much she enjoyed her personality as well. They would study together, slept over in each other's room. Their friends loved them together, and they were inseparable. Saria was a known lesbian to her peers but closeted to her very religious parents.

Her older brother knew that she was gay, and he loved her all the same. He warned her to be careful because their parents would not approve. Saria would tell Nevaeh that she was going to tell her parents about them but always seemed to lose her nerve. Nevaeh vowed to be there for Saria every time Saria promised to tell her parents. Although Nevaeh never pressured Saria to come out, it stung each time Saria lost her nerve. Nevaeh understood that it was

Saria's decision when and where to come out, but it didn't necessarily mean that it made things any easier on Nevaeh's emotional state.

There was no doubt about it that Saria loved Nevaeh, but she was terrified of coming out to her parents and losing everything that she had worked so hard for. They dated all throughout college, and their friends thought they were going to be in it for the long run and were ready to support Saria if her parents disowned her. Nevaeh had met Saria's parents many times, and they loved her. Nevaeh, of course, was Saria's "best friend from school" and would even femme it up when she visited so it didn't raise any flags.

One day, about halfway through senior year, Saria approached Nevaeh in tears. Saria's parents had found a "nice Jewish boy" and they were dead set on them getting married once she graduated from college. Saria thought he was kind and handsome, but of course she was not attracted to him. He, on the other hand, fell for her rather quickly. Nevaeh pleaded for Saria not to do it and to tell her parents about them, but she refused. Saria kissed Nevaeh for the last time and that was it. In an instant, Nevaeh's world changed. She was devastated. She had never felt heartache like she did at that moment in time.

About a year later, Nevaeh received a text message from a number that she hadn't seen in a while. Saria. The instant she looked at the phone and saw her name, she had a rush of emotions. She never deleted her number because she wasn't ready to let her go. She stayed single and detached from other women outside of her friends in hopes Saria would come back to her. The text was a link to an invitation to Saria's wedding. She was getting married to that "nice Jewish boy." Nevaeh's stomach dropped, and her eyes filled with tears at the thought of Saria getting married to someone else, let alone a man. Nevaeh respectfully declined the invitation, deleted, and blocked the number, never to hear from Saria again.

After that text, Nevaeh was able to put Saria behind her. She wasn't sure if Saria sent her that text on purpose or not, but in her mind, it was the closure that she needed to assure that Saria no longer loved her. It was Saria's way of saying I release you. So, Nevaeh moved on, but she vowed never to allow another woman to make her feel that way again. Although Nevaeh understood why Saria left, the pain of losing her was unbearable.

The women finished their lunches, paid the bill, and left. Tiara decided to go home to work on one of her clients' meal and training plans. Imani decided to visit one of the girls she was dating, and Nevaeh went home to relax before her possible big date with Marie later that evening.

EIGHT

"So you hit me up when it's convenient for you, huh?" Simone (one of Imani's girls) said through the receiver of the phone. "When none of your other girls are readily available, you call me," she said with an attitude.

Imani rolled her eyes and sucked her teeth. "It ain't even like that."

Imani knew it was like that. She kept at least one girl as her main but would never fully commit to her. Along with her main girl, she would have two or three other girls she was able to call when one wasn't acting the way she wanted her to. She was smart with her moves and would never date women who interacted with the same people. She was good at playing the field and loved the thrill.

"Well, I feel like it's like that. I hear from you like once a week. And when I do hear from you, it's to hook up. I like our sex, but I don't like the way you make me feel."

"I'm not trying to make you feel any kind of way, but good. I want you. I want to be with you. I'm just not ready to settle down yet. Plain and simple."

"I know you're not ready to settle down. I don't really think I am either. I don't really know what I want."

"I know what you want. Me to come over."

"You're so full of yourself," Simone scoffed. "I hate it but can't help but to like it." She sighed. "Fine, come over. The door will be unlocked."

"Bet."

✳ ✳ ✳

Imani pulled up to Simone's house. Even though Simone told her the door was unlocked, out of habit she knocked, then opened it. "Hello? Simone?" she called out as she peeked her head in.

"Come on in and lock the door behind you, please." Imani did as instructed. She stepped in and locked the door.

"Where are you?" Imani called out. As she stood in the living room, she caught a glimpse of Simone's cellphone sitting on the coffee table. It was 5S with a cracked screen, "And she still hit me back right away." She laughed to herself and did a little dance.

"I'm in the kitchen."

When she walked into the kitchen, to her surprise Simone was sitting on the island, legs wide open. She wore matching ruby red lingerie, a black silk robe that slightly had fallen off her shoulder, and stilettos. Imani's mouth fell open. *Fuck me*, she said to herself.

Simone said nothing. She looked at her seductively and motioned for her to come over. Imani licked her lips as she slowly approached Simone. She pulled her dreadlocks up, so they wouldn't be in the way. As she walked up to her, Imani admired every inch of her body. She loved how the natural sunlight hit her milk chocolate complexion. She envisioned herself sucking on her perky B-cup breasts being pushed up by her bra. She imagined running her hands up and down her freshly shaved legs, kissing her tight abs as she worked her way down. She was mesmerized. She was turned on and her mind ran wild. When she reached Simone, she grabbed her thighs and went in for a kiss. Simone pressed her pointer finger against Imani's lips. That stopped Imani in her tracks. Simone spread her legs wider and motioned for Imani to go down on her with her eyes. Imani was turned on even more by the take-charge attitude and the silent commands.

Imani obeyed and dropped to her knees. She slowly kissed and licked Simone's inner thigh. She reached her spot, slid her panties over, and dove in. She ate Simone until she climaxed. After she climaxed, she kept going. Simone got to the point where she couldn't take it anymore and pulled her face up to meet hers. Their breath was heavy as they kissed deeply. As they kissed, Imani picked Simone up and stood her up. She spun her around. She slowly disrobed her, allowing it to drop to the floor. She then unhooked her bra, releasing the beautiful, perky B-cup breasts. Simone leaned her hands on the counter, as Imani kissed her way down her body. She reached her panty line and slowly pulled them down. Simone stepped out. Imani stood up and kissed her neck. Imani reached around her, running her hand down her abs to her clit. Simone let out a moan. That was Imani's cue, and she began to apply pressure to her clit. Simone's juices dripped down her thigh.

"Fuck, Imani. You feel so good," she moaned. "Do you have your strap-on?"

Imani knew why she came to Simone's house, so she had put her strap-on on before she left the house. "Yes," Imani whispered out of breath in her ear.

"I want you to fuck me with it until I cum."

Imani stopped. Simone turned around. "Come with me." Imani led Simone to her dining table. "Undress me," Imani commanded in a sensual voice.

Simone did as she was told and unbuttoned Imani's shirt. She let it fall to the ground. She then removed Imani's pants.

"Turn around and bend over." Imani instructed.

Simone smirked and bent over the table. She elevated her ass. Imani put some lube on her strap-on.

Simone let out a moan as she slid in. "Shit."

Once Imani was in, she stroked slowly to get her rhythm going and then quickened the pace. They moaned in unison as they panted heavier. Simone's breasts bounced to the pace of the thrusts. Imani reached her hands around Simone, used one to play with her nipple and the other to play with her clit as she fucked her from behind. Simone couldn't hold out much longer and climaxed. Her body shook. As Imani witnessed her, shortly after she did the same. Imani took a minute to compose herself then slowly slid the strap-on out of Simone. Simone twitched as she exited.

"Fuck. That was good." Simone said breathlessly.

"Yeah, that was a lot of fun."

"We should do it again sometime," Simone smirked.

"Yeah, next time don't give me so much pushback," Imani commanded.

"Whateva." Simone rolled her eyes.

NINE

Eliana sat at her desk as she worked on a photography project that she had picked up.

"Eliana," Trisha said softly as she sat on Eliana's bed.

Eliana was so wrapped up in her project that she didn't realize Trisha had called her name.

"Eliana." Trisha paused. "Eliana, I'm pregnant," she said in a disbelieving tone.

Eliana scrunched her face to keep her glasses on. Her mouth was agape as she continued to edit. "What'd you say about a segment, babe?"

"I said I'm pregnant!" she shouted as she held back tears.

Eliana stared blankly at the screen as she slowly closed her mouth. Her back stiffened. The silence was so intense that you could hear a pin drop.

"Whose is it?" Eliana interrupted her in a monotone.

"Why is that important?"

"Whose is it?"

"I don't think that—"

"Damn it, Trisha! Whose fucking baby is it?!" she snapped and spun around in her desk chair to face Trisha.

"Jordan's!" Trisha burst into tears.

"Jordan?" Eliana scoffed in disbelief. "From the bowling alley? The guy you told me I had nothing to worry about? The Jordan that had me feeling like I was going insane because you made it seem like I was making shit up? That Jordan!?" Trisha sat there quietly with the look of guilt on her face. "You don't have to answer those questions. Your face says it all." She paused. "How long has this been going on?"

"Why does that matter?"

"This isn't the time for you to ask questions, Trisha. This is your time to answer. How long has it been going on?!"

Trisha sighed. "You remember that party that Nevaeh, Imani, and Tiara threw a few months back?" Eliana glared at her. "Of course you do. Well after we fought, I stormed out, and I reached out to Jordan for comfort. The intention wasn't there, but we kind of just hooked up. We've been hooking up since."

"Kind of just hooked up?" Eliana asked softly. "But the intentions were obviously there the times after you just kind of hooked up," she said in a mocking tone. "You've been fucking him and then coming to me, making promises like everything was going to be okay, kissing me with that mouth that his dick has probably been in? You know what?" She stood up. "I'm going to need you to get out," she instructed calmly.

Trisha said through tears, "You don't want to talk about this?"

"Talk?" Eliana took a deep breath, closed her eyes, and exhaled. "At this point what could we possibly have to talk about? I'm over here trusting you, ignoring people who I love and trust. They're warning me about you. I'm taking you back time after time, believing you would change, standing up for you like an idiot! All the while you're out there fucking around. Shit, I don't even know if he was the only one. He's just the only one that got you caught up." Eliana took another deep breath to gather herself. "Give me your keys and get out of my apartment, Trisha."

"But, Ellie. I was hoping we would consider raising this baby together. This could be ours. We can have a family. It could help fix us."

"Are you fucking psychotic?" Eliana asked. "I mean you've got to be if you think for a second I would consider parenting a child with you! 'We' don't need to be fixed, Trisha, you do. Get your shit and get out of my motherfucking apartment."

"But I—"

"Trisha," Eliana interrupted, "you are one fucking word away from shitting your teeth out."

Trisha cried as she gathered her things. She placed her copy of Eliana's keys on the table. She opened the door with Eliana behind her. As she stood in the door frame she turned around. "Even through all this, I just want you to know that I still lo—"

Eliana pushed Trisha out of her apartment with one arm and slammed the door with the other. "We can raise the child together," she said to herself in a mocking tone. "I might be an idiot for falling in that trap, but she got me fucked up if she actually thought that was about to happen." She walked over to her bed.

She sat down and put her face in her hands as she replayed in her mind the events that just took place. Eliana began to laugh. She let out a loud deep sigh. That sigh released five years of frustration. Five years of manipulation. Five years of not putting herself first. She was shocked to feel more relief than sadness. *"Now what?"* she said aloud. That was a weighted question for Eliana. She knew she was afraid to be alone, but she knew she couldn't go back to Trisha.

There were so many emotions that flowed through her that tears began to fall from her eyes. She felt as if a weight had been lifted off her shoulders. Like a toxin finally left her system. She felt free.

TEN

"Yes. I have a reservation for two," Nevaeh told the hostess.

"What's the name?"

"Nevaeh."

"Ah. Yes, here you are. Reservation for six o'clock for two. Please follow me," the hostess smiled.

Nevaeh had reserved a table in Geibourne's most romantic restaurant. The overhead lighting was dim, and a live R&B band played as a woman with a sweet, soft, soulful voice sang on a stage. The music was at a perfect volume where you could still talk to your date as well as hear the music. Each table was preset with a tablecloth, silverware, dinnerware, and candlelight, and Nevaeh had called ahead to have a half dozen pink tulips placed in the middle of the table.

"Here you are, ladies. Please have a seat. Your server will be right with you."

"Thank you," the girls responded in unison.

"My pleasure. I hope you two enjoy your evening." She smiled as she walked off.

"Oh wow, pink tulips. They're beautiful." Marie sniffed the flowers.

"I'm glad you like them," Nevaeh smiled.

"Tulips are my favorite flower."

"I know."

Marie glanced around the restaurant. She noticed no other table had flower arrangements. "Did you have them placed here?" she asked.

Nevaeh nodded.

"Aw, Nevaeh that's so sweet. Thank you very much."

The server walked up. "Hello, ladies. My name is Leon, and I will be your server for the evening. May I interest you in a glass of our specialty wine?"

"Do you drink wine?" Nevaeh asked Marie.

"From time to time."

"Sure." Nevaeh turned to the server, "We will take two glasses of your specialty wine, please."

"Sounds great, and will you be having appetizers, or do you need a little more time?"

The girls looked at one another. "We'll take a little more time. When the drinks come out, we should be ready to put in our order."

"Okay. Then I will return shortly with your drinks."

"Wow, this place is pricey." Marie scanned the menu.

"No. Please don't worry about the prices, just get what you want."

"Alrighty. Well, this salmon sounds pretty intriguing."

"Yeah, I was looking at this lobster tail myself."

"Dang, that looks good too! Great, now I can't decide," Marie pouted.

"Well, how about you can try a little of mine if I can try a little of yours?"

"But what if I like yours more than I like mine?"

"I mean you can always just sit there and watch me enjoy my food. I can describe to you what every bite tastes like. I'll describe it in such vivid detail that it'll be like you're the one eating it," Nevaeh joked.

"Well, damn. You wouldn't trade with me?"

"I'm not giving up my lobster tail!"

"I guess that will be a risk I'll have to take because this salmon looks bomb."

Leon returned with their wine. "Alrighty, ladies here is your wine. Are you two ready to order, or do you need more time?"

"No, I think we're ready."

"Awesome, what are we having?" Leon pulled out his pen and pad.

"I will have the lobster tail, please," Nevaeh requested.

"Excellent choice. And for you?" Leon turned to Marie.

"I think I am going to go with the salmon, please."

"Yes. Yes. Another great choice. Okay, ladies, let me get those out of your way." He took their menus. "I will put your orders in and your food will be out shortly."

"Thank you," they responded. Leon smiled pleasantly and walked away.

"So, Nevaeh. I want to get to know you more."

"Uh oh. Okay, what's on your mind?" Nevaeh questioned.

"So, what's your type?" Marie took a sip of her wine.

"In what sense?"

"Hmm, physical."

"Well, at the risk of sounding corny, you are my type physically."

"All right," Marie smirked. "What about personality?"

"Uh, smart."

"Well, I own and run my own business. Successfully, might I add. What's next?"

Nevaeh smiled flirtatiously. "Knows how to party."

Marie raised her hand to get Leon's attention. He made eye contact with her and walked over. "Yes, miss?"

"Hey Leon, do you mind grabbing us two top-shelf tequila shots, preferably silver, before our food comes out?"

Leon smirked. "Of course, miss. Will you be having limes with your shots?"

"We will," she responded.

"Right away." Leon scampered off.

Marie turned back to Nevaeh. "Next."

Nevaeh licked her lips. "Also doesn't mind staying in the house and hanging out from time to time."

"Well, I have a subscription to Netflix, Hulu, and Amazon Prime. I mean no big deal, though," Marie smiled with a shrug.

"Adventurous."

"I've been skydiving before and scuba diving, too. A whale swam by me. It was slightly terrifying, but I would love to do it again."

"Family oriented," Nevaeh continued.

"I love my family. We cool."

"Goes for what she wants."

Leon returned to the table with their shots. "Here you are, ladies. I really hope you enjoy."

They smiled at him. "Thanks."

"Cheers." Leon nodded as he walked off.

"Well, we're here. Still doing this dating thing," Marie continued. "So I think that proves I go for what I want. Cheers." She lifted her shot glass.

"Cheers." Nevaeh followed, and they tapped their glasses together.

They threw the shots back, then proceeded to eat the lime.

Nevaeh cleared her throat. "Damn tequila. Uh, I guess the last, but certainly not the least, thing that I look for is a goofy sense of humor. Somebody I know I can have fun with."

"I know tequila makes your clothes come off," Marie smiled and winked.

Nevaeh chuckled, "Well played."

"Alrighty, ladies." Leon returned with their food. "Here is your salmon." He placed Marie's plate in front of her. "And here is your lobster tail." He placed Nevaeh's plate in front of her. "Here, let me get those out of your way." He picked up the shot glasses. "Is there anything else I may get you? Perhaps another glass of wine?"

"Uh, yes, actually that would be great," Marie responded.

"Right away."

✶ ✶ ✶

Nevaeh and Marie laughed until they had tears in their eyes. They talked and got to know one another on a different level over a fantastic dinner.

"Wow, I am stuffed." Marie sat back in her chair.

"Me too," Nevaeh agreed.

"Oh man, I love this song." Marie closed her eyes as she bobbed her head while the band played one of her favorite slow jams.

Nevaeh smiled. Her beauty never ceased to amaze Nevaeh. "Well, we have time. Would you like to dance?" She held out her hand.

Marie smiled, "I would love to." She placed her hand in Nevaeh's.

Nevaeh stood up and placed Marie's arm in hers as they walked to the small dance floor in front of the stage. Nevaeh took Marie's hand and spun her around.

"Nevaeh. My my my, I didn't know you were such a smooth dancer."

Nevaeh grinned, "I'm sure I can show you a few things that you didn't know I could do." She took a deep breath. It was now or never. "Do you want to be my girlfriend?" she blurted out. "Like, make this official?"

Marie smiled from ear to ear. "I thought you'd never ask."

"So is that a yes?"

"That's definitely a yes." Marie kissed her on the lips.

A few other couples followed their lead and decided to get up and slow dance as well. The girls slow danced into the night.

ELEVEN

Anita had decided a few months earlier that she wanted to spend the rest of her life with Jasmine. She wanted to start a family with her. Raise children in a loving home with two loving parents, something she never had. Before Jasmine, Anita never imagined she would end up being with another stud, but that all changed when she met her. Everything felt so right between them and she had never loved a woman so deeply before.

Anita rode passenger during patrol while her partner, Marcus, drove. "Hey Marcus man. I got something I want to talk to you about."

"What's going on with you, Nita?" Marcus was a 6'5, muscular African American with a deep voice. He was married with three kids, two boys and a girl. He was tough, but he was fair. His spirit was warm and always gave off good vibes. He made a great partner for Anita because she too was tough, but fair. They had a great relationship on and off duty. "Is this about Sarg telling you, you would make a great detective?" Marcus asked.

Anita was caught off guard. "What? No. How'd you know about that? I haven't told anyone but Jasmine."

"People talk, Anita. Plus, we all agree, so word spread fast." Marcus smiled.

"Well, no, that's not what I wanted to talk to you about. Quite frankly, I don't know when I'll be ready to talk about that. I'm comfortable where I am." Anita crossed her arms.

"And that's why you should do it. Do the things that scare you," Marcus encouraged.

"What the fuck. Jasmine pretty much told me the same thing."

"Well, she's a smart woman," he smiled.

"Yeah, she is." Anita paused. "But no, that's not why I wanted to talk to you." She continued, "You're a family man, right?"

"Of course. You know this. I love my wife and kids. Wouldn't trade them for the world. Why do you ask?"

"Well," Anita paused. "Well, I'm thinking about asking Jasmine to marry me."

"What?!" he shouted. The bass from his deep boisterous voice made Anita jump.

"Anita, that's huge! I'm so happy for you." He glanced over at Anita. "Although you seem hesitant. What's running through your mind?"

"I don't know, man. I guess I'm just nervous. She's everything that I've ever wanted plus some. What if she's not ready to get married? What if she says no?"

"Girl, shut your mouth. You're an amazing woman. I know that for a fact. You two make an awesome couple and one day, if you so choose, will make even better parents."

Anita smiled. "Thanks, Marcus. I appreciate that."

"Of course, girl. You know I got you. Have you looked at rings yet?"

"I've actually already asked her parents' permission, and they were so excited. They gave me Jasmine's late grandmother's ring."

"Her grandmother's ring, huh? Is that Jasmine's style?"

"Not really. Her parents and I laughed about that." She chuckled as she had a flashback of the situation. "So I took it to a ring spot and they duplicated it, but to be more of a band style. It looks really cool."

"Wow, Nita. That's awesome. How are you going to ask her?"

The conversation was interrupted by the dispatcher calling out for a domestic disturbance. They were closest to the call, so they responded.

Jasmine was home that Wednesday evening. She was binge-watching a show on Netflix. She got upset and yelled at the television when it asked: "are you still watching?" "Yes, I'm still watching. Damn!" she yelled. Her phone rang. "Hey babe! What's going on?"

"Jasmine," Anita cried, "I've been shot."

Jasmine's breathing stopped. Her worst fear had come true. She took a minute to let those words sink in. Then a million questions came out at once. "What?! How'd this happen?! Who did this to you?! Where are you?! I'm coming to you!"

"Give me that phone," she heard Marcus say in the background.

"Hello?! Marcus?!" Jasmine frantically shouted into the phone.

"Jas, hey, it's Marcus."

"Marcus, what the fuck is going on? Anita has been shot? Is she okay? Where are you guys?"

"Man, Jas, Anita is fine. It's a flesh wound. She's just being dramatic."

"I'm not being a dramatic babe! This shit hurts!" Anita shouted in the background.

Marcus rolled his eyes. "But yes, everything is fine. She's going to live and keep her leg. We are going to go to the hospital, though, to get her checked out and bandaged up."

"What hospital are you guys going to be at? I'm heading out the door now."

"You don't have to come here. I'll make sure she's home safe."

"Marcus!" Jasmine demanded.

Marcus gave her the hospital name and she rushed out the door.

✶ ✶ ✶

"Excuse me, ma'am." Jasmine approached the receptionist. "I'm looking for an Anita Watkins. I was told she's here."

"Hold on, let me check it out." The receptionist paused as she typed away on her computer. "Ah. Yes, here she is. What is your relation to the patient?"

Jasmine dreaded this question. The judgement people passed off when they saw two studs dating was unreal. Most of the time it was silent judgement, but their facial expressions said it all. Regardless, Jasmine proudly but politely stated, "I'm her girlfriend."

To her surprise, the statement didn't seem to faze the receptionist. "Oh, okay. Well, she is in room 303. Do you need me to let you know how to get there?"

"Uh, no thank you. I think I'll be okay. I appreciate it, though," Jasmine responded, kind of caught off guard by how smoothly that interaction went.

"You're welcome. I hope you have a nice day." The receptionist smiled.

When Jasmine entered the room, Marcus was sitting in a chair next to the window. She observed the bare hospital room as Anita lay silently in the bed. Her left calf was bandaged up. She stared blankly out the window.

"Baby?" Jasmine said softly as she burst into tears.

Anita turned her head toward the entrance as she revealed a faint smile. "Hey, baby."

"How are you feeling?" Jasmine sniffled.

Marcus stood up. "Hey Jas, it's good to see you." He walked over and gave her a hug.

"Hey Marcus, thank you for watching after her." She hugged him tightly as she wiped away tears.

"Of course. You know I wouldn't let anything happen to my Nita poo. I'll give you ladies some time." Marcus left the room.

"Anita, you scared the shit out of me. Why would you start off by telling me you've been shot? I thought I was going to lose you." She burst into tears again at the thought of losing her. She hugged Anita for dear life.

"I know, Jas. I apologize for that. That wasn't the best way to start that off. But I am fine, and I will be released in a few hours."

"Well, I'm going to sit with you until they release you. I'll let Marcus know he can go home to his family. And I'll text the girls to let them know what happened."

"Please let them know in a better fashion than how I told you."

Jasmine laughed through her cries. "I most definitely will."

"I love you so much, Anita." Jasmine kissed Anita.

"I love you too, baby."

TWELVE

Tiara was speaking with a potential client about his physical fitness and diet. After they finished business, they sat back and attempted to get to know each other a bit better. Tiara liked to be personal with her clients. She enjoyed being on a level of friendship, so they were comfortable coming to her with any issues they may have. She was very successful in her profession and was able to turn down clients if she didn't like their vibe.

"So do you have a family, Ethan? Husband? Wife? Kids?"

"Uh. I am married. To a woman. We have two boys. Why would you ask about the husband?"

"You never know these days. Hell, I'm a lesbian, and people don't expect me to be." Tiara always tried to work her being a homosexual into the conversation while getting to know her clients. She wanted to see how they would react. If they weren't cool with her loving whom she wanted to love, then she was okay with not doing business with them. She didn't need or deserve their negative judgment and would be just fine without their business.

Ethan was shocked. "You're a lesbian?!"

Tiara nodded.

"I don't understand how you don't like dick. You're so beautiful. Very feminine."

Tiara sighed. "Oh, Ethan," she said in a condescending tone. "Let's put it this way. As a straight male, I'm going to say it's a safe bet you can look at another male and tell if said male is attractive or not. Right?"

"Yeah, but—"

"Right." Tiara interrupted him before he could finish whatever ignorant words were about to come out of his mouth next. "You can say to yourself, because I know you wouldn't dare say it aloud, *man, that is one attractive guy*. Like for instance a Shamar Moore. Everyone knows he's obviously an attractive male. Now with that being said, while having that thought, you don't have that funny feeling in the down south region," Tiara did an in-the-air, open-palm circular motion in his groin area, "that makes your happy parts, well, happy. Happy to the point you either want to kiss him or fuck him. Right?"

"Right."

"Well, I'm like that. In girl form."

"Okay."

"Is my sexual orientation going to be an issue?" Tiara asked politely.

"No, of course not," Ethan quickly replied.

"Cool. I hope you're teaching your sons better than that. Why would you even think that was an appropriate thing to say? I mean you live in Geisbourne. This city is super gay friendly."

"I don't know what came over me," Ethan lowered his head.

"And word of advice. Don't ask another lesbian that question ever again. It's rude and disgusting."

"Right. Sorry about that." Ethan genuinely apologized.

Tiara rolled her eyes. Her phone buzzed. "Oh, my fuck," Tiara stated aloud as she read the group text Jasmine sent out.

Hey you guys. I just want to start this text off by saying everything and everyone is fine, but Anita has been shot. IT WAS JUST A FLESH WOUND. She has been discharged, and we are back at the house if you guys want to come over. Love y'all.

"What's wrong with you?" Ethan asked.

"One of my really good friends, she's a cop—was shot at work. I have to go." She started to pack up her things.

"Oh, my goodness! Okay, well, I hope your friend is all right."

"Yes. Thanks. Uh, I will be in contact with you soon about getting your routine and eating habits down. Hope you have a great night."

Tiara responded in the group text, *I'm about 30 minutes from your house. I'm on my way.*

Shortly after, the group chat blew up.

Nevaeh: *I'm out with Marie right now, but I'm going to end the date and come over.*

Imani: *WHAT. THE. FUCK. I'm omw!!!*

Cassidy: *FUCK! I'm at work right now but get off in about an hour. I'm going to head over as soon as I'm done.*

Eliana: *Yup about to head over!! Grabbing my keys now.*

Jasmine: *All right. See you guys in a bit.*

Tiara: *Somebody about to have to get got!!! SQUAD!!!*

Tiara put on some music and took off to go check on her wounded friend.

When Tiara arrived, Imani and Eliana were already inside. She rang the doorbell. Jasmine opened the door. "Hey, T."

"Hey Jas." They hugged. "How's Nita doing?"

"Girl, she is fine. Thank God. She just scared the crap out of me. Come on in."

Tiara stepped into the house. Anita was reclined back, relaxed. "Hey girl. Who I got to go fuck up?" Tiara asked playfully as she hugged Anita.

"Girl, it's not even like that. I'm just happy to be alive and well, honestly. Definitely put a new perspective on things."

"Yeah, I feel you on that," Tiara agreed. "Hey Ellie."

"Hey T."

"Hey knucklehead." Tiara turned to Imani who sat on the floor.

"What up?" Imani smiled.

They all sat and talked for a while as the rest of the gang showed up.

THIRTEEN

"Nita, how are you?" Cassidy asked. "I mean, with all things considered."

"Man. I'm going to be honest with you guys. I don't think I'm ready to talk about how I'm feeling about this yet. Let's just hang out and act as normal. You all make me laugh and I need that right now. For real." Everyone could see the hurt in Anita's eyes and obeyed her wishes.

"Well, I got something to tell you guys." Eliana broke the silence as everyone sat around in Anita and Jasmine's living room. "Trisha and I broke up."

"Oh goodness," Imani responded sarcastically. "Y'all will be back together in a few weeks."

Everyone laughed, even Eliana.

"No, really. We broke up. For real this time. Guess what happened?"

"Oh shit, serving up some hot tea." Tiara was excited.

"She told me she was pregnant."

Everyone was taken aback. They sat there silently as they looked around at one another.

"What?!" Tiara finally shouted. "That's foul even for her. By who?! Do we know him?!"

"Jordan James. That dude that works at the bowling alley, not too far from my apartment. The one I confronted her about, and she told me I had nothing to worry about."

"Oh hell no!" Tiara said.

"Yup. And then guess what she had the audacity to recommend."

"What, bitch?" Tiara was deep into the story.

"She said that she was hoping we could raise the baby together. Start a family. She told me I was her rock and she didn't know how she is going to do it without me."

They all burst out into laughter along with Eliana.

"You're her rock?" Tiara laughed. "That bitch can go kick rocks."

The laughter erupted even louder. Once everyone calmed down, Nevaeh asked, "But really Ellie, how are you holding up? Are you all right?"

"Yeah man. I'm all right. I feel like a weight has been lifted off my shoulders, ya know?"

"Please don't go back to her," Imani pleaded.

"Yeah, real shit, she's the worst," Cassidy chimed in.

"I'm so serious right now. I don't want anything to do with her."

"I hope her actions don't cause you to look badly at bisexuals," Cassidy added. "We're not all like that."

"Nah girl, it's not even like that. I just blame her as an individual. She crazy," Eliana laughed.

"Well, shit, now you can go out boo huntin with me!" Imani teased. "Since Nevaeh got all boo'd up, and Tiara isn't about that life, I haven't had a partner in crime."

"Boo huntin?" Tiara rolled her eyes. "Don't you have enough boos?" she snarked.

Imani sucked her teeth. "Whateva."

"Actually, I think I'm going to take some time and focus on myself for the time being. That was one hell of a rollercoaster ride I was on and lasted way too long. I need some time to breathe," Eliana admitted.

"I can respect that," Imani said.

"Hey! You guys, you know what I think we need?" Tiara jumped in. "A weekend at the beach. You know my parents have a beach house a few hours south of here. we can crash in over the weekend."

Everyone's face lit up.

"Yeah, that actually doesn't sound like a bad idea!" Jasmine responded. "A couple of days to get away from it all. Wake up to the sounds of waves crashing."

"Martinis on the beach with our toes in the sand," Eliana added.

"Beautiful ocean sunsets." Cassidy nodded her head.

"Sounds like we have a weekend girls' trip!" Everyone's face lit up.

"Are we bringing significant others or no?" Nevaeh asked.

"Uh, significant others?" Imani shot a look over to Nevaeh. "Are you trying to subtly tell us something?!"

"Oh. Yeah. I guess in the mix of everything going on, I forgot to tell you guys. I asked Marie to be my girlfriend and she said yes."

They all screamed. Tiara, Imani, Cassidy, and Eliana dogpiled on top of Nevaeh.

"This is great news, Nevaeh!" Cassidy said as they climbed off her. "I'm so happy for you guys."

"Hell yeah, Nevaeh!" Eliana said.

"Oh yeah, my girl finally grew some balls." Imani playfully punched Nevaeh in the arm. "I'm so proud of you."

"With the exception of our role model couple, Anita and Jasmine, we'll just make it a framily trip," Tiara suggested.

Jasmine flashed a goofy smile at the use of the word framily.

"Is that cool with everyone?" Tiara asked.

Everyone agreed and they excitedly planned their beach weekend.

FOURTEEN

"Good morning, baby." Anita rolled over to see Jasmine awake, staring at her laptop screen, zoned out. "Hey babe, you okay?" she asked.

"Yeah, I'm fine, just thinking," Jasmine responded.

"Uh oh. What are you thinking about?" she asked sleepily.

"Are you happy with us?" Anita looked at her, confused. "I mean I know you're happy, I'm happy too, but we've been together for such a long time. Do you think we've got that lesbian bed death thing going on that everyone talks about? Ya know, with long term lesbian couples?"

"Huh?" Anita rubbed her face with both hands.

"I mean we haven't had sex in like three weeks, I just want to make sure we're okay."

Anita sighed, "Baby, we're good. I mean technically I can't speak for you, but I'm happy and I couldn't see myself with another person. I love you."

"I love you too, that isn't the point. The point is we haven't had sex in quite some time." Anita groaned. "Hear me out. I mean, it's been a little over a week since your shooting scare and you seem to be healing up fine. That day just put into perspective how precious life really is. Enjoy it while we can."

"Do you want to have sex right now or something?"

Jasmine chuckled to herself. "No, you romantic son of a bitch, I don't. I'm just having a discussion."

"Well, what exactly is it you want to discuss?"

"You promise you won't get mad?"

"No," Anita replied bluntly.

"Well, then I'm not sure I should bring it up." Jasmine crossed her arms.

"Jasmine, it's too late for that, you already brought it up."

"I suppose you're right." Jasmine paused for a few seconds. "Well, you know that chick who lives down the street from us?"

"Uh, there are a few of those."

"You know, the one who always flirts with us and tells us that we are cute."

"Ciera?"

"Yes. Her."

"Of course I know her. We have both agreed that Ciera fine as fuck." Anita grinned at the thought of her.

"Well, what if," Jasmine cleared her throat, "what if we approached her about that threesome she has offered us a few times?"

Anita sat up, "Is this some kind of test or something? Because guaranteed, baby, I will fail this test."

Jasmine laughed. "No, Anita. It's not a test. I'm being so serious right now."

Anita glared into Jasmine's eyes. Jasmine glared back. "Well, I mean I'm down if that's something you would be into."

"Really?" Jasmine was surprised.

"Why do you sound so shocked?"

"Well, I mean we've always been monogamous and you've never really seemed like the type to branch out like that."

"I mean I never thought you were the type either, yet here we are. That's why I love the relationship we have. There isn't anyone else in the world I could think of that I would want to experience something like this with. I just want both of us to be happy."

"I am happy, but I think maybe we should do something out of our ordinary. See if we like it. I mean we both think she's bad, and she was the one that offered."

"That is definitely out of our ordinary." Anita paused. "You don't think it would cause like drama or problems, do you?"

"No. We've been through a lot together over the past nine years. I believe we are secure enough in our relationship to allow this to go down. We just have to continue to be open and honest with one another like we've always been."

"This is true," Anita agreed. There was a pause and then she spoke up, "Are we really going to do this?"

"I mean. Yeah," Jasmine said with a sly grin.

"Smack me so I know that I'm not dreaming."

Jasmine smiled, "How about I just kiss you?" Anita nodded and Jasmine went in for the kiss. "So when would we ask her about it?"

"I mean it's a Sunday," Anita responded. "We can't ask her on the Lord's day," she said with a straight face.

"True. Well, would it be weird to like, schedule a threesome? Is that how it goes down? Do people set up threesome appointments? Should we Google it?"

"Girl, your guess is as good as mine. I have no clue. Do we just knock on Ciera's door and be like, hey, so about that threesome?"

"I mean we could ask her tomorrow. But Mondays seem like an odd day to have a threesome. They seem like more of a weekend activity to me."

"Oh! What about on a Thursday? Then we can label it Threesome Thursdays." Anita was excited about her creative alliteration.

Jasmine gasped, "Threesome Thursdays, I like that." They high fived.

Jasmine and Anita tossed ideas back and forth because they really had no clue how this was going to play out. They didn't even know if Ciera was serious about the threesome thing or if it was just friendly flirty banter. They laughed at themselves because of how they must sound as amateurs planning a threesome.

"Should we tell the girls?" Anita asked.

"Hell yeah, we should tell the girls! I bet they would lose their shit if they found out we had a threesome! I know they think we're this innocent, boring, monogamous couple. We have to show them that long term relationships can be fun too. Especially Imani. My goodness, that girl is a trip."

"I know she be running through girls," Anita agreed. "And they know she's a player and they just keep letting her do it! That's the thing that kills me."

"She must have that crack vag, man," Jasmine stated.

"That what?" Anita quickly turned her head to look at her girlfriend.

"You know crack vag?"

"Jas, what the fuck is a crack vag?"

"Well, you know that pussy is playing with your mind and is bad for you, but you just can't stay away from it. It's like it's laced with crack or something."

"What the hell?" Anita laughed. "Tiara's right, you do be making up shit. Either way I like it. I'm going to start using it."

"You should. Spread it around. Hashtag it."

"So do you want to try and get this threesome going before our girls' getaway next weekend? It'll give us a fun story to tell."

"Yeah. I'm down," Jasmine responded a little nervous. "Let's get it going."

"Let's try your Google idea."

They started their research to plan the perfect threesome approach.

FIFTEEN

The crowd roared. Cassidy had tears in her eyes from laughter. She was in awe at how great Deja was on stage. It was quite different from her personality off stage. About once a month, Deja performed at an open mic comedy night at a local nightclub.

Cassidy knew Deja was funny, but on stage it was like she transformed into this totally different person. It was a turn-on for Cassidy. She loved a woman with a good sense of humor. It was even more mesmerizing to watch the transformation. To know her personally and how she acted off stage, then to see her switch and shine on stage drove her wild. Cassidy laughed along with the crowd as she watched her friend with benefits deliver her punchlines flawlessly as if she were born to be on stage.

"I've had a great time with you all tonight! Thank you so much for having me!" Deja said into the microphone. She received a standing ovation. She humbly bowed and blew kisses to the crowd. "Thank you all!" she said again, as she waved and walked off stage.

"Man, what a performance!" the emcee said as he walked onto the stage. "Please give it up one more time for Deja!" The crowd clapped and cheered again.

Cassidy waited impatiently after the show for Deja to walk out. "Cass." She spun around when she heard Deja's voice.

"Oh my goodness, Deja, you did such a great job!" Cassidy said as she hugged her.

"Yeah? You think so?" Deja inquired, slightly self-conscious.

"Are you kidding me? Yes! Holy crap, you had everyone, including me, in tears. You got a standing ovation!" Cassidy was so excited for her.

"Yeah, that was pretty cool." Deja chuckled to herself.

"Oh Deja, is this Cassidy?" One of Deja's fellow comedians asked as he looked Cassidy up and down.

"Yeah, this is her." Deja smiled at Cassidy.

"Ooouu, she is cute, girl. Good for you," he said. "A few of us are going out for some drinks if you two ladies would like to join."

"Uh, maybe. We'll talk about it and see."

"Okay, boo. Well, you have my number, so just hit me up. You know how us gays are, I'm sure we'll be partying until the sun comes up. Haaaay!" he said as he shook his ass.

"I know you will be, baby," Deja said as she playfully slapped his ass. "I'll hit you up."

"Okay, girl, I'll holla at you later. Bye, Cassidyyy," he said as he walked off.

"Who was that?" Cassidy asked as she grinned from ear to ear.

"One of my homeboys, he's a riot. I love him. We've been doing standup with one another for years." Deja paused. "What's that grin?"

"You know what this grin is about." Cassidy playfully nodded her head and pointed to her smile.

"I really don't. What? That he knew your name?"

"Don't play coy with me. So, you've been telling people about us?"

"So we're an us now?" Deja flirtatiously asked.

"I don't know, you're the one going around telling everyone about me."

"I wouldn't say, everyone. I mean I might've mentioned you once or twice to a person or two," Deja responded. "Don't let that shit go to your head." She playfully pushed Cassidy.

"Right," Cassidy said. She couldn't wipe the smile off her face.

"You want to come back to my place?" Deja asked.

"You don't want to go out with your fellow comedians and celebrate your standing o?"

"Girl, I ain't going out with them. Deshawn was not lying when he said they party until the sun comes up. I'm not even trying to be about that life tonight. I'd rather just have you all to myself."

Cassidy's grin grew bigger, "Yeah, I'm down for that. I'll have to run back to my apartment first to grab my uniform, though. I work tomorrow."

"That's cool. I like seeing you in your uniform anyway. It's sexy."

"That uniform can be a lady-getter at times, man. I love it," Cassidy joked.

"First of all, I better be the only lady that you're getting."

"The only lady, huh? So does that mean we're an us?" Cassidy asked.

Deja gazed into Cassidy's eyes. "C'mon, let's go." She turned to walk off and Cassidy smacked her butt.

✶ ✶ ✶

They drove in separate cars back to Cassidy's place.

"I could've just met you at your apartment. You didn't have to follow me here if you didn't want to," Cassidy told Deja as they exited their cars.

"I know I didn't have to, I wanted to. Now c'mon, let's go get your stuff so we can head back to my place."

"All right," Cassidy smiled.

Cassidy opened the door to her apartment. "C'mon in and have a seat. It shouldn't take me long to grab my stuff."

"All right." Deja sat down on the couch as Cassidy disappeared into her room.

Cassidy was gathering her things. She jumped when she felt a hand on her back. "Fuck, Deja, you scared me," she said.

"My bad, that wasn't my intention," she said as she stared into her eyes.

"Then what was your intention?"

"This." Deja grabbed Cassidy's face and kissed her. Their kiss was deep. Passionate. A lot more passionate than their normal kisses. Cassidy's heart raced. She pulled away from Deja.

"Wow," Cassidy said breathlessly. "That was…" she cleared her throat, "that was different."

"Different bad?" Deja asked.

Cassidy shook her head, "No, definitely not in a bad way. I really, really liked it."

"Me too." Deja went in for a kiss again. It lasted longer, followed up with roaming hands.

Cassidy pulled away again. "Hold on," she told Deja.

"Is something wrong? Why do you keep stopping?"

"Just give me a minute. Sit down on the bed." Deja did as she was told and Cassidy walked off into the bathroom. About ten minutes later she walked back in. "You said it was sexy to see me in uniform, right?" Cassidy asked. She only wore her pants and blouse. Her blouse was open, exposing her breasts.

Deja's mouth was slightly opened, and she seductively ran her tongue across her lips. "Yeah. I like that. Come here."

Cassidy obeyed, walked over and sat down next to Deja on the bed. Deja straddled her. Deja slowly pulled Cassidy's hair tie out. Cassidy took her hand and shook out her hair to allow it to lie naturally on her shoulders.

Deja stood up. "Stand up," she ordered.

Cassidy obeyed. "Yes, ma'am."

"Damn, you look good in your uniform with your hair down like that," Deja said as she studied Cassidy's frame. The light from her lamp hit her perfectly.

This time Cassidy went in for the kiss. She grabbed the back of Deja's neck with one hand and pulled Deja into her. Deja pushed Cassidy onto the bed. Cassidy lay back, perched up on her elbows, as Deja did a little strip tease for her. Cassidy couldn't think of anywhere else she'd rather be. She watched as Deja swayed to the beat of her own music, yet it was silent. It was so sensual. Cassidy loved every moment of it. Deja made her way over to the bed and got on top of Cassidy. Cassidy sat up so Deja could pull her blouse off. Deja ran her fingers through Cassidy's hair as she admired her beauty.

"You're so beautiful," she told Cassidy and went in for a kiss. Before she knew it, Cassidy was completely naked. Their hands were roaming, not a body part was left unkissed. After they were done, they lay there in silence as they held one another. They both ran their fingers up and down one another's back.

"I could fall asleep right now." Cassidy broke the silence with a whisper.

"Really?" Deja asked.

"Yeah. Why do you ask?" Cassidy's eyes were closed.

Deja smiled, "To be honest with you, I could go for round two."

Cassidy opened her eyes and grinned. "Hold on, I don't want to oversleep in the morning." She set her alarm, then dove in for another round.

SIXTEEN

It was a Thursday afternoon, and Nevaeh decided to make a stop by No Man's Land to see Marie. She observed a few regulars as she walked in and sat down at the bar.

"Hey baby, what are you doing here?" Marie asked as she leaned over the bar to give her a kiss.

"Oh, nothing. I don't have anything scheduled for the day, so I thought I would stop by and make an appearance. I wanted to see my favorite girl before the girls and I head out on the weekend trip tomorrow. Hopefully brighten your day a little bit."

"Well, my day always becomes better when I get to see your shining face." Marie's compliment made Nevaeh smile. "Actually, baby, there is something I wanted to talk to you about."

"Oh goodness, nothing bad, I hope," Nevaeh said, a little worried.

"No, nothing bad, but not out here. It's a private matter." She turned to one of her bartenders. "Hey Ken, you mind tending the bar yourself for a few? I need to talk to Nevaeh in the office."

"Yeah, of course, go do what you need to do."

"Cool, thanks. Come with me to the back." Marie led Nevaeh to her office and shut the door behind them.

"Okay, babe, what's so important? You got me a little worried."

Marie locked the door. She seductively looked into Nevaeh's eyes.

"Oh. Oh!" Nevaeh slyly smiled. "In your office, babe? Ooouu, you nasty. I like it."

Marie sat on the desk. She hiked up her skirt and spread her legs. "I've missed you."

Nevaeh needed no more instruction. She said nothing as she kissed Marie and made her way down.

✶ ✶ ✶

There were only a few customers in the bar at the time. Ken knew what they were doing in the back and turned up the TV, to hopefully drown out the very vocal Marie. He laughed to himself and shook his head. He had his back to the bar entrance as he watched the TV. He heard someone sit down at the bar. He turned around and was astonished by this woman's beauty.

He cleared his throat. "How's it going?" he asked.

"I'm pretty good," the lady answered back.

"Getting some day drinks in on a Thursday afternoon? I like it," he joked. She smiled. "Are you new in town? I haven't seen you around before."

"Uh, you can say I'm new. I used to live in the city, moved away for a bit, and now I'm back."

"Well, welcome back! What can I get for you?"

"Thanks. Uh, I'll have a Guinness on tap, please."

"Sure thing." He grabbed a chilled glass.

"Man, it sounds like someone is having fun back there, huh?" the lady laughed, referring to the faint moans coming from the office.

"Yeah, I know. Two love birds doing their thing. My homeboys would clown me if they knew a beautiful lesbian couple was back there gettin it on, and I didn't try and join in on their sex shenanigans. Instead, I'm out here attempting to drown their sounds out by turning up the TV." He laughed.

"Well, as a lesbian, hell, actually just as a woman in general, I will say that it is very much appreciated that you don't try and insert yourself where you're not wanted. Pun intended. Cheers." She did a single nod and lifted her glass.

Ken and the newcomer sat and chit-chatted for about twenty minutes. "You want another beer?" he asked when he noticed hers was low.

"Uh, actually I better not. I just wanted to come out and see what this bar was like. I saw great reviews. If it's anything like what's going on in that back room, I'm definitely going to have to come back," she told him with a smile.

"Yeah, I would suggest it. This is one of the most popular lesbian/gay bars around. If you're out fishin, I'm sure you'll get a catch. Just watch out, these ladies can get pretty wild," he advised. "It's actually really entertaining." He chuckled.

"I bet they do, but thanks. I think I'll be able to handle myself. I recently ended a long-term relationship, and I am looking to have some fun."

As she paid, the sound of the office door opened. "Well, looks like the love birds are done," she joked. Ken nodded with a smile.

Nevaeh and Marie walked out trying to act as if nothing had happened. Nevaeh turned the corner, stopped dead in her tracks. She looked like she had seen a ghost.

"Saria?" she managed to choke out. Nevaeh's heart sank as her forehead wrinkled. It was as if all those emotions from their abrupt college breakup had flooded in. She was stunned, but surprisingly calm.

"Nevaeh?" Saria's eyes widened. She was shocked to see Nevaeh's face. Tears immediately filled her eyes. She scrambled to pay, gathered her belongings, and rushed out the door as fast as she could. She didn't want to cry in front of anyone.

Nevaeh stood there for a moment, stuck, as she stared intensely at the bar's front door. Once Nevaeh composed herself, she chased after her. Saria fumbled with her keys at her car as she tried to open the door.

Nevaeh walked up to the car with her head cocked to the side. "Saria?" she said softly as she got closer.

Tears flowed down Saria's face. "Nevaeh. I'm sorry. I didn't know you were going to be here. I have to go." She finally managed to make her way into her car.

"Shit," Nevaeh said to herself as she watched Saria drive away.

SEVENTEEN

Eliana lay on her back in her bed as she stared at the ceiling. It was so quiet in her apartment. She loved her new-found peace that she felt, being Trisha-less. She had her moments of weakness where she considered calling her to see what she had to say but stood her ground and stayed strong. She knew she deserved better than the drama and chaos Trisha brought into her life. She thought she would hate being single, but it turned out it was a nice change of pace. She was able to do what she wanted when she wanted, she didn't have to answer to anyone, and most importantly, the toilet paper was always placed correctly on the holder.

Eliana was excited for the journey to get to know herself all over again. She could hardly remember who she was before Trisha. Trisha had such a toxic hold on her that she lost herself in the process. Eliana knew that she was afraid of being alone, but she knew she had to be in order to accomplish self-discovery. She was ready to find out. As she lay there, her phone buzzed. It was a message from a potential client. Eliana took advantage of some of the freelancing websites that were available to get her name out there, and it was working.

She and the client were in the same city, not too far from one another, so they decided to meet up for lunch that day to talk more in detail about the project. Eliana liked to make sure she was the right fit for the job before accepting a task. She hated feeling as if she shortchanged one of her clients. A few hours after they messaged back and forth, Eliana found herself at Sammitches. It was Geibourne's most popular sandwich shop, owned by two men named Sam and Mitch. They decided to meet up there so they both could have lunch as well as discuss business. Eliana had arrived first. She ordered a mango juice to sip on. She scrolled through social media as she waited. She chuckled to herself as she scrolled past a few memes and watched some short videos.

"Eliana?" She heard a voice that sounded soft and sweet say her name. She looked up from her phone and saw her client. She was stunning. She appeared to be about 5'10 with tan skin and wore makeup that made her bright blue eyes stand out. She wore green, thick-framed glasses that seemed to fit her perfectly. Her fiery red hair draped over her shoulders. She had a tattoo on her neck and full sleeves on both arms. Eliana instantly thought her profile photos did her no justice.

"Hi, yes." Eliana stood up and extended her hand. "Scarlett, right?"

"Yup, that's me." Scarlett shook her hand. "Thank you so much for meeting up with me in person. I would really like to get personal about this project because it means so much to me."

"Yes, of course, I'm happy to do it. Please sit down." They both sat down. "Do you want to order something to eat or drink first? Or start discussing the project and then order some food?"

"Uh, I would like to just start talking and see where it leads us."

"Sounds good to me," Eliana smiled. "So," she began to talk as she got a notebook and pen out of her bag, "tell me more about the project. I know we discussed it on Messenger, but I would like to hear about it in person."

"Most definitely!" Scarlett said excitedly. "So, as I told you I'm a tattoo artist. I wanted to do like a person-behind-the-tattoos kind of project. For some reason, some people still see people with as many tattoos as I have as scary or unapproachable. I wanted to portray us tatted people as more of the family-oriented, fun-loving people that some of us are."

"I love that," Eliana said as she took some notes. "Family-oriented? So, you're married?" Eliana fished. She didn't look up as she wrote because she didn't want her facial expression to give away her curiosity.

"Yeah, I am." Eliana was disappointed, but was able to look up from her notebook now that she knew the answer. "My wife and I have been married for a little over seven years now and have a set of twin girls."

"Oh wow, a house full of women. That must be interesting."

Scarlett laughed, "Yeah, it's something, all right."

"Okay, so tell me more about your passion with tattoos."

"Well, my mom and dad both have a bunch of tattoos. They're not as tatted up as I am, but they raised us to believe that it's my body, and I can do what I want. I can't help that people are too afraid to find out more about what they don't know."

"Definitely. I like that way of thinking," Eliana smiled. She still was disappointed about the fact that Scarlett was married, but happy to be in the company of a fellow lesbian. "You said your parents raised us? You have siblings?"

"Sure do! An older brother and younger sister. They also have tattoos. My sister owns her own gym, and my brother is a teacher.

My brother usually wears long-sleeve shirts, so his tattoos aren't exposed while at work, which is definitely understandable. Some parents can be a tad judgey."

Eliana nodded in agreement. "So, do you have any ideas of how you would like the photoshoot to go?"

"I would love to just have photos taken while doing everyday, family-oriented stuff. I'm not sure of what, but things that portray us to be the loving people that we are."

"Hm." Eliana thought for a minute. She began to toss out ideas. "Okay, so what about starting off with a picture of you and your wife and daughters getting ready to start the day? Have me take pictures of the everyday morning routine? Maybe have a family photo of you, your parents, and siblings as a happy family, perhaps in front of your childhood home? And maybe try taking a photo with the entire family at the dinner table, laughing, enjoying one another's company? And a picture of your brother teaching with short sleeves on and the kids being interactive as if to say the tattoos don't bother them? Definitely have a photo of everyone in it. Have a few black and white photos, but have the tattoos in color?"

"I love all those ideas!" Scarlett's face lit up.

"Awesome. I have a few others that I would love to discuss more, but I need to get my train of thought together and get back with you on that. If that's okay with you."

"Yes, of course. I'm really excited to do this project. I feel like I picked the right person for the job."

"Well, I'm happy you feel that way." Eliana blushed. "Would you like to order some food? I'm getting kind of hungry."

"I'm glad you asked because I am too."

The women placed an order for their sandwiches. They continued to get to know one another and talk about the project.

"Wow, that was delicious," Eliana said.

"Yeah, I'm stuffed," Scarlett agreed. "So, when would you like to meet up again for the project? I'm free this weekend if you have the time."

"I am actually going on a little girls' trip with my friends this weekend. We all need to get away for a bit."

"I can understand that! Well, my schedule is pretty flexible."

"How does Tuesday sound for you?"

"Tuesday sounds great." Scarlett stood up. "Well, I have to get going. It was great meeting you, Eliana, and I am looking forward to working with you."

Eliana stood up and shook her hand. "I'm looking forward to working with you as well. Seems like a very interesting project!"

"Great. See you soon!" Scarlett waved as she walked away.

"Bye." Eliana sat back down. She jotted down some more notes before she packed her things up and left.

EIGHTEEN

"I think I'm going to throw up," Jasmine confessed.

"What is wrong with you?"

"I'm so nervous!"

Anita walked over to her girlfriend. "Babe, everything is going to be fine. The worst thing she can say is no," Anita paused, "and then possibly never speak to us again and tell everyone that we attempted to seduce her and then we will probably have to move."

Jasmine groaned as she buried her face in her hands.

"Babe, I'm kidding!" Anita laughed. "Look, just relax. Once we all get together and talk, I'm sure everything will be okay. She seems like such a fun-loving person that even if she doesn't want to, she'll be able to joke about it."

Jasmine exhaled with relief. "Yeah, I guess you're right. You don't think it's kind of wrong that we're inviting her over in hopes that we have a threesome?"

Anita thought for a second. "I mean, no? Right? People invite other people over that they're attracted to all the time hoping that they get some action. Isn't that like 80% of what being single is about?"

"I guess. Just seems, I don't know, weird."

"Jasmine, this was your idea." Anita gave her the side eye.

"I know."

"Look, if you don't want to do this we can cancel. We don't have to do this. I'm happy with just being with you. I don't care." Anita kissed Jasmine on the lips.

"Aw, baby, that's sweet, but no we're going to do this. We leave for the beach house tomorrow, and we need this story to tell." Jasmine was serious. "Plus, I think it's a good way to explore our sexuality together."

"I agree. Let me get you a glass of wine." Anita got up to pour two glasses of wine, then came back into the living room and sat down next to Jasmine. "Here you go. Maybe this will help you relax."

"Thank you." Jasmine gave Anita a kiss. "Here, let's make a toast."

"What are we toasting to?" Anita asked.

"To our first Threesome Thursday. Maybe this is the start of something new, or maybe just a one-time thing, or maybe it won't even happen, who knows. I'm just glad I'm experiencing it with you. Cheers."

Anita smiled, "Cheers."

Just as their glasses clinked, the doorbell rang.

"Ah fuck." Jasmine was nervous again.

"Damn, it's three o'clock on the dot." Anita looked at her watch, "This girl is punctual. I like her already. Jasmine, you got to calm the fuck down or it's going to get weird."

Jasmine nodded at her as she chugged her glass. "Right," she said with an exhale.

The doorbell rang again.

"Coming!" Anita shouted. She turned and looked at Jasmine. "I'll get the door; you get it together."

123

"I'm cool." Jasmine sat back awkwardly.

Anita opened the door. "Ciera! Hey!"

"Hey Nita!" She leaned in for a hug. Anita was turned on by the scent of her perfume.

"Come on in, Jasmine is inside."

Ciera walked in. "Hey Jas!" Jasmine stood up as Ciera greeted her with a smile and a hug.

"Hey Ciera, it's great to see you." Jasmine nervously smiled. Anita silently mouthed *keep it together* from behind Ciera's back.

"This is the first time I've been in you guys' place. It looks great."

"Aw, thanks. Please have a seat." Jasmine said.

"Oh, you guys are participating in a little day drinking, I see." Ciera came in and sat down.

"Yeah, do you want a glass?" Jasmine asked as she attempted not to sound nervous.

"Actually, I would love some."

Jasmine went in the kitchen and brought out the entire bottle. She poured Ciera a glass before she set the bottle down on the table. "Here, so if we want more, it's conveniently there," she smiled. They sat around and laughed, drank, and snacked. It wasn't at all awkward like Jasmine thought it was going to be. As a matter of fact, she was very relaxed.

After a couple of hours and two bottles of wine, Ciera very bluntly stated, "So, did you guys really just invite me over here just to joke around and day drink?"

Jasmine choked a little.

"What do you mean?" Anita asked.

"Look, guys. We're all grown here. I've offered to do the threesome thing multiple times and out of nowhere y'all decide to invite me over to kick it? Jasmine was mad nervous when I first came in, drinks, I mean all signs point to it." Ciera stood up. "I'm not sure if you two thought I was playing when I made those offers," she continued to talk as she slowly started to unbutton her shirt, "but I can assure you I was not." She let her shirt fall to the ground. "I think both of you are sexy as hell. If I'm wrong, please stop me. If not," she paused and looked between Anita and Jasmine with seduction in her eyes, "then what are we waiting for?"

Anita and Jasmine were instantly turned on by her forwardness. They both studied the shirtless Ciera standing there with her damn near flawless milk chocolate skin tone and beautiful C-cup breasts. The two looked at each other. Anita nodded to Jasmine as if to say you go first. Jasmine smirked; the alcohol had her feeling more relaxed than earlier. She stood up and walked toward Ciera. As she inched toward her, Jasmine could feel the intensity of Ciera's stare, and it sent an electric shock through her body. She put her face up to Ciera's but pulled away when Ciera went in for the kiss. Jasmine grinned before she dove in for the kiss. Ciera instantly melted. Jasmine's hands roamed Ciera's body. She grabbed a handful of her ass. Ciera let out a little moan. Anita sat in the chair wildly aroused as she watched her girlfriend make out with this other woman. Anita discovered a side of herself she never knew existed. Ciera panted as she pulled away from Jasmine.

She made her way over to Anita and straddled her. Anita allowed her to make the first move. Ciera began to kiss Anita. Jasmine got behind Ciera. She ran her hands over Ciera's body as she kissed her neck.

"That feels good," Ciera moaned.

"Stand up," Anita commanded. Ciera obeyed.

When she stood up, Anita pulled Ciera's shorts and thong down to expose her beautifully maintained pussy. "Oh, you knew what you came here for," Anita smiled.

Ciera giggled. "I know what I want, and I go for it."

"Jasmine. Undress," Anita demanded.

Jasmine liked the forcefulness that came from her girlfriend and took her clothes off, allowing each piece of clothing to fall to the ground individually.

Both Jasmine and Ciera stood in front of Anita naked. Anita didn't ask, she just decided to take charge of this situation. Neither Jasmine nor Ciera minded. "Here's what I want to happen," she spoke as she stripped down to her boxers, still sitting down. "Ciera, I want you to come over here and put one leg up on the arm of the chair. I want to eat you out while you and Jasmine kiss. I also want you to play with Jasmine's pussy while doing that."

"Yes ma'am." Ciera did as she was told. She put her leg up on the arm of the chair placing her pussy in Anita's face. Anita dove in. Ciera moaned. Loudly. "Fuck," she blurted out. Jasmine began to suck on Ciera's nipples. This made Ciera's body jerk. Jasmine brought her face up to Ciera's and they began to kiss. Ciera moved her hands down on Jasmine. She placed her fingers on Jasmine's clit. The heat and wetness were such a turn-on for her. Ciera bucked against Anita's face. As her breathing became choppier, Jasmine stopped kissing her and moved her mouth back to her nipples. Anita grabbed on to Ciera's ass to push her face deeper inside her. Ciera grabbed Anita's head; she couldn't take it anymore and she came. Hard. She screamed. Her body shook. She saw stars.

"Oh my god." Ciera's body went limp.

"We're not done yet." Anita stood up. "You want to taste Ciera?" she asked Jasmine. Jasmine nodded. Anita kissed Jasmine passionately. "Now I want you to cum." Anita started to play with Jasmine. Jasmine moaned into Anita's mouth as they kissed.

Ciera sat down in the chair. As she watched the couple, she began to fidget from excitement. She got down on her knees, pulled Anita's boxers down and ate her out from behind. Jasmine and Anita both simultaneously came. Breathlessly all three of them flopped down on the couch. They sat there in silence for a bit. The only sound that could be heard was the three of them breathing heavily.

"Holy shit." Ciera wiped her mouth. "So that happened."

They all looked at each other and laughed. "Yeah, it did," Anita said.

"I mean Anita for the win, right? How she took charge like that." Jasmine hyped up her girlfriend.

Ciera clapped.

"Thank you. Thank you, ladies. Please, no photographs." Anita joked around. They all laughed.

"So our first Threesome Thursday was a success," Jasmine said.

"Threesome Thursday?" Ciera asked.

"Yeah, that's what we named it."

Ciera giggled, "You guys are dorks. Hopefully there won't be too many other women. I really enjoyed myself and would like to do this again sometime. Would love to see what else the three of us can do together."

Jasmine and Anita looked at each other and smiled. "Nah," Jasmine assured Ciera. "If we do this again, you're the only woman we'd want in our bedroom. I can assure you of that."

"Yup," Anita agreed. "Plus, we haven't even dipped into our toy box yet!"

"The toy box? Hell! We didn't even make it to the bedroom!" Jasmine chimed in.

"You guys have a bedroom?" Ciera joked.

They all sat on the couch naked, as they laughed and enjoyed each other's company. Anita and Jasmine could both agree that they had an amazing first Threesome Thursday and would love to do it again.

NINETEEN

It was early Friday morning when the girls agreed to meet at Anita and Jasmine's place. They felt safer leaving their cars at their house because Anita's cop car would be parked out front. They all pitched in and rented a van, so they could all ride in the same vehicle. The beach house was about a three-hour drive away. Everyone was excited to get on the road and start the weekend. Anita and Jasmine had an extra pep in their step from their Threesome Thursday. They wanted to tell the girls and the anticipation was killing them, but they wanted to wait for the right moment to reveal their good news.

Cassidy noticed they were extra cheerful, "You two seem to be in an extra good mood this morning," she said to Jasmine. "You guys had a good night?" She nudged Jasmine as she implied that they had sex.

Jasmine smirked, "It wasn't anything out of the ordinary," she lied. "Just another Thursday night in the Anita Jasmine household."

"Yeah, I don't believe that worth a shit," Cassidy joked.

"All right, ladies!" Anita shouted, as she unintentionally interrupted their conversation.

"We're going to finish this conversation," Cassidy told Jasmine with a smile on her face. Jasmine nodded in agreement.

Everyone gathered by the car in front of Anita. "So, we're about to get on the road in a bit. Since nobody wanted to drive, looks like I'm going to take care of that."

"Thank goodness," Tiara said under her breath.

"If we don't make any stops," Anita continued, "we can be at the house by elevenish. So, I'm going to ask this because it always happens. Does anyone have to use the bathroom?" Anita darted her eyes at Imani.

"What the fuck is that supposed to mean?" Imani was defensive.

"Imani, you are always the first one that has to go pee when we go anywhere," Nevaeh specified.

"I can't help it that I have a sensitive bladder." Imani crossed her arms. "You guys are assholes." Anita continued to stare at her. "Fine! I'll go pee! Not because y'all told me to, I'm going to go pee because I want to!" Imani stormed off into the house.

They all laughed. "I hope everyone remembered to grab everything. Jasmine and I packed some snacks for us all to share on the way up there."

"Aw," the girls all said.

"Our momma bears looking out for us. Thanks, guys," Eliana said.

Imani came out of the house and they all piled into the van. Anita set the house alarm and locked up before she hopped into the driver seat. "Are we all good to go?"

"Yaaaaaas!" The girls were excited.

"All right then, let's ride!"

Anita put on some music, and they drove off. On the way up to the beach house, the girls sang and talked about random things.

They joked around and reminisced. They arrived at the beach house on schedule.

* * *

"We made it!" Imani shouted as she hopped out of the van. "Now hurry up and open the door, T! I've been holding my pee for like twenty minutes now because I didn't want y'all to make fun of me!"

Tiara laughed, "Aw, poor baby!" She went to the front door and unlocked it; Imani pushed past her to rush to the bathroom.

"Where the fuck is the bathroom in this big ass house?!" Imani screamed as she opened and closed doors.

"Last door on the left!" Tiara shouted.

"Why is it so far away from the front door?!" Imani shouted as she found the bathroom and slammed the door.

Tiara chuckled and shook her head. She took a deep breath as she immersed herself in the smell of the beach house. It had been a while since she had been there, and it was still as beautiful as the last time she was there.

The house was gorgeous. It was an 8,000-square-foot, single story home. There were seven bedrooms and six bathrooms. It had floor to ceiling windows, an open floor plan, and the back wall opened to the patio for an indoor-outdoor feel. There was a pool out back, with steps that led directly to the beach. Her parents knew the girls were coming, so as a gift they had fully stocked the fridge with alcohol, snacks, and various foods.

"Phew." Imani sighed with relief as she snapped Tiara out of her daze. "I needed that!"

"I bet you did, come on, let's go get our stuff."

The girls all grabbed their belongings from the van and claimed their rooms. They told Tiara to take the master bedroom since it was her parents' house, but she insisted that Anita and Jasmine sleep there.

That day they all had drinks, danced around the house, laughed, and played a few games. At sunset, they decided to have a fire on the beach. They started up the fire, brought a cooler of beer out with some snacks, and relaxed.

"Man, this is so relaxing," Cassidy said. "Tell your parents thanks for letting us crash here for the weekend and for stocking up the fridge."

"Oh, it's not a problem, girl. My parents love to show this beach house off. As long as they don't have anything booked, we can come here as often as we like. The only thing they ask is we clean up after ourselves."

"Shit, that's not an issue," Cassidy said.

"Hey ladies, I want to make a toast." Anita lifted her beer. "To the best damn group of friends anyone could ever ask for. I love us because we can keep it real with one another, you guys make me laugh, and make me feel loved. With my upbringing, it's nice having y'all out here. You and my brothers are all I have. Seriously, you guys are my family, excuse me, framily." Jasmine smiled. "And I love you guys. Cheers."

"Cheers!" they all said.

"Hey Nevaeh, you doing all right?" Imani asked, concerned. "You seem kind of out of it."

"Ugh," Nevaeh said. "I don't want you guys to freak out."

"Ah shit," Tiara said.

"It's nothing. Don't worry about it," Nevaeh said.

"Just spit it out, Nevaeh," Imani pried.

"I saw Saria!" Nevaeh blurted out.

Everyone froze, wide-eyed, as they looked around at each other.

"I went to see Marie yesterday, so I could spend some time with her before this weekend. We went into her office, did what we do, we walked out, and fucking Saria was sitting at the bar."

"What the fuck?" Imani said, surprised. "Well, what did you do?"

"I was stuck. It was like I saw a ghost. Couldn't believe it was her. She left in a frenzy, and I chased after her. She was fumbling with her keys. She was a nervous wreck trying to get into her car, and all I could do was stand there and stare at her. That's all I could do," she sniffled. "I mean what the actual fuck? Saria? Are you kidding me?"

"Holy crap," Jasmine said.

"You all right?" Eliana asked.

"I don't fucking know," Nevaeh sighed.

"What the fuck do you mean you don't know?" Imani asked. "Marie. Remember her? Remember how happy she makes you?"

"Of course I remember her, Imani. You think I like feeling like this?"

"So what are you going to do?" Tiara asked.

"I think I'm going to hit her up. I want to talk to her. Seeing her in person stirred up a lot of emotions I thought I had moved past. I need answers."

"I think that's a bad idea, Nevaeh," Imani insisted. "It's not worth it; stay faithful to Marie."

"Yeah? What the fuck do you know about being faithful, Imani?" Nevaeh joked.

Imani gasped as she placed her hand up to her chest as if she were shocked. "Well, I never!" she laughed. "Nah, but really I just saw the damage hurricane Saria did, and it wasn't pretty. I see how happy you are now, and I don't want you to make an impulsive decision based on your emotions. It's all out of love. I know you're probably going to see her anyway because that's what you fucking do. Just know whatever you decide to do, we got your back."

They all nodded in agreement.

"Thanks, guys."

Cassidy cleared her throat. "Uh, I have some news."

"Ah shit," Tiara repeated.

"Well, I got an assignment to Korea."

"What the fuck?" Imani repeated.

"Yeah. I leave in six months." Cassidy paused. "I don't want to go, but I'm not able to deny it."

"So what the hell does that mean? You're leaving us forever?" Eliana asked.

"You can't leave us. We need you. Balance the universe out and shit," Tiara said with a serious face.

Cassidy laughed, "Well, hopefully not forever! I get to put in bases on my dream sheet to hopefully get stationed at after Korea. I'm going to put this base as my number one choice."

"I will go straight up to whoever the hell issues bases and let them know they need to bring your ass back here afterwards. They can't split our family like that," Imani said.

Cassidy sighed as she ran her hand through her hair. "Man, I wish it were that easy. You know in any other circumstances I'd be thrilled to go to Korea, but I don't want to go. I always thought I wanted to get stationed overseas and stay, but after being here and finding my physical, spiritual, and mental home, those plans have changed. I love you guys, and I have Deja, I'm settled here. I'm comfortable. Happy. I don't think I've ever felt this happy and at home before, even with my blood family. I mean they're great, don't get me wrong, but they're not you guys."

"Well, we will be right here WHEN you get back," Anita assured.

"Yeah, we'll keep sending positive vibes out to the universe that you come back," Jasmine chimed in. "Shoot, we might even try and make a family trip out to Korea and visit you!"

"That sounds like a great idea. I've been needing a getaway, especially after Trisha's crazy ass!" Eliana agreed.

"That would be amazing. Okay, enough about me and Korea! It's going to make me sad." Cassidy waved them off. "I would actually like to get back to why Anita and Jasmine have been jollier than usual today," Cassidy pried.

"Yeah, y'all have been extra loving today," Nevaeh added.

"Well," Anita started.

"Ah shit," Tiara said again.

"We had a threesome!" Jasmine blurted out then quickly covered her mouth.

They all sat there in shock as they stared at the women.

"What the fuck?" they all shouted, mimicking Imani. They laughed.

"What in the wooooorld?" Eliana was stunned.

"What... I mean how... I mean who... huh? You two?" Imani pointed between the two. "Y'all are the most monogamous couple we know!"

"I think what Imani's trying to say is who, what, when, where, and how?" Cassidy said.

"That's right, ladies, spill the tea!" Tiara said.

Anita and Jasmine looked at each other and smiled. Jasmine nodded at Anita because she knew how much she wanted to tell the story.

"Well, Jasmine brought up the idea to do something a little out of the ordinary. She came to the realization of how precious life is after that shooting incident. We've been together for some years now, and we both agreed that our relationship is strong enough to explore a little. Y'all remember that Ciera chick we told y'all about?"

"Oh shit! Ciera? That bad chick that live down the street? That kept offering y'all to invite her in your bedroom?" Imani got excited.

"Yeah. Well we took her up on that offer," Anita said.

"Holy shit." Eliana was in disbelief.

"Yeah, and it was fucking phenomenal," Jasmine enthused. "I mean I was nervous as fuck at first, but after we chilled, and I had several glasses of wine, it was smooth sailing."

"Her body is on point," Anita said. Jasmine nodded in agreement.

"Well, I'll be damned," Nevaeh said.

"Yeah. I mean it was a great time. So much so that we might even do it again," Jasmine said.

"See, that's what the fuck I need." Imani was hype. "A girlfriend who we both can pick up girls together. Y'all give me hope. You the real MVP." She wiped a fake tear from her eye.

Tiara rolled her eyes.

They all sat around and joked for about another hour.

"All right, ladies, I think I'm going to call it a night tonight," Jasmine confessed.

"Aw boo!" they all playfully hissed.

"Yeah, I know I'm lame." She leaned over and kissed Anita. "I just want to lie down and relax for a little bit."

"Okay, baby. I'll be up in a bit. I'm going to chill for a little longer."

"Yeah, no worries. Goodnight, ladies." Jasmine smiled and did the Buckwheat wave with her hand under her chin. All the girls waved back the same way.

Jasmine went inside.

"Guys!" Anita made sure Jasmine was in the house, then she spoke in a whisper yell to the group. "I have big news, and I need your help!"

"Shit, you the cop, we supposed to be asking you for help to hide the body!" Imani whisper yelled back.

"What? No. I want to propose to Jasmine."

"Aaaaahhhh!" they all whisper screamed.

"Oh my goodness, this is great!" Cassidy was excited.

"Yeah, and I want you all to help me," Anita whispered. "So this is what I was thinking…"

TWENTY

Everyone was ecstatic for the big day. They all played it off so Jasmine wouldn't catch on. Imani and Tiara woke a little earlier than everyone and fixed breakfast. They had a good spread with fried eggs, bacon, waffles, chopped breakfast potatoes, fresh fruit, and mimosas.

"Man, Imani and T, you guys have outdone yourselves," Anita said. "This breakfast was delicious."

"Yeah, it really was," Nevaeh agreed. "Hey Nita, do you mind going to the store to pick up some marshmallows? We were thinking about doing some s'mores today. If you go, me, Ellie, and Cass will clean up everything."

"Uh, sure, I can do that. Hell, I hate cleaning the kitchen anyway." Anita knew why she asked but played it off. "You want to come with me, baby?" Anita asked Jasmine. Inside she prayed she would say yes because if she didn't it would mess up the plan.

"Ya damn right I'll go! I hate washing dishes." Jasmine was enthused.

"All right, y'all, we'll be back," Anita said as she grabbed the keys. They went out the door.

Once the door closed, the girls rushed to the window to make sure they drove off.

"All right, ladies, gather up!" Nevaeh instructed. They all put their hands in the middle as they huddled up. Nevaeh began to give out tasks. "I will clean this kitchen up as fast as possible; Imani and Tiara, I want you two to go set up the back patio; Cassidy, go get Anita's outfit and make sure it is ready for her to go when they get back so she can change as fast as possible; and Ellie, set up the cameras so they have good angles to get as many shots as possible. We want to make sure we get as much as we can on video! We only have about thirty minutes so we need to fucking move! Ready?"

"Break!" they all shouted and clapped at once as if they were in a football huddle before they dispersed.

Anita had spoken with Tiara's parents prior to the weekend trip. She asked if she sent them some money could they get all the supplies she needed for the proposal. They agreed but refused to accept her money. They loved Anita and Jasmine and wanted to do what they could to help.

On the back porch Imani and Tiara vigorously worked to place the elegant decorations Tiara's parents had purchased. The pool had a waterfall attached, and they figured out how to turn that on as well. Cassidy ran up to the room and found Anita's outfit. She went over it with an iron, so it wouldn't be wrinkled. Eliana set up three hidden cameras that were all able to be controlled by an app on her phone. She set them up to catch every angle. She also set up a video on the TV that Anita made for Jasmine. Nevaeh cleaned the kitchen as fast as she could. Once Cassidy finished with the outfit, she came into the kitchen to help Nevaeh finish up.

Anita attempted her best to buy time because she knew the girls were back at the house scrambling to get everything set up.

"Here are the marshmallows, now let's get back to the house and enjoy the rest of our day," Jasmine insisted.

"Hold on, let me call Nevaeh and see if we need chocolate and graham crackers or anything else."

"Yeah, that sounds like a good idea. We don't want to get back to the house, get situated, and then have to leave again."

Anita called Nevaeh.

"Hey Nita," Nevaeh answered the phone.

"Hey Nevaeh, do we need anything else for the day?"

"Nope, you guys are all clear," Nevaeh said.

"You sure?" Anita questioned.

"Yup! Let's do this!" Nevaeh was excited.

"All right, homie, we'll be back in like fifteen."

"Sounds good, see you then."

"Bet." They hung up. "Well, Nevaeh said we are all good, we don't need anything else, so let's pay and get back." Anita instantly became nervous. It felt like metal butterflies were clunking around in her stomach, she could feel that her palms became clammy, but she tried to play it off.

Jasmine noticed Anita's sudden change in demeanor, no matter how hard she tried to hide it. "Hey babe, you okay?" Jasmine asked.

"Oh yeah, I'm good," Anita lied, "just a little warm. I'm sure I'll be fine once we get back and I can sip on a drink by the pool."

Jasmine shrugged it off. "All right then, let's ride." They made their way to the register.

Anita anticipated this life-changing moment. She didn't know why she was so nervous. She knew Jasmine loved her. She knew that they were meant to be together and she knew that Jasmine would say yes, but it was still a huge deal.

We're heading to the car, Anita texted Nevaeh.

"All right, ladies, it's almost show time!" Nevaeh screamed throughout the house. "They're in the car on the way back!"

"I'm so exciteeeed," Tiara sang as she shimmied.

Jasmine and Anita pulled up to the house. Right on cue Anita's phone rang.

"Hey Jas, you can go ahead inside, I'm going to take this call real quick."

"Everything okay?" Jasmine sounded concerned.

"Oh yeah, no worries," Anita smiled.

"Okay, well, I'll see you inside." Jasmine hopped out of the car and went toward the house.

"Nevaeh? Jasmine is on her way in."

"Word. Cassidy is out back with your clothes, hurry up!"

Anita hung up the phone and rushed to the back of the house. Cassidy stood off the the side of the backyard as she waved Anita over. "Hurry hurry! I have your suit right here."

"Thanks, Cass. I'm nervous as fuck," Anita said in a shaky tone.

141

"Girl, don't be. Jasmine loves you and this is about to be the sweetest shit I've ever witnessed," Cassidy reassured her with a hug and led her away so she could change.

✶ ✶ ✶

Jasmine walked into the front door to a smile on Eliana's face that was ear to ear. She was holding a red rose.

"What in the world are you smiling about? And why are you holding a rose?" Jasmine was confused.

Eliana said nothing as she continued to smile and handed her the rose. Jasmine continued to walk slowly. Next up was a smiling Nevaeh. She held an orange rose and handed it to her. Next was a smiling Tiara, she held a yellow rose. As Jasmine walked on, butterflies began to flutter in her stomach, she had a feeling what was coming. Next up was Imani and she held a green rose; Cassidy held a blue rose. Before she exited out the back door, an indigo rose lay on the counter with a note underneath.

Come out back. Jasmine looked up from the paper. Before she walked out back, she turned around to see her friends as they smiled at her. Tears began to form in her eyes. "Guys?" she asked.

"Go," they all simultaneously whispered as they shooed her out the back door. Eliana grabbed her camera so she could take pictures of this joyous moment. Jasmine turned the corner. The scenery was beautiful. The sounds of classical music played lightly, the pool waterfall, and waves crashing in the distance were heard. There was a tiki torch path that led to Anita standing at the end of it. She wore white pants, a white button up shirt, and violet suspenders, and held a violet rose.

"Baby?" Jasmine said as she broke down in tears.

"Come here." Anita's voice was warm. Soft.

Jasmine walked slowly toward Anita as tears streamed down her face. The girls followed; all gathered around them at a distance with their phones out to get this beautiful moment on film. Eliana moved a little closer so she could get some good shots. When Jasmine walked up to Anita, she handed her the last rose.

"It's all the colors of the rainbow," Jasmine finally realized. "You know how much I love rainbows," she said through tears.

"I know, baby," Anita chuckled. "Jasmine," she continued, "you and I have been through some shit together. No matter how hard I fall, you are always there to dust me off and to tell me just keep swimming." Anita sniffled. "The issues that I've had with my parents, man, you've seen me at my worst and yet you still loved me through all of it. From the slammed doors and ugly cries to singing at the top of our lungs in the car with the windows down and binge-watching trashy television with even trashier food, it has all made me fall in love with you more as each day passes by. I couldn't imagine spending my life with anyone else. I am so grateful to have you in my life, and I look forward to spending the rest of my life with you. You're my person." Anita reached in her pocket. "So on this day, in front of our closest friends I want to ask you," Anita got down on one knee. "Jasmine Matthews. Will you do me the honor of becoming my wife?"

Jasmine nodded her head yes rapidly as she said, "Yes!" Anita jumped up to hug her.

"Yaaaay!" everyone screamed for joy, they had the confetti poppers ready and waiting. They pulled the string so confetti exploded on them as they kissed. There wasn't a dry eye in that house. All the girls gathered in for a group hug.

"Babe, is this my grandmother's ring? You had it customized?" Anita nodded. "I'm so happy!" Jasmine shouted. "I love all of you guys!" She wiped away her tears.

"Hey now! Let's celebrate!" Imani shouted. She changed the classical music to a party playlist she had on her phone.

The girls drank and danced into the night. Later that night, Tiara noticed Anita and Jasmine had disappeared. She looked out the window on the beach. "Hey guys, come look at this," she said to the girls. They all came over and piled up to look out the window. On the beach they saw Anita and Jasmine slow dancing under the moonlight with the waves crashing behind them.

"Gah, they are amazing," Eliana said.

"Yeah, they give me hope to one day find true love," Imani agreed.

"I think I'm in love with Marie," Nevaeh blurted out.

They all were a little taken aback by her outburst.

"No shit?" Imani asked.

"No shit," Nevaeh smiled.

"Good for you, Nevaeh," Imani encouraged.

TWENTY-ONE

Later that night after everyone turned in for the evening, Tiara lay in bed wide awake. She was so happy for her friends, and just couldn't seem to shake the joyous vibe that drifted through the air. It could've also had something to do with the number of drinks she had. She sat up in her bed. "Ugh," she groaned to herself. She crawled out of bed, left her room, and quietly shut the door behind her. She tiptoed to Imani's room and stared at the closed door as she debated with herself whether to open it or not. Eventually she knocked. A few seconds later Imani opened the door.

"I was hoping you would come," Imani whispered with a smirk.

Tiara rolled her eyes and brushed past her. Imani quietly closed the door.

Tiara had her back turned toward her as Imani walked up and put her arms around her from behind. Imani began to kiss Tiara's neck.

"You know that's my spot," Tiara whispered.

"I know," Imani said through kisses.

Tiara turned to face Imani and they began to kiss. Imani wasted no time as she threw Tiara on the bed. Imani climbed on top of her and they continued to kiss.

"Did you bring the strap?" Tiara panted.

"Of course. Never leave home without it." Imani got excited.

"I want you to fuck me with it."

Imani jumped up. "Okay." Tiara ripped her clothes off as Imani was getting situated.

Imani stood at the foot of the bed. She took a moment to admire Tiara's body. She grabbed Tiara's legs and pulled her toward her, so her waist was at the edge of the bed. Tiara gasped. Imani licked her lips. "You might want to grab a pillow," she suggested.

"Gah, you're so cocky," Tiara scoffed. "I think I'll be okay," she said in a sarcastic tone.

Imani smirked. She got down on her knees, put Tiara's legs on her shoulders, and dove in. Tiara's back arched as she gasped. "Oh shit," she let out. She immediately reached her hands above her head in search of a pillow. She found one and shoved it over her face. Imani could hear muffled moans and intensified her mouth. Tiara climaxed.

Imani wiped her mouth as she got up. She was extremely turned on and was ready to fuck Tiara.

"Scoot back," she instructed, and Tiara obliged. Imani turned Tiara over and lifted her butt in the air. Imani rubbed Tiara's butt as she admired it. She was ready. Tiara wiggled and groaned into the pillow from pleasure as Imani slid inside. Imani started off slow. Her breathing became choppy as she picked up the pace.

"I want to get on top," Tiara whispered.

Imani rolled onto her back as Tiara slid the strap-on inside her. Tiara wasted no time as she began to ride Imani. Imani's hands explored Tiara's body. She loved seeing Tiara from that position. Imani sat up and sucked on Tiara's nipples. That caused Tiara to quicken the pace. Tiara clutched onto Imani. They both came simultaneously. Tiara got off Imani and lay down on the bed next to her.

"Fuck you, Imani," she said.

"What did I do?"

"Why do you have to feel so good?"

Imani laughed. "I guess it's a natural born gift. I don't know." She paused. "Tiara, I'm going to be real with you. I don't know how much longer I'm going to be able to keep this up," she said with concern in her voice.

"What do you mean?"

"Ugh, I can't believe I'm about to say this," Imani admitted. "We've been doing this for a few months now, and I think I'm starting to catch feelings."

"What?" Tiara was shocked.

"Yeah."

"Imani, I thought—"

"I know what you thought," Imani defeatedly interrupted. "You've known me since college and you always thought I was some player who never caught feelings." Imani paused. "The reason I've never caught feelings is because none of them were you." She made a gagging sound. "Oh God, I can't believe I just said that. I think I just threw up in my mouth a little bit."

Tiara chuckled, "So why bring it up now? Does the proposal have you feeling some kind of way?" she asked.

"No, it's not that. We've been fucking for the past few months, and I don't know how much longer I can keep this up. It's driving me insane that I can't tell one of my best friends how much I care for her more than just a friend because I'm afraid that I might lose this connection that we have."

"Why me?" Tiara wondered. "What makes me so different than the other ones?"

"Tiara, honestly, I don't think I can even find the right words to describe why it's you. You're spontaneous, yet boring at the right times. You make me laugh yet piss me off. You're intelligent, caring, and a fighter. You're my best friend and I don't want to fuck this up."

Tiara fell silent. She gathered her thoughts. "Imani." She chose her words carefully. "I've seen too much. I don't know if I can trust you in a relationship after all the things I've witnessed you do. I'm not ready for you and your..." she paused, "history."

Imani sat up. "Look, I know how the world sees me. Some mannish dyke with commitment issues. Yes, a chick has actually said those words to me, but I'm more than that."

"I know you're more than that, Imani. You're one of my best friends. That's not the issue."

"Look, I know that I don't deserve you. You're such an amazing person, and I don't want to half-ass these feelings. I will cut every single one of them hos off." She was serious. "If that is what I have to do to prove my feelings for you, consider them gone."

"It's that easy for you to cut women off, huh?"

"If it means that I get to have all of you, then yes."

"I'd have to think about it." Tiara got up and put on her clothes. She walked toward the door.

"I mean what I say, Tiara."

Tiara self-consciously brushed her hair behind her left ear. "Prove it," she whispered, and quietly slipped out the door.

TWENTY-TWO

The ladies arrived back to Anita and Jasmine's house Sunday afternoon. They all said their see you laters and got into their cars.

Nevaeh hopped into her car. She sat in the driver's seat and stared at her phone. *I'm on my way.* She finally sent a text out. She pulled up to the park. She observed the outside surroundings and spotted Saria sitting on a bench. She seemed nervous as she waited there.

Nevaeh stared at her. *What the fuck are you doing, Nevaeh?* She eventually got out of the car and made her way over to the bench. Saria spotted Nevaeh and immediately stiffened up from nerves. They made eye contact. Neither of them smiled. It was as if they were both in shock. As Nevaeh got closer, Saria stood up. They stood an arm's length apart from one another. They locked eyes.

"Saria," Nevaeh eventually said softly.

Saria sobbed softly and wrapped her arms around Nevaeh. "I'm so sorry, Nevaeh. I'm so so sorry," she said between sniffles.

Nevaeh returned the hug, but she said nothing.

"Ugh," Saria scoffed as she wiped her tears away. "I told myself I wouldn't cry and fucking look at me." She laughed. "Please sit down."

They sat next to one another on the bench. Their arms slightly touched.

"So how have you been, Nevaeh? It's been so long," Saria questioned.

"I've been good. Finally happy." she exhaled. "You?"

"I'm not too bad. I'm working on becoming happy," she replied.

There was an awkward silence.

"So," Saria started, but Nevaeh interrupted.

"How could you leave me like that, Saria?" Nevaeh asked as she turned to Saria. "You were my everything. I was willing to move mountains for you. You knew that. I thought you felt the same, then you just… left."

"I do apologize for leaving so abruptly, but it wasn't that simple."

"Sure." Nevaeh was aware that the situation was not simplistic, but it didn't make it hurt any less.

"It wasn't, and you know that. I was about to graduate from college and my family was all I had."

"You had me and the girls," Nevaeh snapped back.

"So you're telling me, that if I had come out to my parents, and they disowned me, you would've supported me even if we didn't work out?"

Nevaeh was silent.

"I didn't think so," Saria exhaled. "I was scared, Nevaeh. I was a young, broke, frightened little girl who wasn't ready to stand on her own yet."

"On your own? So, you're telling me, you didn't feel as if I had your back? Like you didn't really love me or something?"

"Of course I loved you, Nevaeh!" Saria snapped. "If you didn't know that I loved you after all we went through, then this is a bigger problem than me leaving. Do you think it was easy for me to leave you?! My heart felt like it shattered that day. It felt as if someone ripped half of my soul away. I was never the same." Saria tried to hold back tears.

Nevaeh fell silent again.

Saria sighed, "When we broke up, I tried to play as if I were happy. I even married that nice Jewish boy. I was married to him for eight years." Saria wiped away her tears and sniffled. "I fell into depression because of the lie I was living. Everything started to catch up to me and I just couldn't handle it. Well, during one of my happy episodes, I felt as if having a baby would fix my depression. I thought if I could focus all my energy on making that baby happy, that it would in turn make me happy. Well, it didn't. After Malik was born, I was still miserable."

"Really?"

"Yeah. Now don't get me wrong, I love that boy with all my heart, and he has brought me so much joy. But deep down inside it felt like something was missing. Finally, one day I told my now ex-husband what was wrong. I told him I couldn't live a lie anymore."

"I bet that was difficult," Nevaeh sympathized.

"It was. At first, he was upset. He told me that he didn't want to parent a child with some dyke, and he was going to fight for sole custody. That hurt, a lot actually, but then some time later he came to me and told me he understood. He supported me. He apologized profusely for the way that he had lashed out. Told me he was just hurt. I moved into one of the guest bedrooms of our house and started therapy. Eventually, I moved in with my brother, Noah, and that's why I'm back in the city. Malik was still too young to fully understand what was going on, thank goodness. My ex would even go to family functions with me to pretend we were a happy couple. He's my biggest supporter. He told me he couldn't stay angry at me because he discovered that it wasn't a choice to feel how I felt. He said that if my being with women would allow me to be a better mother to our son then he supported that. I love that man. He is still one of my best friends. He moved back to Morocco, though. He video calls and sends money for Malik and me, but it's not the same as if he was here. I've been single parenting for a while. If it weren't for my brother, I'd be lost. He's been a savior."

"Wow, Saria. I didn't know." Nevaeh tried to wrap her mind around all of the information Saria provided.

"You couldn't have known, Nevaeh, and I do not blame you for anything whatsoever. You were great. So patient with me. Those were all me and my decisions, but it was something I had to go through to be the person I am today. But there is," Saria paused to gather her thoughts. "There is one thing out of all of that I still regret to this day, and that is leaving you. I shouldn't have done that. At least not the way that I did. You deserve more than that. You were my first love and the only person I have been in love with since." She was hesitant with the words that followed. "And if I'm being honest, I'm still in love with you."

Nevaeh looked at her with a confused, shocked expression.

"I just needed to get that off my chest. I'm still in love with you, Nevaeh, and I can't seem to shake that shit. No matter how hard I try, no matter what I do."

Nevaeh, "I don't know what to say, Saria."

"You don't have to say anything. I'm fine now. I've come to terms with knowing that I fucked up by letting you go, and I'm living with it now."

Silence fell.

"So what did your parents say when you told them?" Nevaeh asked.

"Oh man, they flipped shit," Saria laughed. "They were not happy about it; I will say that. Eventually, they came around, though. I think my brother had something to do with it even though he denies it. My parents told me that they didn't want to miss out on the joys of being grandparents nor did they want to miss out on being in their daughter's life. It was a relief, to say the least. It was like I could finally breathe."

"Yeah, I bet."

Suddenly Saria kissed Nevaeh. For a moment Nevaeh kissed her back; she missed the way her lips felt, her scent, the electricity between them. She fell into the days when they were together. Once Nevaeh realized what she was doing, she pushed herself away from Saria.

"I'm sorry," Saria said, embarrassed.

Nevaeh took a deep breath to compose herself. "Look, Saria. It took me a very long time and a lot of women to get over you. I turned into another person after the breakup happened as well. I'm finally getting back to being whole again, and I don't need you doing shit like that to mess it up," Nevaeh sternly admitted. "I have a girlfriend now. Actually, that was her bar we were at when I saw you. Her name is Marie. She's smart, makes me laugh until my belly hurts, successful, gorgeous, and after you I didn't know that I was capable of loving so deeply again until I met her."

Saria nodded her head with tears in her eyes. "She sounds fantastic," she said in a broken voice.

"She is. She truly is. And that's why you have to understand that that kiss cannot happen again."

"I understand."

"If you're okay with it, I would love to be friends, though. You're back in the city, it must be lonely without anyone here."

"Yeah, it is. I mean I have my brother and his girlfriend, but ya know. A lot of people pretty much stopped talking to me after we broke up. Kind of sucks."

"Yeah."

"I'm not going to lie, it might be hard for me to only have you as a friend, but I would rather that than not have you in my life at all." She paused. "I would love to meet Marie someday."

"I'm sure you would like her. She's a great person. A little feisty, but I'm sure you guys would get along great."

"Yeah, I bet she is feisty. You've always had a thing for women like that," Saria smirked.

Nevaeh chuckled, "Yeah, I do. Hey and I would love to meet Malik someday. We can all go to his recitals, plays, games, or whatever it is that he decides to do."

"He would love the attention. He eats that shit up."

"Gets that from his momma I see," Nevaeh joked.

"Hey." Saria playfully punched Nevaeh in the arm.

"I'm kidding," Nevaeh smiled.

"You said we. You think your friends would be okay with me being back?"

"Eh." Nevaeh shrugged. "You let me handle them. They'll come around."

"Yikes. Sounds a little intimidating."

"Yeah. Like I said I was pretty messed up for a while and they were there to pick up the pieces. I think it was more so from its ending so abruptly than anything. It'll be okay, though. We'll figure it out. You've been through a lot over the years. Ultimately I understand why you left. It was your choice to make and I want you to know that I respect you for that. As much as I was hurt, I know you were hurting even more."

"Thanks, Nevaeh. That really means a lot coming from you."

Nevaeh smiled, "But hey, I should probably get going."

"Same here."

They stood up and started walking toward their cars.

"It was great seeing you again, Saria. I'll hit you up. Maybe you can come hang out with the girls on one of our Friends' Friday nights."

"Friends' Friday?"

"Yeah, we're kind of into alliterations. Makes us feel smart and shit," Nevaeh smiled.

Saria giggled. "Right. Well, maybe."

They hugged. Nevaeh went to pull away, but Saria pulled her in a little tighter, and sniffled. They finally separated. "All right, now get out of here, you're holding me up," Saria joked.

Nevaeh could see the tears in Saria's eyes. "Yeah," she said softly.

"All right, hit me up." Saria hopped into her car and drove off. Nevaeh did the same.

Nevaeh drove to Marie's place without even realizing she did.

"Hey baby. How was your trip?" Marie asked as Nevaeh entered the door.

Nevaeh said nothing. She dropped all her stuff on the floor and aggressively kissed Marie.

Marie pushed her off. "Whoa, baby. Everything okay?"

"Yeah, I'm fine." Nevaeh said as she went in for another kiss while she started to unbutton her shirt.

Marie pushed her away again. "What the fuck is going on with you?"

Nevaeh exhaled, "Forget it." She started picking up her stuff as she headed toward the door.

"What the fuck is going on here?" Marie asked as Nevaeh continued to gather her stuff. "Wait, Nevaeh! What is going on?"

Nevaeh stopped in her tracks. "I met up with Saria!" she said without turning around to face Marie. "And she kissed me," Nevaeh said as she held back tears.

Marie was stunned. She stood there blinking rapidly as if her brain was trying to process what was just said. "Excuse me?" she was finally able to cough up.

Nevaeh turned around with tears rolling down her face. "She kissed me," she said through tears.

"Saria?" Marie asked as if she needed reassurance. "Your first love Saria?"

"Yeah," Nevaeh responded defeatedly.

"She," Marie paused as she held back tears, "she kissed you?"

"Yeah."

"What the fuck?" Marie's sadness quickly began to turn into anger. "Why didn't you tell me that you were meeting up with her?"

"Because I didn't want it to be a big deal."

"Didn't want it to be a big deal?" Marie made air quotes as she said big deal. "Well, was it?"

"Was it what?"

"Don't play dumb with me, Nevaeh. Was it a big deal?"

Nevaeh walked over to the couch and sat down. She sighed, "I don't know."

"You don't know? Motherfuck…" She paused. "Well, you know what I don't know? I don't know if I can be with someone who kisses their ex and then tries to come fuck me. Get your shit and get out," Marie demanded.

"Marie, can you chill for a minute? I want to talk to you about this."

"Talk? There aint shit to talk about. Seems like you and Saria did enough fucking talking. Matter of fact, I'll get your shit for you." Marie started angrily gathering Nevaeh's belongings.

"Marie, sit the fuck down! I'm trying to talk to you about some deep shit right now! You keep telling me how guarded I am, then I try to talk to you about something that is truly bothering me and you blow the fuck up. This is why I didn't want to tell you about meeting up with her!" Nevaeh shouted.

Marie glared at Nevaeh, but she obeyed and sat down.

"Thank you." Nevaeh was relieved. "Now I will apologize because I went about this situation all wrong. I should've told you about going to meet up with her. I didn't because I was afraid of the backlash that I might've gotten from it, but honestly, curiosity got the best of me. You know how much I loved that girl, we've had the ex-discussion. I just felt like I had some unanswered questions. Unresolved issues. I needed to talk to her. It was weighing heavy on my mind since I saw her that day in your bar. I needed to do it for me."

Marie sniffled. "Did you kiss her back?"

Nevaeh exhaled, "For like a millisecond I got caught up in it, but then I realized what I was doing and pushed her away."

"So you're telling me you don't have feelings for her anymore?"

"No. I really don't. Her kissing me made me realize how in love I am with you." Nevaeh sniffled. "I discovered how deeply I'm able to love again. How important you are to me. I wanted nothing more than to rush here and tell you everything that happened. Unfortunately, it didn't play out exactly how I wanted it to," she chuckled.

"No, it did not." Marie laughed. "You came about that all wrong. You almost got cut."

"I know and I'm sorry about that. There were just so many things running through my head at once that I didn't know how to handle it."

"Yeah. I can understand that." Marie paused. "So you love me?" Marie smirked.

"Yeah, I do," Nevaeh smiled, "like a lot. It's kind of gross how much I do."

Marie leaned in and kissed Nevaeh on the lips. "I love you too." There was a slight pause. "I guess that's why I was going to flip out on you. It made me mad that somebody else shared something intimate with you. Especially a woman that I know how much you loved. It made me feel angry, abandoned, betrayed, and sad all at once. But I also want to apologize."

"What are you apologizing for?"

"That you didn't feel comfortable enough to come to me about meeting up with your ex. I can understand why you did it, and for real I'm glad you did. I'm glad you got the answers you were looking for. I know that was something you needed to do."

"Thank you." Nevaeh was relieved.

"So what'd you guys talk about?"

"Well, she told me she got divorced and came out to her parents." "Damn. I bet that took some balls."

"Yeah, she said that after some time her parents came around and her ex became one of her biggest supporters. She has a five-year-old son. And she told me one of her biggest regrets was letting me go."

"Oh, she better chill."

"There's nothing to worry about," Nevaeh smiled. "Oh and I told her that I would love for her to meet you," she said quickly.

"What the fuck?"

Nevaeh laughed. "She doesn't have any friends here and I figured it'd be good for her to hang out with all of us. Plus, she said her son is starting little people sports. Figured it'd be cool to go cheer the little man on."

"Ugh," Marie scoffed. "I will do this because I'm a nice person and I love kids, but I tell you what, if she try me, I'm smacking the dog shit out of her."

"She shouldn't. I made it very clear how happily in love I am with you and she respects that."

"Yeah, okay. We'll see."

"Thank you, baby," Nevaeh smiled.

"For what?"

"Just for being you and so understanding. Most people would be quick to judge and not listen to the reasoning behind the situation. I really do love you."

Marie and Nevaeh cuddled on the couch and talked into the evening. That day they became even closer; oddly enough, Saria was to be thanked.

TWENTY-THREE

Two weeks after the weekend getaway, Anita and Jasmine invited all the girls over to their house, so they could plan the wedding. They provided a platter of cheese, crackers, grapes, and finger sandwiches, along with red and white wine, spread out on the coffee table for everyone to eat and sip on as they planned.

"Okay, everyone." Jasmine was excited. "We have come to the conclusion that we would love to help keep your businesses alive. I know y'all have successful business lives, but this is our way of saying thank you for being so great to us and allowing us to have a family away from family. We will be paying each and every one of you for your services if you so accept. We would like Imani's company to cater."

"Oh, you know I'm there!" Imani responded with joy.

"Nevaeh, we would love to hire you to help us plan the wedding of our dreams," Jasmine continued.

"Anita. Jasmine. I would be honored," Nevaeh responded sincerely.

"Eliana, we would love for you to photograph our bridal photos, but since we want you in our wedding, if you have a recommendation of someone who would be great at taking pictures of the wedding and ceremony, that would be awesome."

"I got y'all, no doubt," Eliana reassured.

"Tiara, we would like to use your parents' beach house as the venue. Why not get married where we said yes to the rest of our lives?" Jasmine said as she looked into Anita's eyes.

"Oh my goodness, yes! I'm sure my parents would love to host the wedding there." Tiara spoke excitedly.

"Speaking of wanting you all to be in our wedding," Anita added, "Ellie and Imani, I would like for you two to be my female version of groomsmen as well as my best women."

Eliana and Imani smiled with excitement.

"T and Nevaeh, I would like for you two to be my bridesmaids as well as maids of honor."

"Yay!" Nevaeh clapped.

"And Cassidy. Our beautiful Cassidy. Since you are leaving us," Jasmine paused and looked at Anita with a smile. She then turned to look at Cassidy again and sighed, "It breaks our heart that you have to go because you have become an important part of our family. We are so glad that Nevaeh, being the fearless flirt that she is—" Everyone slightly chuckled together. Nevaeh took a bow while sitting down. "...we are so glad that she decided to hit on you that night at No Man's. Even more glad that you turned her down."

"Hey!" Nevaeh shouted playfully.

"Hey nothin, Nevaeh!" Anita joked back. "If she would've said yes, y'all would have hooked up and Cassidy would not be sittin here today."

Nevaeh and Cassidy looked at one another and nodded in agreement. "You right," Nevaeh agreed.

Jasmine continued, "Anyway we are glad that you are part of the family and we are so sad to see you go. We would like to ask you to officiate our wedding."

Cassidy teared up, "Aw, you guys! I would love nothing more than to officiate it. Thank you." Cassidy stood up and hugged Jasmine. Everyone smiled at the beautiful moment.

Nevaeh cleared her throat. "Anita and Jasmine, I hope you guys know that I won't be charging you for my services. Consider it a wedding gift."

"Same here," everyone agreed. "Yeah, I think I can speak for everyone when I say y'all are family. Chosen family at that, which is better than the family that's forced onto us," Imani chuckled. "For this occasion, your money is no good here."

"Yeah, my parents and I will feel the same way," Tiara chimed in.

Anita and Jasmine were both greatly touched by the kind gestures; Anita started to tear up. "I know we say this a lot, but it's important for the people who matter to you, to know that they matter. So, I will continue to tell you all how much you mean to me, no matter how corny it might be. Y'all mean the world to us, for real. Like to the point where if we all ended up moving away from one another, we would have to have mandatory annual family reunions."

"What?" Eliana chimed in. "If we all move away from one another? Is that a hint at something? Is another one of you bitches moving?" Eliana looked around the room.

"No," Anita laughed, "it was hypothetical, love."

"Mmmhhmm. Better be hypo-damn-thetical." Eliana sipped her wine.

"Anyway," Anita continued, "we just want to say thank you. You guys have been there for us from our lows to our highs. When I got shot…" She paused.

Jasmine leaned over and kissed her shoulder. "It's okay, baby, you got this," she whispered in her ear.

Anita cleared her throat. "I know the gunshot wasn't a serious one, but it definitely allowed me to look at life differently. I knew that life could be taken away from us at any moment, but I didn't REALLY know. With that being said, I just wanted to take the time to tell you all how much I love you guys and how much each and every one of you means to me."

There wasn't a dry eye in the room. "To framily," Tiara managed to choke out as she raised her glass.

"To framily," everyone said and raised their glasses. "Cheers."

TWENTY-FOUR

"Ugh baby, I'm nervous," Marie groaned.

"On some real shit, baby, so am I, but I think this is for the best. If it doesn't play out well, we don't have to do it again."

"Fine."

Nevaeh stood up, leaned in and kissed Marie on the lips. They smiled at one another. They were at No Man's Land. Marie was behind the bar, and Nevaeh sat on the customer side with a beer.

"Tequila?" Marie asked.

"Tequila." Nevaeh nodded her head.

Marie poured the shots. "May this awkward encounter not be so awkward. Cheers."

"Cheers." They tapped glasses and threw the shots back.

Ken walked in from the back carrying clean glasses. "Damn, ladies, y'all planning on having another 'meeting'?" he asked sarcastically, using air quotes around meeting.

"Shut up," Marie joked and playfully smacked him with a dish towel. "No. I am meeting Saria for the first time."

Ken asked, "Saria? Why does that name sound familiar?"

"You remember that gorgeous girl who came in here a while back when Nevaeh and I were having our 'meeting' in my office? Then when we came out Nevaeh followed her out of the bar?"

"Oh shit! Saria! Your ex?" Ken asked Nevaeh.

Nevaeh nodded.

"What the fuck is up with that? I mean like why?"

"Because she doesn't have friends out this way. I'm just trying to help," Nevaeh ensured.

"The three of you together, though? FIRE," Ken suggested.

"Ugh," Marie scoffed. "Stop being such a dude."

"He's not wrong, though," Nevaeh said as she sipped her beer with one hand and high fived Ken with the other. Marie glared. "I'm kidding, babe!"

"Whatever." Marie turned away to clean the shot glasses.

"No, I'm not," Nevaeh mouthed to Ken. Ken smiled.

"Oh shit, she's here," Ken said as he saw Saria walk in the door.

"Fuck," Marie whispered.

"Hey Saria!" Nevaeh said nervously with a hug.

"Hey Nevaeh," Saria responded back with a hug.

"Saria, this is Marie. My amazingly wonderful girlfriend I told you about, and Marie, this is Saria."

Saria outstretched her hand to shake Marie's. Marie shook Saria's hand and glared at her. "If you kiss my girlfriend again, we're going to have some serious problems," Marie instructed.

Nevaeh closed her eyes and placed her face in her hands; Saria's eyes widened from shock. "Oh no," she assured. "That will never happen again. Trust and believe me."

"Bet not." Marie softened her glare. "Anyway with that out of the way, it's a pleasure to meet you. I can see why Nevaeh was attracted to you, you are gorgeous," she complimented.

Saria blushed. "Thank you. That's very sweet of you. You are stunning as well."

Marie smiled, "Yeah, I do all right." They both laughed. "Please, let's all three go back to my office so we can talk in private. Ken, are you going to be all right by yourself for a little bit?"

"Oh yeah, I'll be fine for now. We're not busy at all. You three go handle your business," Ken assured with a smile.

The three ladies walked back to the office.

"Please have a seat." Marie gestured to the chairs in front of her desk. "So Saria, Nevaeh tells me you've got a son? I love kids."

Saria smiled, "I do! His name is Malik. He's five, and he's the light of my life."

"That's sweet."

"Nevaeh tells me this is your bar? That's impressive."

"Thanks," Marie smiled. "Yeah, this is my baby, and I worked my ass off to get her up and running."

"Well, you've done an amazing job," Saria complimented. "I must ask, why the name No Man's Land?"

"Well, originally, it started out as a lesbian only bar, but it wasn't doing so well. Lesbians as a whole have this tendency to come out, find a girlfriend, then hibernate. We always complain about not having enough lesbian bars around, but then don't frequent them enough so they stay open. I don't know, anyway it doesn't do well for business. So I decided to switch it up. It's still technically a lesbian bar but open to everyone. People loved the name regardless of gender, so I kept it."

"That's awesome."

The three of them talked and laughed for about an hour.

"Oh wow, look at the time," Saria finally said. "I should probably get going."

Marie seemed upset. "Aw, really? We were just warming up."

"Yeah, Malik has a play coming up, and I have to get him to rehearsal."

"A play? That sounds cute. When is it?"

"Friday after next."

"Well, maybe we can come support?" Marie offered.

"Malik and I would both love to have you."

"Awesome. Well, just let us know the details."

"Sounds like a plan. Thanks, you two. For real. This was nice." Saria gave both Marie and Nevaeh a hug. "I'll see you guys." She went out the door.

"So what'd you think?" Nevaeh inquired.

"Damn, Nevaeh, I have to give it to you, the girl isn't at all what I expected."

"Well, what did you expect?" Nevaeh was curious.

"You know, I'm not exactly sure what I expected. I just know I didn't expect for us to get along like we did. I thought I was going to have some deep-seated anger or jealousy there, but I didn't."

"Is that right?"

"Yeah," Marie continued, "I can definitely see why you fell for her."

"You seem intrigued," Nevaeh observed.

"I might be," Marie responded with a smirk.

TWENTY-FIVE

A few weeks had passed. Nevaeh, Marie, and Saria's friendship grew stronger. One day, Saria invited the couple to Malik's school play and the two enthusiastically accepted her offer.

"Malik, put your shoes on or else we're going to be late!" Saria fussed at her son as he wanted to do everything else but put his shoes on.

"Mom, I'm trying!" Malik shouted back.

"Well, try harder! You have people that are coming to watch you in your play tonight!"

"People are coming to watch me?" His eyes lit up.

"Yes! Now we don't want to disappoint them, do we?"

"Of course not, Mom." Malik came into the living room with his shoes on. "Let's give the people what they want."

"Good grief, boy, where did you hear that fr…" She paused and waved it off. "You know what? Never mind. Let's go." Saria gathered everything and headed out the door. She buckled Malik into his seat in the back and then hopped in the driver's side. When she turned the ignition, her phone buzzed. It was a text from Nevaeh.

Hey Saria, Marie and I are on our way to the school. We're looking forward to meeting Malik and watching him perform!

Great we're on our way too. See you guys there! Saria responded before she pulled out of the driveway.

By the time Saria and Malik arrived, Nevaeh and Marie were already there. They walked into the auditorium and Nevaeh and Marie waved them down from their seats.

"Hey you two," Saria said as she gave them a hug. "It's good to see you guys again."

"Good to see you too," Marie smiled.

Saria gazed at the two of them for a few moments, then broke the stare and cleared her throat. "Malik, sweetie. This is Ms. Marie and Ms. Nevaeh." Malik hid behind his mother with a shy grin. "Marie, Nevaeh, this is Malik."

"Hi," he said in a timid voice.

"Hi, Malik." Nevaeh and Marie waved.

"We're really looking forward to seeing you perform today," Marie said.

Malik's grin grew.

"Okay, I'm going to take him on stage, and I'll be right back to sit with you two."

"Sounds good," Nevaeh nodded. Marie and Nevaeh found their seats.

"He is adorable!" Marie exclaimed.

"I know, right! I cannot handle his little dimples. Too cute," Nevaeh responded.

"Hey, you know what I was thinking?" Marie asked.

"What's that?"

"Maybe we should see if Saria wants to join for Friends' Friday tonight."

"You think so? You don't think it might be too late to find a sitter?"

"Yeah, that's a strong possibility, but there's no harm in asking, right?"

"That's true," Nevaeh agreed. "Okay, let's do it."

Saria sat down next to them. "Hey you two, thanks for coming. It means a lot to both of us." She smiled. "It takes a village, right?"

"Of course. We are happy to be here." Nevaeh smiled back.

"Hey, so we both were wondering, how would you like to come and hang out with us and the girls tonight? For Friends' Friday?"

"Really? Wow, I would love to." Saria paused. "Wait. Are Tiara and Imani going to be there? Last I heard they weren't too fond of me."

Marie and Nevaeh glanced at each other. "Let me worry about that," Nevaeh assured.

"Oh boy." Saria's tone saddened. "It's okay though, maybe next time. It's kind of late to find a last-minute sitter anyway."

"No. Not maybe next time. Definitely," Marie demanded.

"We meet every Friday night, so you've got a heads up," Nevaeh informed her. "And if you do happen to find a last-minute sitter, please let us know. You are welcome to come."

"Thanks," Saria smiled.

The play started. There were laughs and applause as proud parents watched their children on stage. Saria took videos and pictures of Malik and his co-stars. She was so excited for him. Overwhelmed to see that he had made friends. She teared up from joy, but quickly brushed them away. After the play Saria, Nevaeh, and Marie went up on stage to congratulate Malik and his friends.

"Mom!" Malik shouted with a huge smile on his face as he ran to his mother's arms.

"Malik! You did so good, baby!" She gave him a squeeze. "I'm so proud of you." She kissed him on the cheek.

"Yeah, you did so good," Nevaeh said.

"Thanks!" Malik said with his chest out. "Did you guys see my solo?"

"We sure did! You were fantastic!" Marie exclaimed and put her hand out for a high five. Malik gladly gave her one.

"You know what?" Saria asked Malik. "You did so well today, how does ice cream sound?"

"Yaaaaaay!" Malik was ecstatic. "Ice cream!"

"Great!" Saria turned to Marie and Nevaeh. "What about you two? Would you like to join us for ice cream?" Saria wasn't sure why, but she developed butterflies in her stomach as she anticipated their answer.

"Please! Please!" Malik begged.

Nevaeh and Marie glanced at each other. "We'd love to," Marie responded as they both smiled.

"Great," Saria smiled.

"So what kind of ice cream do you want?"

"Bubble gum!" Malik shouted excitedly.

"Bubble gum?" Nevaeh and Marie asked in unison with a look of disgust on their faces. Malik nodded enthusiastically.

"Yeah, that's his obsession right now. Bubble gum ice cream. It's gross." Saria shook her head.

"It's not gross, it's delicious, Mommy!" Malik defended his ice cream.

"It sure is, sweetie," Saria fake smiled.

Marie and Nevaeh laughed to themselves.

✳ ✳ ✳

"Hi, what can I get for you?" the cashier asked Saria.

"Yes, may I get a kid's bubble gum, a Strawberry Deluxe, and then whatever they want?"

"Oh, we can get ours," Marie responded.

"No. Please." Saria insisted. "Let me get this. It's the least I can do for you two taking time out of your day to make it to Malik's play," she smiled.

Marie smiled back, "Uh, sure, I'll get the Mango Mayhem," she told the cashier.

"And I'll have the Cookie Crusher." Nevaeh put in her order.

"Great, that will be $21.63. What's the name on the order?"

"Saria."

"Saria? Beautiful name attached to a gorgeous woman." The lady flirted from behind the register.

"Oh, thank you very much." Saria blushed, grabbed the receipt and walked off.

"Oh snap," Nevaeh teased as they sat down. "Looks like Saria has an admirer."

"Nah, she was just being kind." Saria continued to blush.

"No, she was not just being kind. She was shooting her shot," Marie chimed in.

"Well, we're not here for that today." Saria brushed it off. "Today we're here for Malik." Saria quickly glanced back at the cashier. She was busy helping other customers.

"Right. So Malik, what do you like most about school?" Marie switched the subject.

"I like when we draw."

"Oh yeah. Drawing is a lot of fun." She continued, "Do you have a favorite color?"

"Yellow!" he smiled.

"Yellow? Why yellow?"

"Because it's bright and happy like the sun! And me!"

They all smiled at his response.

"Saria!" The staff shouted her name to go pick up their order.

"I'll be right back."

Nevaeh, Marie, and Malik continued to talk as she went to get their ice cream. She walked up to the counter and glanced over at the cashier once more, this time the cashier made eye contact with her and winked. Saria smiled at her and blushed as she grabbed the ice cream and hurried back to the table. Before she sat down, she took a moment to observe the interaction between the women and Malik. It brought her warmth as she watched Malik interact with the pair with genuine excitement. It once again brought those butterflies that she wasn't sure where they came from. *Why do I get so nervous around these two?* she asked herself. She brushed off the feeling, assuring herself that she was just nervous because Nevaeh was her ex. She sat down. "Here you go, guys." She passed out everyone's orders.

"I think you have a little something written on your cup," Nevaeh pointed out.

"Huh?" Saria looked at her cup. The cashier had written a note with her number attached on her cup: *Give me a chance?- Kennedy.*

Saria glanced at the cashier again, this time she stared directly at her with a grin. Saria smiled, but didn't have the butterflies.

"All right, you two. Y'all are worse than Malik." Malik smiled at Marie and Nevaeh.

"You deserve to be happy, Mommy." Malik stated.

"Let's just enjoy our ice cream. Okay?"

They all nodded. They joked, laughed, got to know one another, and had a great time over ice cream.

"Well, this has been a blast," Saria exhaled. "I really needed this, so thank you, guys."

"No," Marie responded. "Thank you. We truly enjoyed ourselves."

"Yeah, and Malik is an amazing kid. You're doing such a great job," Nevaeh input.

Saria sighed, "Thanks. I'm trying my best. My brother helps out a lot." There was a slight pause. "Anyway, we should get going," Saria said with sadness. She didn't want to leave them, but she knew she had to. She wasn't sure where the feelings were coming from and they confused the hell out of her, but she couldn't stop them.

"Yeah. I guess we should get going too," Nevaeh said. They all stood around and stared at each other for a few seconds, as if Nevaeh and Marie felt the same as Saria.

Saria broke the pause with a hug. "All right, well I guess I will talk to you guys later."

"Right. Hey, don't forget about Kennedy now." Nevaeh teased as she gave her a hug. She also felt a little jealous.

Saria rolled her eyes. "Yeah. Right."

"And if you find a last-minute sitter, please join us tonight," Marie reminded her.

"Yeah, of course. I would really like that." Saria gave her a hug.

They walked off.

* * *

"Hey Saria! Is that you?" her brother shouted from the back as she walked in the door.

"Yeah, it's me! Hey Noah!" she shouted back.

He came into the living room and greeted her with a hug.

"Hey Malik! Oh man, buddy, I'm so sorry I missed your play today! I had to work."

"It's okay, Uncle Noah, I understand."

"How'd you do?"

"I did so good! And Mommy took me out for ice cream afterwards! And I met Mommy's friends Ms. Nevaeh and Ms. Marie!"

Noah made eye contact with Saria. "Is that right, buddy? That sounds so great!" He stood up. "Hey how about you go play and I'll be there in a bit to join."

"Okay!" Malik ran off.

"Saria," Noah said sternly.

"Don't." She rolled her eyes and walked off.

"Nevaeh? Really?" Noah asked. "And who's Marie?"

"Her girlfriend."

"Her girlfriend." Noah paused and took a breath. "You still have feelings for her?"

Saria groaned. "I don't know. It's hard, Noah. I don't want to have feelings, but something is definitely still there. And Marie?" she exhaled. "My goodness. She's amazing too. I wouldn't want to do anything that would cause me to come between them. Sometimes

I do feel like I get this vibe from them both, but I chalk it up as me reaching for something that isn't there."

"What do you mean vibe? Like a sexual vibe or they're both into you, like relationship vibe?" Noah inquired.

"I don't know, Noah. This shit is crazy to me. Nevaeh has been the one that got away for me. Maybe I have these feelings for Marie because of Nevaeh? I don't even know. It's all so confusing," Saria exhaled. "They invited me to go out with them tonight. Well, not just them, their group of friends. They meet up every Friday to catch up, drink, and blow off steam. I told them I couldn't make it."

"Why is that?"

"I told them that I wouldn't be able to find a last-minute sitter."

"Well, I know that's a lie because I love hanging out with my nephew and I'd be glad to watch him for you."

Saria sighed, "Yeah, I know. Nevaeh's best friends from college, Imani and Tiara, are going to be there, and they hate me for how things ended with us."

"Well, sis, if you want to truly at least be friends with these two, you're going to have to face Imani and Tiara eventually."

"Yeah, I know, but I don't want to," she pouted as she flopped down on the couch.

"Saria," Noah exhaled and placed his hands on her shoulders, "you know all I want for you is to be happy, baby sis. You need that. You deserve it. You've been doing such a great job with Malik, I think it's okay if you take a little time for yourself. I don't know about trying to come between the two of them because that's like playing with fire, but you never know. A glorious friendship could form from it and maybe you can find love again through the group of friends."

"Yeah. I guess." Saria continued to pout. "You're so wise."

"Call them. I will watch Malik tonight. I will also watch him for your hangover tomorrow," he chuckled.

"I don't want to inconvenience you, Noah," Saria pushed back.

"You're not. I'm offering. Maybe I will invite Liz over. She loves Malik and he has gotten in the habit of already calling her Aunt Liz," he smiled. "We'll watch movies, eat junk food, and play games. It'll be a fun night."

"I really like you and Liz together. She's good for you," Saria smiled.

"Yes, she's amazing. And this group of friends will be good for you." Noah got the conversation back on track.

"Are you sure?"

Noah shook his head. "No, But there's only one way to find out." He handed Saria her phone. "Call them."

"Okay, okay." Saria teased, "So pushy." She walked off into her bedroom and shut the door.

What the hell are you doing right now, Saria? she asked herself as she paced back and forth. *What if Imani and Tiara still hate me? What if Nevaeh told her other friends about me and they hate me too? So I'm just supposed to go in there with a bunch of hatred thrown in my face? I can't handle that pressure right now. Then again Marie likes me, and that is Nevaeh's current girlfriend, so maybe there is hope.* Saria sighed. *Well, here goes nothing.*

Her heartbeat quickened as the phone rang.

"Hello?" Nevaeh's voice came through the receiver.

"Hey," Saria responded nervously.

"What's going on, Saria? Everything all right?"

"Yeah, everything's all right. Great, actually. Noah said he'd watch Malik for me tonight, so I'll be able to meet up with you guys for the Friends' Friday."

"Really?" Nevaeh's voice perked up. "Well, that's great!"

"What happened?" Saria heard Marie ask in the background.

"Saria's brother said he'll watch Malik tonight so she can make it."

"Awesome!" Marie was enthused.

"Great, so No Man's Land around eight o'clock," Nevaeh instructed.

"No Man's Land around eight. Got it. I will see you there," Saria said.

"Can't wait."

The call ended. *Oh boy. I really hope this does not turn into a shit show,"* Saria exhaled.

TWENTY-SIX

Eliana's phone binged uncontrollably. "What the hell is going on?" she mumbled. Suddenly, it rang.

"Hello?" Eliana answered with a spoonful of cereal in her mouth.

"Eliana!" Scarlett screamed into the phone. "Google 'Good Souls'! Girl, our project went viral!"

"What?" Eliana was caught off guard. She quickly put her bowl of cereal down and raced over to her laptop. She pulled up Google and typed in "Good Souls by Eliana Morgan." Article links popped up for her website, project, and social media accounts. Collectively, she had over one million shares and retweets. "What the fuck," she said in disbelief.

"I know, right! This is crazy." Scarlett was just as amazed.

"I wonder what happens now?" Eliana asked.

"I don't even know."

"Maybe we can all go out and grab some drinks in celebration?"

"Yeah, that's a great idea." Eliana was still in disbelief.

"Well, I already told people on my end and tomorrow evening works for us."

"Uh, yeah. I should be able to swing that."

"Awesome, just let me know."

"Will do. I'll talk to you later."

"Later."

Holy shit Eliana. You finally did it, she said to herself as she continued to scroll through the links. Once she read enough reviews, positive and negative, she got up to go shower.

She stood there and allowed the warm water to flow down her face. She was still in shock that one of her projects had reached so many people. It amazed her that some people still thought tattoos were so taboo in this day and age. Her project had reached guys, girls, and everyone in between in the small towns where people weren't as open minded as they were in Geibourne. There were even young lesbians who responded to her, thanking her. They were so excited to see another publicly out lesbian in the art world. It was all a humbling experience for Eliana.

When she got out of the shower, she looked at her phone and she had over 300 notifications. There were texts from her girls, missed calls from family members, a few messages from popular YouTubers and bloggers, girls trying to get with her in her DMs, and more responses on her social media accounts. There was one notification in particular that took her by surprise. It was from Arlie, the creator of her favorite art YouTube channel *Arlie's Art*. She asked if she wanted to make an appearance on her channel. Eliana was elated.

As she continued to scroll through her phone, another notification caught her full attention. Scott. Scott was the owner of a popular local art gallery. He wanted to know if she wanted her photos to be the main event at an upcoming showing. Now that "Good Souls" went viral, all her other photos were getting attention as well. She could no longer hold her excitement in.

Eliana screamed, "Yes!" as she jumped and danced around her studio apartment. The dancing was not flattering to say the least, but she didn't care. "Oh my goodness," she said in relief as she flopped down on her bed. Breathlessly, "I can't believe this is happening to me." She pulled out her phone and finally hopped in the group text with her girls. The group went crazy because they were all so excited for her. They agreed to discuss it more later that night at Friends' Friday.

Next, she called her mom. "Ellie!" her mom screamed into the phone.

"Hey Mom!" Eliana smiled.

"The younger kids around the neighborhood kept telling me you went viral! I finally was able to look at your project. My goodness, Ellie. It's amazing."

Eliana teared up. "Thank you so much, Mom."

"Are you crying?"

"I'm so happy!" she blurted out. By this time, it was a full-fledged ugly cry. "I never thought something like this could happen to me."

"Oh baby," her mom said in a soft tone. "I did. I always knew you had it in you. Even though it hurt to see you go, I knew I had to let you move away from home. You've always had that drive in you."

Eliana calmed down a bit. "But I thought you wanted me to go to college?"

"Of course I did because I'm your mother. I worried. That's what we do as mothers. But I never for a second doubted you. I'm always in your corner, Ellie."

Eliana laughed as she wiped away her tears. "Ugh, I can't believe I'm over here crying like a little baby."

"I think you're allowed an emotional outburst at a time like this," her mother encouraged.

"Thanks, Mom," Eliana smiled. "How's Dad?"

"Oh you know, he's being your father." Eliana felt her mom roll her eyes through the phone. "How are you doing now that you've had some time away from Trisha?"

"Mom. I cannot express to you how good I feel. Like I knew Trisha wasn't good for me, but I didn't fully grasp how bad she was for me until she was out of my life for good. My mind is clearer. I'm getting to know me again. I'm learning how to be by myself, and that being alone doesn't necessarily mean I'm lonely. I'm facing my fears, Mom."

"That's so good to hear, Ellie. I love to hear that you're doing well. You're an awesome chick, you should want to get to know you." Her mom's voice was sweet and nurturing.

They caught up on the phone for about an hour before hanging up.

Eliana then decided to respond to Arlie. Arlie instantaneously responded to her message asking if they could speak on the phone, and provided her number. Eliana stared at her phone, once again in disbelief. She couldn't believe that Arlie James gave her her number! After she had her fangirl moment, she calmed herself down and dialed the number.

"Hello?" Arlie answered.

Eliana attempted to sound as calm as she could. "Hey Arlie, it's Eliana."

"Hi, Eliana. I was hoping you would call! Please call me AJ," she insisted.

Eliana's smile was so big it felt as if her face was going to get stuck that way. "Okay, AJ." She blushed.

"Yeah, so I wanted to link up with you because I really enjoyed your project," Arlie continued. "It was thought-provoking even for today's society. It still amazes me how some people view tattoos."

"I was just thinking the same," Eliana agreed. "But really I have to give the credit for the idea to Scarlett. She and her family are the models in the project. She gave me the idea."

"Yeah, but you were the one who made it happen," Arlie assured her. "But if it's okay with you, I'd love to have you make an appearance on my channel, and Scarlett too if she'd be cool with it."

"I would love that. I'll bring it up with Scarlett. Actually, we're supposed to get together for drinks tomorrow night in celebration of the project. I'll ask her then."

"Really? That sounds like it will be a good time."

"Yeah? Would you like to join us?"

"I wouldn't want to impose."

"Trust me. You would not be imposing. I'd love to have you. You can be my plus one," Eliana smiled.

"All right then. Yeah, I'm in."

"Great. I will text you later with the details."

"Can't wait to hear from you."

"Awesome."

They hung up.

Next up was Scott. She wanted to have her project display at his next showing. Scott also wanted her to give him a call. She wasn't as giddy as she was with Arlie. Eliana knew that was because she had a thing for Arlie.

"Hello?" Scott cheerfully answered the phone.

"Scott? Hi, it's Eliana."

"Eliana! Yes. Thank you for calling."

"Are you kidding me? No, thank you for reaching out to me."

"I had no choice; your project was amazing. So like I said in the message, I would like to show off your artwork in my next showcase. It's not for another few months, but I like to have everything organized beforehand." Scott continued, "I was hoping we could meet up for lunch sometime next week and discuss the details."

"Sure, which day are you thinking?"

"Tuesday works perfect for me."

"Tuesday it is then."

"Great! I'll see you then. Bye bye."

"Bye." Eliana could feel the excitement rising in her again. Her dreams had started to come true.

TWENTY-SEVEN

"Baby!" Marie screamed from the bathroom.

"Yeah?" Nevaeh screamed back as she lay on her bed.

"Hit up Saria and ask her if she wants to ride with us to the bar," Marie suggested. "I know this has to be weird for her, meeting Tiara and Imani again after all these years and what happened. I mean you saw how freaked out she was at the mention of them."

"Yeah, she did seem pretty nervous. You sure, baby?"

"Yeah, of course." Marie peeked her head into the bedroom. "Why? Do you think it's a bad idea?"

"No. Not at all. I mean we invited her; I think it would only be right of us if we showed up together."

"Something is up with you." Marie sat down on the bed and placed her hand on Nevaeh's stomach.

Nevaeh propped herself up on her elbows. "Nothing is wrong, baby. I promise."

"Okay, but if there is, please talk to me."

"You know I will."

Marie leaned in and gave Nevaeh a kiss. The kiss deepened and hands began to wander. Marie pulled away from the kiss. She stared passionately into Nevaeh's eyes. She rose to her feet. She slowly pulled her skirt up as she intensely stared at Nevaeh. Nevaeh loved when Marie did this. She slid off the bed and onto her knees. She placed one of Marie's legs over her shoulder. Marie grabbed onto the bedpost for balance. Nevaeh began to devour Marie. Marie's body jolted as she felt the warmth of Nevaeh's mouth on her.

"Yes, baby." She let out a moan. "I've been needing this." Marie rubbed her head and pulled it deeper into her pussy. Nevaeh's motion quickened and Marie moved her hips to the motion.

"Oh shit, baby, I'm close," Marie said through breaths.

Nevaeh knew what that meant. She slid a finger into her girlfriend and found her G spot. Marie couldn't hold it in any longer. She let out a scream, "I'm cumming!" Her body jerked and her knees began to weaken. Nevaeh didn't allow that to stop her. She kept going until Marie practically ran away from her.

"Stop! Stop!" Marie managed to breathlessly blurt out as she pushed Nevaeh's face away. Nevaeh wiped her mouth. She gently pulled Marie's skirt down and straightened it. She stood up. Marie pulled her girlfriend in for another passionate kiss.

"That was unexpected," Nevaeh smiled.

Marie kissed Nevaeh and began to roam her body.

"No baby, it's okay," Nevaeh insisted.

"Are you sure?"

"I'm positive. Sometimes I just like getting you off," Nevaeh smiled. "You want to finish getting ready or what?" she teased.

"Yeah, I should probably do that. And you hit up Saria."

"Okay." Marie gave Nevaeh another quick kiss before she scurried back to the bathroom.

Nevaeh lay back down on the bed and called Saria.

"Hello?" Saria answered.

"Hey Saria. Marie and I were wondering if you wanted to ride with us to the bar tonight. We know you were a little nervous about going. We didn't want you to have to show up by yourself."

"Oh man, really?" Saria sounded relieved. "Yes, actually that would be great. Thank you so much."

"Of course."

"I'm almost ready, I can head over in about twenty minutes if that's cool?"

"Yeah, that sounds good. I'll text you Marie's address."

"Great, see you soon."

"Bye bye."

"Hey baby!" Nevaeh shouted.

"What's up?"

"Saria will be here in about twenty minutes. We'll catch a ride from here to the bar."

"Cool!"

✶ ✶ ✶

The doorbell rang. "I'll get it!" Marie shouted as she opened the door.

"Saria! Hey!" She opened her arms and gave Saria a hug. "Please come in!"

Saria walked into the apartment. "Wow, this is nice, Marie."

"Oh, thank you very much." Marie led her into the kitchen. "Come on in the kitchen, we're taking a few pre-game shots."

Saria chuckled, "Oh man, I don't know if I'm ready. It's been a while since I've drunk."

"No pressure. We're not playing keep up. Just drink what you can handle."

Saria smiled. They had a stare that lingered, but was interrupted when Nevaeh walked into the kitchen. "Hey Saria!" Nevaeh smiled and gave her a hug. "You look amazing."

"Oh please. I feel like I look like crap. It's been so long since I've been out without Malik, I hope I remember how to function around adults."

"Girl. You're going to be fighting off the women with a stick," Marie chimed in as she poured three tequila shots.

"The first time I drank with Marie, I told her tequila makes my clothes come off. She has not stopped feeding it to me since," Nevaeh joked.

"That's because," Marie passed out the shots with lemons, "I like it when your clothes come off, baby." She smiled and gave her girlfriend a quick kiss.

Saria gazed at them. "I love that you two are happy. You guys make a beautiful couple."

They smiled. "Well, cheers to a great night, and that Tiara and Imani won't punch you in the face," Nevaeh said jokingly. Saria glared at her. "I'm kidding, I'm kidding! It's going to be a great night."

"Cheers." They took the shots.

"All right, ladies, Uber will be here in about five minutes. Let's wrap this shit up!" Marie said enthusiastically.

✶ ✶ ✶

When they pulled up to the bar Saria let out a nervous sigh.

"Hey. It's going to be okay," Marie assured her.

"It might be a little rough in the beginning, but it'll all work out. Trust me," Nevaeh comforted. "You ready?" she asked.

Saria looked at her. "Absolutely not."

Nevaeh smirked, "Sounds about right. Let's do this."

Marie entered the bar first.

"Hey Marie!" The girls shouted as she walked in. She waved at them. She held up a finger so she could have a minute to go check on her staff. Even though she wasn't working, she always made sure her people were good.

Next, Nevaeh walked in. "Nevaeh! We've been waiting for y'all!" Imani shouted out as she threw her arms in the air. Nevaeh did a head nod and smiled. She stood there as she held the door open to give Saria some time to get her bearings and enter the bar. After about a minute with the door held open, Saria finally decided to enter. Marie stood behind the bar as she darted her eyes back and forth between Saria and the table.

"Yo, what the fuck is she doing here?" Tiara stood up and announced.

"Huh? Who is it?" Imani turned around. "Oh hell nah! Saria? Absolutely fucking not! We're not doing this today! In your girlfriend's bar, Nevaeh? That's some triflin shit!"

"I already know about it. And I approve," Marie stated as she walked up to the table with the pair.

Cassidy and Eliana looked at one another. "Daaaaaaamn," they said under their breaths and gave each other a sly fist bump.

"That's Saria?" Eliana whispered to Cassidy as she stared at her in shock.

"Shit. I guess so," Cassidy responded. "No wonder Nevaeh fell so hard for her."

They looked at each other. "Dibs!" they whisper shouted at the same time.

"No!" they whisper shouted again. Everyone's focus was on Saria, so they didn't even realize what was going on between Cassidy and Eliana.

"The fuck you mean dibs, Cass?" Eliana challenged. "You have Deja."

"Damn," Cassidy said as she turned her head. "Don't tell Deja about this." She paused. "I'm not proud of this moment."

"Yes. I get dibs by default." Eliana did a mini celebration. "I'll take that."

"You're cool with this?" Tiara asked Marie. She nodded. "Do you know how in love your girlfriend was with her?" Tiara instigated. "And then how heartbroken she was when Saria just left?" Tiara was getting upset.

"Yeah, and how we were the only ones there for her to pick up the pieces?" Imani was upset too.

"Yes. We've talked about it. Many times," Marie assured. "All three of us have been hanging out. I've gotten to know Saria over the past couple of weeks, and she's not the villain you two are making her out to be."

"Please. Tiara. Imani. Give her a chance," Nevaeh pleaded. "For me."

Tiara rolled her eyes, sneered, and sat down.

"Fine. For you." Imani wasn't happy about it and took a seat.

"Thank you," Nevaeh exhaled. "So if you haven't realized already," she started to introduce Saria to the rest of the group, "this is my ex turned friend, Saria."

"Hi. I'm Eliana." She quickly stood up and extended her hand.

Anita snickered at the sight of Eliana throwing herself at Saria. "Hi." Saria nervously shook her hand.

Eliana held onto Saria's hand a little longer than she should have. Anita inconspicuously squeezed Eliana's leg. Eliana picked up on the cue and realized what she was doing. She sat down.

Cassidy snickered. "Rookie," Cassidy whispered to Eliana when she sat down. Eliana rolled her eyes.

"Right. And this is Cassidy, Anita, and Jasmine." They all waved, and Saria waved back with a smile. "These are my girls. My family."

"It's nice to meet all of you," Saria greeted.

Tiara and Imani rolled their eyes.

"Please have a seat." Marie pulled up a chair for Saria.

"Thanks," Saria said softly.

"Can I get you something to drink, Saria?" Marie asked.

"I'll take a Modelo, please."

"Sure thing. Baby, you want something?"

"Yes. Can I get a Corona?"

"Of course." Marie leaned over, smiled, and kissed her sitting girlfriend. She walked off.

"So, Saria." Tiara sat forward in her chair. "How's your husband?" she asked in a matter-of-fact tone.

Saria shifted in her chair. "If you're referring to my ex-husband, he moved back to Morocco to take care of his sick parents."

"Oh." Tiara sat back in her chair.

"Yeah, we split after I went through years of depression due to the fact of my being gay."

Tiara and Imani looked at one another, a little ashamed.

Saria caught everyone up. She filled them in on her depression, relationship, Malik, parents, moving in with her brother, and how sweet Nevaeh and Marie had been to her. She told them how she needed friends and they were kind enough to allow her to hang out. She also told them how nervous she was to meet back up with Tiara and Imani.

"Look," Tiara said. "I apologize for the way I came off. You have to understand how much we care for Nevaeh. The way she shattered when you left was not pretty, and from then on we vowed to collectively hate you."

"Yeah, I'm sorry too, man. I didn't realize you went through all that. Sounds like it was rough," Imani apologized. "It's your right to come out when you are ready. I guess it was just hard to see Nevaeh hurting like that."

"I hope you can forgive us." Tiara's voice was compassionate.

"I forgive you guys," Saria smiled. "I get it, though. It was a difficult and confusing time for all of us. I've apologized profusely for how abruptly I ended things. It wasn't right, but I was young and scared. I felt like that was my only option at the time. I'm just glad to be here and healthy again."

They all smiled. "Hey." Imani held up her beer. "Here's to being healthy again."

"To being healthy again." They all held up their glasses to the toast and took a sip.

✴ ✴ ✴

They all hung around the bar. Saria fit right in with the gang. They loved her personality. Saria was hit on repeatedly by other women. She was flattered, but continued to turn them down. Anita noticed how close Saria, Nevaeh, and Marie were getting. She thought it looked a little odd. To the point where they appeared to be flirting with one another, but she left it alone.

"Phew, it's getting late," Jasmine yawned.

"Yeah, we should probably get going," Anita agreed. They got up and gave everybody a hug. Anita pulled Nevaeh off to the side. "Hey Nevaeh, everything good with you three?"

"Yeah, what do you mean?"

"Uh, I don't know. Just wanted to check in." She didn't want to insinuate anything.

"Oh. Yeah, we're good, Nita. I appreciate it."

"No problem, girl." They hugged.

"All right, guys. We'll see y'all later!" Jasmine and Anita left the bar.

"Yeah, I should probably head out too," Cassidy agreed.

"Shit. Yeah, it is late. I guess it is time to call it a night," Eliana chimed in and everyone agreed. The girls all gave their hugs and said their see you laters. Saria stayed back with Marie and Nevaeh.

"Wow, tonight was really fun," Saria said as she sat down at the bar. "Thank you both so much for inviting me out. I really needed this."

"Of course." Nevaeh placed her hand on Saria's. "I told you it would all work out."

"Yeah, they loved you," Marie chimed in. They all had another moment where the three of their stares lingered amongst one another.

Saria cleared her throat and pulled her hand from under Nevaeh's. "Well, I guess I should get going too."

"Hey, why don't you just crash on my couch?" Marie insisted. "I mean your car is already there, you can just drive home in the morning." Inside she hoped that Saria would accept her offer.

Saria thought about accepting the offer. She also knew that the feelings she had for Nevaeh never really went away, and she had begun to develop feelings for Marie as well. She wanted to go home with the couple, but she knew alcohol mixed with the attraction she had for them would not lead to anywhere good. Surely, she wasn't the only one with these feelings, but she didn't want to embarrass herself if she was. "Uh, I really do appreciate it. You guys have done enough. But I think I'm just going to catch an Uber home and come by in the morning to get my car."

"Nonsense," Marie insisted. "You're coming home with us. My couch is so comfortable, you won't even miss your bed."

Saria was reluctant, but she accepted. "All right, thanks. I'll just text Noah and let him know I'll be home in the morning."

Marie opened the door to her apartment. Saria felt butterflies in her stomach. She wasn't 100% sure what to do with these feelings. Marie made the couch up for Saria.

"All right, here you go," she said. "The bathroom is right there, and if there is anything you need, my room is right there. Doesn't matter the time, wake me up and I'll help."

"Thank you, but this is plenty. I'll be okay."

"Alrighty, well, goodnight." Marie gave Saria a hug.

"Goodnight." Nevaeh gave her a hug as well.

"Goodnight. Don't let the bedbugs bite!" Saria said, embarrassed. "Sorry, it's something I say to Malik all the time."

They chuckled and walked off.

"So that went really well," Nevaeh said to Marie after she closed the bedroom door behind them.

"I know! I'm so happy that it did." Marie began to undress. Nevaeh looked at her as she undressed as well.

"You know," Nevaeh walked over to her and helped her undress, "we could pick up from where we left off earlier."

Marie slightly moaned. "I would like that." She kissed Nevaeh. The kiss quickly picked up and clothes began to come off faster. "I want you to fuck me with the strap-on tonight," Marie managed to blurt out.

"Okay." No questions asked as Nevaeh agreed and put the strap-on, on. As she did that Marie lay on the bed. Once Nevaeh had it on she started to eat Marie out. Marie's back arched and she let out a moan.

* * *

In the living room Saria lay on the couch wide awake as a million thoughts ran through her head. She couldn't sleep. Suddenly, she heard faint moaning noises coming from the bedroom and sat up. The moaning noises got a little louder. All her senses were officially awakened. Saria slid off the couch. She walked toward the room as if she were in a trance. Once she got to the door, she placed her hand on the handle. She quickly pulled it away. *What the fuck are you doing?* she asked herself. She put her ear to the door. As she listened to the noises from the other side, she began to rub on her breasts. She couldn't handle how aroused she truly was. She had never done anything like this before, but the attraction she felt for the two of them was undeniable. Once she couldn't take it anymore, she slid her hand onto her clit and started to play with herself. She closed her eyes and imagined she was in the room with the couple as she listened to them. As her motion quickened, her chest began to rise and fall faster. Her breathing became choppy. *Am I really about to cum this quick??* she thought to herself. It had been so long since she had sex, and she was so horny that it didn't take her long to orgasm. As she reached the point, she placed her hand over her mouth and came. Hard. She almost fell onto the floor.

She went into the bathroom and washed her hands. Saria splashed some water onto her face. She stared at her reflection as she dried her face off with the hand towel. She lay back down on the couch. *What the fuck have I gotten myself into?* Saria asked herself. She could no longer deny the feelings that she had for Marie and Nevaeh.

TWENTY-EIGHT

Arlie and Eliana showed up at the bar at the same time. Arlie went in for a hug from Eliana. "Eliana, it's good to meet you."

Eliana returned the hug. "It's nice to finally meet you as well. And please, call me Ellie," she smiled.

"Wow, you're even more gorgeous in person," Arlie complimented.

"Oh." Eliana blushed. "Thank you so much."

Arlie smiled. "Shall we go in?" she asked as she motioned toward the entrance.

Eliana led the way into the bar. They were meeting up with everyone from the project. Her eyes scanned the bar in search of Scarlett. Finally, the two made eye contact and Scarlett waved them over.

"Ah!" Scarlett squealed as she hugged Eliana. "It's so good to see you. I'm glad you were able to make it."

"Same!" Eliana returned the hug. "Hey Scar, this is Arlie. Arlie, this is Scarlett. She's the brains behind the project."

"Arlie." Scarlett outstretched her hand. "It's so great to meet you. Ellie is the one who got me into your channel. I really like your art reviews. Watching your channel has made me more interested in art."

Arlie placed her hand in Scarlett's. "Wow, thank you very much. I love to hear that I help inspire people."

"Well, c'mon, ladies, let's go hang out and Arlie, let me introduce you to the rest of the gang."

"Let's do it," Arlie enthused.

All the adults from the photoshoot were there that night—Scarlett's wife, brother, his wife, her sister, and her husband, as well as her mother, father, and her in-laws. They had a big group. Eliana went around and gave everyone a hug and introduced Arlie as she did.

"So Arlie," Scarlett's brother spoke, "what made you want to interview Eliana and my sister on your channel?"

"Well, I don't have many tattoos myself, but I love that people have them. I enjoy hearing the stories behind tattoos. I love seeing people express themselves. When I ran across the project online and saw the reactions to it, I knew I had to represent it on my channel."

"Cool," Todd responded. "Well, I'm excited to watch that episode," he smiled.

They all took shots, laughed, played games, and ate for hours. Eventually Scarlett's parents wanted to go home.

"Hey, we can't be hanging around you young kids all night. We need to get going," Scarlett's dad admitted.

"Actually we should probably get going too." Scarlett looked at her wife and she agreed.

Everyone decided to take off, but Eliana wasn't ready to call it a night. "I think I'm going to stay out a little longer," she told Scarlett.

"You sure? By yourself?" Scarlett worried.

"Not by herself. I'll stay out with her," Arlie chimed in. "I'm not quite ready to turn in either."

Scarlett smirked, "Well, all right then. Okay, ladies, you two don't get into any trouble." She hugged Arlie. "Goodnight, Ellie." She leaned in to give Eliana a hug. "Good luck, girl," she whispered in her ear. Eliana blushed.

"Goodnight, Scar, I had a blast tonight."

Scarlett waved as she walked out of the bar. Eliana and Arlie grabbed drinks and found a table in a dim corner.

"Wow, they were a lot of fun," Arlie admitted.

"You sound surprised," Eliana responded.

"It's not that I'm surprised, I guess it's just a different pace of people than what I'm used to interacting with. Hanging out with you all was like a breath of fresh air I needed."

"Yeah, they're great." Eliana paused. "So what kind of people are you used to interacting with?"

"I don't know about you, but there are hundreds of people around, but it still seems to feel lonely. A lot of the people I meet are so unreliable that it makes it difficult to actually make and keep friends, especially within the lesbian scene. Usually the single ones are looking for a relationship, for a quick hook up, or just got out of a relationship and have a bunch of baggage I'm not looking to sort through. I just want a few good friends."

"Yeah, that does suck," Eliana sympathized. "I lucked out and met a group of friends of my dreams years back. They are my go to for everything, without them I don't know where I'd be."

"You're lucky." Arlie lifted her glass to her lips.

"So you don't want to be in a relationship?" Eliana genuinely asked. "That's kind of weird as a lesbian," she joked.

"Yeah," Arlie chuckled. "It's not that I don't want to be in a relationship, it's just I'm not trying to rush into anything. I've done the typical lesbian 48-hour date and by hour 72, you're in a relationship. I know it's not what I'm looking for."

"Yeah, I get that. So what if you run into the right girl? Then what? Are you not going to pursue her?"

"I didn't say all of that. I just said I wouldn't want to rush into anything." Arlie looked Eliana in her eyes. "Why? Are you interested?"

Eliana blushed. "Maybe," she flirted as she stared back.

Arlie smirked, "What about you? Are you looking for a relationship?"

"Not necessarily. I guess I fall under the recently got out of a relationship with baggage category. My ex and I broke up a few months back, and she was fucking crazy. She cheated on me, got pregnant, and then said she thought we could raise the baby together," Eliana laughed.

"Wow." Arlie joined the laughter.

"Yeah, it was pretty great. I told myself after that I wanted to take some time for myself before getting into another relationship, but if the right girl comes along, I wouldn't push her away."

Arlie lifted her glass. "Cheers to the right one coming along."

"Cheers." Eliana tapped her glass to hers.

"So your ex got pregnant, huh? You fall in love with a straight girl or something?"

"No, she was bi," Eliana said. "I'm not the kind of lesbian that doesn't date a woman because she's bi. I have no issues with it, but when you cheat on me that's another story."

"Did she put a sour taste in your mouth about bisexual women?"

Eliana chuckled, "No. Just a sour taste in my mouth for women named Trisha." Eliana paused. "But in all seriousness, I feel bad for bi women when it comes to the lesbian community. Lesbians can be so fucking judgmental at times. I don't think all bi women are cheaters. I don't think all bi women are going to leave their girl for a man. I think that's a personal thing. If I met a bi woman that I'm interested in, I would pursue her like I would any other lesbian."

Arlie smiled, "Well, that's good to know."

"Why is that?"

"Because I'm bi."

Eliana was taken aback. "Really?" she inquired. "I'm not going to lie, I just always assumed you were a lesbian."

"Yeah, a lot of people do. It's funny reading the comments on my channel, but I identify as bisexual. I don't really focus on my sexuality on my channel. I'd rather people focus on the art, than who I'm sleeping with."

"Well." Eliana was impressed. "You learn something new every day."

"I like you, Eliana," Arlie admitted.

"Really?" Eliana asked shyly.

"Yeah, and not just on a physical level. I mean don't get me wrong, I think you're gorgeous, but your project allowed me to catch a glimpse of what goes on in your mind and I liked it. I want to dig deeper and get to know you better."

Eliana was speechless.

"Of course if you don't want to, I apologize for making this awkward."

"It's not that," Eliana managed to spit out.

"I'm sorry, I won't—" Eliana interrupted Arlie's sentence with a kiss.

"So does that mean you like me too?" Arlie asked.

Eliana smiled, nodded, and kissed her again.

"So what'd you like most about the project?" Eliana asked.

"Honestly, I like it all. I like how all of the photos are in black and white with the exception of the tattoos. The photo of Todd teaching his class? Beautifully done. Just the detail in it. How it was taken from behind the class with the kids eagerly raising their hands. His sleeves were rolled up displaying his tattoos and the kids didn't even care. Todd's smile said it all."

"I really enjoyed that one. The kids were great."

"What about you? What was one of your favorites?"

"It's hard to pick just one. If I had to, though, I think it would be the whole family at the dinner table. It was great catching everyone laughing, the kids running around, and the genuine love they all shared for one another. I thought that was beautiful. Also, the one of Scarlett breastfeeding was full of beauty. The look in her eyes when she looked at her daughter was something I couldn't put into words. It was something only a camera could catch."

"Yeah, those were great too. They were all amazing, well thought out. It was a great project," Arlie complimented.

"Thanks, AJ," Eliana smiled.

PART III
(FOUR MONTHS LATER)

TWENTY-NINE

It was a beautiful day at the beach house. The weather was about 75°, there was a slight breeze, but not hard enough to disturb anything. The sounds of seagulls flying and the ocean waves crashing added to the romantic atmosphere.

"Why the fuck am I so nervous right now?" Anita placed her face in her hands. "Calm down, Nita," Eliana insisted. "Imani and I got you."

"Yeah," Imani chimed in. "Jasmine loves you, and you love her. In the end, that's all that matters. You two are meant to be with one another," Imani encouraged. "I can only dream of the kind of love the two of you have. It's like a real life fairytale."

Anita lifted her face from her hands. "Oh. I'm not nervous about marrying Jasmine. She's my heart. I think I'm just nervous because there are so many damn people out there!"

"Oh shit." Imani waved her hand. "Girl, that ain't nothing a tequila shot can't fix. Three tequila shots coming right up!" Imani disappeared from the room before anyone could protest.

✶ ✶ ✶

"Jas, why are you pacing?" Tiara inquired.

"Because I'm nervous, T. Can I not be nervous?" Jasmine snapped.

"Woah." Tiara put her hands up. "You have every right to be nervous. I'm not trying to argue that. It's your day."

"I'm sorry." Jasmine dropped down on the couch. "I just have a lot of things running through my mind right now."

"Oh, Jasmine," Nevaeh comforted her. "You and Anita are meant to be, you have nothing to worry about."

"It's not marrying Anita that makes me nervous," Jasmine admitted. "It's all these damn people! I mean what if I fall? What if I stumble over my words? What if someone speaks up when they say speak now or forever hold your peace? I'm going to pass out." She put her hand on her knees.

"Oh girl!" Nevaeh said. "I think we all can use a tequila shot." Nevaeh rushed out of the room.

Nevaeh and Imani ran into each other at the bar. "What are you doing out here?" Imani asked.

"Tequila shots," they said at the same time.

"Jasmine nervous about getting married?" Imani asked as she poured the shots.

"Not at all. She said she's nervous about all the people that are here. Which is weird because she knows everyone," Nevaeh shrugged.

"Bruh what?" Imani was hype. "Same thing with Nita! She can't wait to marry Jasmine, but she's nervous because of the people."

"They are so cute. I love them," Nevaeh awwed.

"They're truly a match made in heaven," Imani agreed. "Hey, you want to take a quick shot with me?"

"Do I?" Nevaeh poured the shots. "So what are we toasting to?"

"I have an idea." They lifted their shot glasses. Imani took a deep breath and said very quickly, "I think I'm in love with someone, but I'm not ready to tell you who it is." She threw the shot back.

"What?" Nevaeh exclaimed.

"Okay, byyyyyeeee," Imani said as she gathered her shots and rushed off.

Nevaeh stood there dumbfounded. She had no idea Imani was in love with someone and why couldn't she tell her about it? She took the shot, and went back to the room. Tiara and Jasmine waited. "Here we go." She gave them their shots.

"Cheers to a beautiful day." Tiara lifted her glass.

"Cheers." Jasmine and Nevaeh did the same. They all took the shots.

"Woo!" Jasmine shouted. "Damn, I needed that," Jasmine said as she placed the shot glass down.

"Did you guys know that Imani is in love with someone?" Nevaeh wiped her mouth and asked.

"Love?!" Tiara questioned. Then corrected her expression.

"Excuse me?" Jasmine asked. "Our Imani? In love? Who told you these lies?"

"Her. The news came straight from the source."

"Is she dating someone?" Jasmine asked.

"I mean I don't think so. I haven't heard anything." Nevaeh paused. "Come to think of it she hasn't been bringing any girls home lately. She's been chill."

"Wow, she told you she's in love, and she hasn't been bringing girls home? That's major." Tiara made her best attempt to sound shocked. "Did she say who it was?"

"No." Nevaeh shook her head. "She said she wasn't ready to say who it was, yet."

"Well," Jasmine continued, "it was bound to happen eventually. This girl must be pretty special if she brought it up. Imani might be rough around the edges, but she's a great person and any girl would be lucky to be with our girl."

"And that's real," Nevaeh agreed.

"Yeah," Tiara slightly smiled.

"Hey, you ladies almost ready?" Cassidy popped her head into Anita's doorway. "Everyone is seated. Nita, your brothers are so excited and ready to walk you down the aisle."

Anita took a slow, deep breath and nodded her head. "I'm ready."

Cassidy smiled. "Okay, I'll send your brothers up."

✶ ✶ ✶

Just off the back porch of the beach house was where the wedding was set up; there were chairs filled with people. In front of the chairs stood an elegant white arch with the waves crashing behind it.

Tiara spotted Imani and abruptly pulled her to the side. "You told Nevaeh you're in love with someone?" she whispered. "You're in love with me?" Tiara whisper yelled.

"Damn, Nevaeh got a big ass mouth." Imani knew Nevaeh could keep a secret, but she knew something like this Nevaeh would pry. Imani wanted Tiara to know. "I didn't tell her who it was. Chill the fuck out," Imani demanded.

"You ready, Imani?" Eliana asked.

"I sure am. Let's get our two lovebirds married," Imani smiled.

Everyone turned and looked at Eliana and Imani as they stepped up. They wore red suits and looked beautiful in them. As they walked down the aisle, they smiled. Once they reached the altar, they took their appropriate places.

Next up were Tiara and Nevaeh. They rocked yellow suits. They linked arms and proceeded down the aisle. They smiled at people as they walked. Nevaeh made eye contact with Marie and winked at her. Once they got to the altar, they took their appropriate spots as well.

Then out came the ring bearer. It was Jasmine's seven-year-old niece. She insisted that she would much rather carry the ring than throw out flowers. She walked down the aisle with a gigantic smile on her face. She was proud to carry the rings.

Jasmine's five-year-old nephew was the last to come out. Just as his sister wanted to carry the rings, he wanted to throw the flowers. Jasmine's sister, Jenna, wouldn't dare try to force them to do anything else. She wanted her kids and her sister to be happy. Seeing the two young kids break through societal boxes made Jasmine's heart smile. She always told the kids to do what made them happy and don't allow society to put you in a box and slap a label on it.

Anita stepped up with her younger brothers, Jamir and Darrion, on each arm. Despite being younger, her brothers were two of the strongest men she had ever known. She didn't want anyone else walking her down the aisle.

The band began to play an R&B rendition of the Bridal Chorus. Everyone rose. Anita wore a dapper white tailcoat tuxedo with a red pocket square to match Eliana's and Imani's red suits. As she walked down the aisle, her smile was contagious. Once they reached the altar, her brothers both kissed her on the cheek, then sat down. She took her place at the altar.

Finally, Jasmine stepped up with her father. She wore a beautiful tailored white suit with a yellow pocket square to match Nevaeh's and Tiara's yellow suits. Both Anita and Jasmine teared up as soon as they locked eyes. They were in awe of one another. Jasmine's dad kissed her on the cheek once they reached the altar, then took his place in the front row next to her mother and sister.

"Please be seated," Cassidy instructed the audience. "Friends, family, framily…" Jasmine smiled at Cassidy. Cassidy winked. "…and loved ones. We have all gathered here today to share with Anita and Jasmine a very important moment in their lives. In the years they have been together, we have witnessed their love for one another grow stronger each day. Watching them love one another as deeply as they do has taught me what I want in a relationship."

As Cassidy spoke, Nevaeh caught Imani and Tiara gazing into one another's eyes. Nevaeh's eyes subtly darted back and forth between the two. She tried her best to keep her facial expressions under control. Eventually their gaze broke.

"Oh shit," Nevaeh whispered.

"What?" Tiara whispered to Nevaeh with a confused expression.

"What?" Nevaeh whispered as she returned the confused look.

Tiara awkwardly looked away.

"By the power vested in me by Officiate My Wedding dot com, I now pronounce you wife and wife. Now kiss each other already!"

Anita and Jasmine kissed and the guests cheered. Tiara shimmied. The band played Stevie Wonder's "Signed, Sealed, Delivered, I'm Yours." Anita and Jasmine locked hands and danced down the aisle. The wedding party followed behind them as they danced to the song as well. It was a beautiful day.

THIRTY

"Do you want to go and get some ice cream today?" Arlie asked Eliana.

"Yeah, actually that sounds nice."

"Great." Arlie gave her a kiss. Eliana pulled Arlie's face back into hers for a deeper kiss. Both of their hands wandered. Eliana began to pull up Arlie's shirt. "Stop." Arlie pulled away.

"I'm sorry." Eliana composed herself. "That was too much. I'm just so attracted to you that I get caught up sometimes."

"Don't apologize. I want you too."

"Right." Eliana kissed Arlie on the cheek. "Well, let's go get that ice cream so I can cool off because I am hot and bothered right now," she joked. She hopped off the bed. "Are you thinking soft serve? Because that's what I'm thinking."

"Wait," Arlie whispered. She stood up. "Wait," she said again with more confidence in her voice.

Eliana turned and looked at Arlie. Arlie stared back at Eliana. Her eyes screamed for Eliana to touch her. Without words, Eliana walked over to Arlie. Eliana slowly ran her hand down the side of Arlie's face. Arlie closed her eyes and kissed Eliana's hand. She then kissed Eliana's lips. It was full of uncertainty.

"You sure?" Eliana asked Arlie. She knew she didn't want to do anything Arlie was not ready for. She liked and respected Arlie too much to screw it up.

Arlie said nothing as she took her tee shirt off and threw it across the room. Eliana took that as her green light. She took her shirt off as well. Eliana waited for Arlie to make the first move. Arlie went in for another kiss. This time the kiss was deeper, slower, and full of confidence. Eliana laid Arlie down on the bed. She got on top of her, and they continued the kiss. Arlie's breaths were rapid, the more stimulated she became. Arlie wrapped her arms around Eliana and pulled her closer. She ran her hands up her back to her bra and unbuttoned it. Eliana stopped kissing Arlie. They kept eye contact as Eliana slid out of her bra.

Eliana pushed herself up on her knees so she straddled Arlie. Arlie lay there and looked over Eliana's beautiful body. She sat up. Arlie ran her hands over Eliana's breasts. She took Eliana's right nipple into her mouth and played with the other one with her hand.

Eliana closed her eyes, threw her head back, and let out a moan. It had been a while since Eliana had been touched like this, and it felt amazing. Eliana enjoyed her nipples being played with for a bit, but then she grabbed Arlie's face and brought it up to hers. Eliana reached around, unlatched Arlie's bra, and threw it on the floor.

Eliana pulled away from the kiss and stood up. She stared into Arlie's eyes with intensity. Without breaking eye contact, she slowly pulled her sweatpants down, exposing her lace panties. Arlie sat up on the bed as she leaned back on her hands. She was mesmerized as she watched Eliana undress in front of her. "You're so beautiful," she whispered.

Eliana slowly slid her panties down and stepped out of them. Arlie slid out of her sweatpants and panties. Eliana climbed back on top of Arlie. Arlie grabbed the back of Eliana's neck. Their clits touched. It was like voltage flowed through them both. They stopped kissing as they both lost their breath for a minute. Eliana began to move her hips and grind against Arlie.

"Fuck," Arlie exhaled as she reached down and grabbed onto Eliana's butt. She moved her hips to match Eliana's rhythm.

The pace quickened. The headboard knocked against the wall. Arlie couldn't hold it in any longer. She came, but Eliana hadn't finished yet.

"Keep going. I want you to cum," Arlie panted into her ear. Eliana kept going. Arlie's body jerked as she orgasmed again. As Eliana watched Arlie orgasm again that took her over the edge, and she came too.

Eliana breathlessly rolled over next to Arlie. Once Arlie caught her breath, she rolled to her side. She ran her fingers over Eliana's body. Arlie leaned in and grabbed another quick kiss. "You still want to go get that ice cream?" she asked.

Eliana smiled, "I do."

✶ ✶ ✶

The girls had their ice cream and were walking to find a bench in the park. As they walked down the sidewalk, the hair on the back of Eliana's neck stood up.

"Eliana?" She stopped dead in her tracks. That voice made her skin crawl. She turned around to a very pregnant Trisha.

"Trisha," she said, displeased.

"The Trisha?" Arlie whispered into Eliana's ear. Eliana nodded. "Ooouuu," Arlie whispered and stepped back.

"Ellie," Trisha started.

"Don't call me that," she interrupted.

"Okay. Eliana," Trisha shamefully said, "I tried to call you."

"I know," Eliana bluntly responded.

"Right." Trisha cleared her throat. "I saw your work. It was phenomenal, but I expect nothing less from you," she complimented. "Look, I truly am sorry. For everything," she pleaded. "You're all I think about. I miss everything about you, about us. I'm still in love with you." In that moment, Jordan walked up and put his arm around Trisha.

"Eliana." He attempted to sound intimidating.

Eliana burst into laughter. That made Arlie laugh a little. "I can't make this shit up," she managed to say as she threw her hands up. She composed herself and wiped away her tears. "Phew!" she exhaled. "Arlie, this is Trisha and Jordan. Jordan, Trisha, this is Arlie."

"Who's she?" Trisha asked with a slight attitude. "Wait, she's that YouTuber you used to watch all the time," she realized.

"I wouldn't say all the time." Eliana tried to brush off the embarrassment.

"I'm her girlfriend." Arlie stepped up with confidence.

Eliana bit her bottom lip and smiled as she looked at Arlie. Trisha cleared her throat, which caused Eliana to break her gaze. "Jordan. Thank you. Thank you for helping me dodge a bullet." She paused. "Bye, Trisha." She laughed to herself and shook her head. She put her arm around Arlie's neck. Arlie placed her arm around Eliana's waist. They walked off.

"Girlfriend, huh?" Eliana asked.

"I mean it felt right in the moment. She really did seem every bit of awful you made her out to be."

"She really is." Eliana paused. "So did you just say that to help me out or what?"

"Yeah, but I wouldn't be opposed to it."

"Neither would I," Eliana smiled "In the spirit of taking it slow, maybe it's something we can talk about later on down the line."

"Deal," Arlie smiled.

THIRTY-ONE

This Friends' Friday was a going-away party for Cassidy's soon departure to Korea. Before they headed out for the night, the gang decided to go with Saria to Malik's Little League game to cheer him on.

"Malik, you remember Ms. Marie and Ms. Nevaeh?"

"Yes!" He smiled and gave them a hug. Nevaeh high fived him. "Man, Malik, you act, play sports, is there anything you don't do?" she asked him with a smile.

"Nope! I do it all!" Malik bragged.

Saria smiled, "Well these are friends that also want to come and support you. This is Ms. Cassidy, Ms. Eliana, Ms. Anita, Ms. Jasmine, Ms. Imani, and Ms. Tiara."

"Hi!" Malik waved. He gave everyone a hug individually.

"All right, Casanova, go on over there to your team." Saria gave him a hug and a kiss. "Good luck, baby!" Malik ran off.

"Oh my goodness, you guys, thank you so much for coming out here today. I know y'all have your Friends' Friday tonight."

"We have our Friends' Friday tonight," Imani corrected her with a smile.

216

"Yeah girl, this is what we do for family. We show up," Tiara chimed in.

Saria teared up with a smile.

"Oh, c'mon now, don't do that." Imani hugged her.

"I know, I'm sorry. I'm just so happy. You guys don't understand how hard it has been. If I didn't have Noah I don't know where I'd be, and now you guys." Saria exhaled. "What I'm trying to say is, thank you."

"Of course," Cassidy smiled and rubbed her arm.

They all sat down on the bleachers. They cheered on Malik's team. When it was his turn to bat they cheered so loud that the other families seemed jealous, but they didn't care. The support made Malik shine. When he stepped up to bat, the bases were fully loaded, and Saria could tell he was nervous.

"Strike one!" the umpire belted out.

"It's okay, Malik! Shake it off and get back up there!" Nevaeh clapped.

"Strike two!" the umpire's voice rang out.

The girls could see the look of despair slowly creeping up on Malik's face.

"Malik!" Saria screamed out, "Don't you admit defeat yet! You have another chance! Now get up there and do the thing!" she encouraged.

"Do the thing," the girls started to chant. "Do the thing!" They progressively got louder. "Do the thing!" They were hype at this point. They danced as they chanted. Malik smiled and stepped up to the plate. The pitcher threw the ball. Crack! Malik hit the ball!

"Run, baby!" Saria screamed in excitement.

Not only did Malik hit the ball, he hit a home run—the final hit that caused his team to win the game!

* * *

"I'm so proud of you, baby!" Malik ran into his mother's arms after the game. "You did such a great job!"

"Thanks, Mommy. I was so scared up there. I thought I was going to strike out, and my team was going to lose."

"I know, but you held in there and handled your business."

"Aye Malik!" Tiara shouted out. The girls all crowded around him giving him high fives, hugs, and compliments. Like always, he loved the attention. Saria placed her hand on her face and smiled. It brought her so much joy to see this group of women welcome her and her son like they were family. She had been guarded raising Malik on her own, but she slowly realized she could let her guard down around these ladies. It was overwhelming in a good way.

"Okay, Saria, we are going to go ahead and get going to get ready for tonight," Eliana stated.

"Yeah, of course, I need to get him home anyway and get ready myself."

"Okay, cool. We'll see you at No Man's at nine?" Cassidy asked.

"I wouldn't miss it for the world," Saria smiled.

Saria kneeled down in front of Malik. "Okay baby, so I already told Uncle Noah about your big win today. He told me that he and Liz want to take you out to celebrate. Is that okay? He wanted it to be just you three."

"You're not going to come?" Malik asked with a slight sadness in his voice.

"Well, I wanted to go hang out with the group of ladies that came to see you play today. Ms. Cassidy is going away to Korea for a whole year. We wanted to do something special for her tonight, but if you want me to go with you guys tonight, I will. I will cancel my plans. You always come first."

Malik thought about it for a minute. "No, Mommy. I want you to go have fun. I really like those ladies. They're fun. I want you to have friends." He smiled. "Plus, I like spending time with Uncle Noah and Auntie Liz. They're so fun!"

"You're such a kind kid and very considerate. I love you, Malik." Saria closed her eyes and kissed him on the forehead.

"I love you too, Mommy."

"All right, come on, let's go get you cleaned up and get you ready for your celebration evening!"

"Yay!" Malik shouted.

THIRTY-TWO

Marie hung a sign on the entrance of No Man's Land, *Closed For Private Event*. All the girls, significant others, and friends celebrated Cassidy's last weekend before she left. They all pitched in so Marie was able to afford to close the bar for the evening for the event. The girls requested some alone time with just the seven of them so they could do their weekly catch up. Everyone respected that and spread out throughout the bar as they drank, played games, laughed, and enjoyed each other's company.

"Hey Nita and Jas, y'all ever end up doing that threesome thing again?" Imani whispered loudly enough for the group to hear as she cocked her head over to Ciera.

"We actually have been considering it," Anita confirmed. "We've brought the topic up with Ciera and she said as long as she's not in a relationship, she'd be down to link up anytime." She smiled from ear to ear.

"Damn, man!" Imani shouted as she hit the table. "That's amazing. I love how y'all are cool about it."

"Yeah, Nita and I are confident in our relationship, and Ciera is confident in her own skin. We really don't have any issues," Jasmine said as she rubbed Anita's hand. "We've been open, communicating, and honest. We've actually been talking more than we ever have before. I guess that's what the key is."

Anita smiled, "Yup."

"Threesomes are key to a happy, healthy relationship. Got it," Imani jokingly took a mental note. Tiara rolled her eyes. Nevaeh witnessed her response, but didn't say anything.

"I saw Trisha today," Eliana blurted out.

"What?" Imani, Nevaeh, Anita, Jasmine, Tiara, and Cassidy all managed to say in unison.

"Yeah, she tried to hit me with the I'm still in love with you bullshit with a belly that looked like it was holding a baby hippo. Fuck out of here."

"Got damn, Ellie! A baby hippo?" Tiara chimed in.

"Yeah." Eliana shook her head.

"So what'd you do?" Nevaeh asked.

"What the fuck do you think I did? I slapped the fuck out of her and walked off." Eliana attempted to sound as tough as she could.

"Girl," Tiara challenged, "get real. We all know damn well you did not do that."

Eliana chuckled, "Yeah, you're right, but I thought about it, though." Eliana took a deep breath. "Well, as she was confessing her love to me, Jordan walked up, put his arm around her, and stared me down like I was supposed to be intimidated by him." Eliana laughed. "I looked at them both and laughed in their faces. I didn't know what else to do. After I laughed, I actually thanked Jordan for helping me dodge a bullet. Then I said 'bye Trisha' and walked off. That was the end of that." Eliana purposely left out the fact that Arlie said she was her girlfriend. She knew the girls would make a big deal out of it.

"Oh man, that's great," Tiara said. "I love that. *Bye Trisha,*" she mimicked Eliana.

"I see Trisha is still the worst." Cassidy rolled her eyes.

"Yeah, she definitely sucks," Eliana agreed. "You know what, though. Now that it's all said and done, I'm glad it happened. I feel like that needed to happen in order for me to grow as a person. I needed to fall in love with myself again, and I needed to grow some balls and learn how to stand up for myself and not allow a significant other to walk all over me. So even though Trisha is a gawd-awful person, I appreciate her and everything she taught me about myself. Now I'm taking my time with a girl who truly appreciates me."

"Amen, you philosophical bitch! I can drink to that!" Tiara lifted her glass and took a sip.

"Okay ladies, I think it's time we go interact with the masses. It is my going-away, after all." Cassidy smiled and stood up. The ladies followed her lead. Without anyone noticing, Tiara cut a look over to Imani and walked to the bathroom. Imani played it off and continued to talk but then broke away soon after to meet with Tiara.

✶ ✶ ✶

Imani opened the bathroom door. Tiara stepped out of the stall. Imani slowly walked over to Tiara.

"What the fuck are we doing, T?" Imani asked.

Tiara didn't answer as she dove in for a kiss. The kiss became heavier. As Imani picked Tiara up and sat her on the sink, the bathroom door flung open. Cassidy's smile faded into pure confusion as she attempted to make sense of what she witnessed. She stared at them like a deer in headlights. Tiara hopped off the sink as they pushed away from one another. They adjusted their clothes and wiped their mouths. Cassidy stood there, mouth agape, as Tiara and Imani stared back. There was a two-minute moment of awkward silence as they stared at one another. Finally, Imani cleared her throat.

"So what's up, Cass? We good?" she asked but didn't wait for a reply and slipped out of the bathroom. Tiara followed behind her and softly squeezed Cassidy's arm in reassurance on the way out. Cassidy snapped out of the daze. "What the hell?" she asked herself, then went to the bathroom.

✶ ✶ ✶

Nevaeh wandered over to the booth where Saria and Marie chatted. "What's up, ladies? You two look like you're having a good conversation. What are you two talking about?" she inquired.

"Oh, nothing. I was just telling your girlfriend here how much Malik loves you guys. He told me he wants to participate in everything the school has to offer just so we all will go cheer him on." Saria was joyous.

"Oh, wow," Nevaeh smiled. "Well, Malik is a special kid. I'd love to go to whatever he's got going on."

"Hey, I'm going to grab another drink, you guys need anything?" Marie asked.

"No. Please." Saria placed her hand on Marie's shoulder. "Let me get it." She stood up. "What do you want?"

"Modelo," Marie said.

"Nevaeh?"

"Vodka Red Bull."

"No problem." Saria scurried off.

"You two look chummy." Nevaeh sat next to Marie and gave her girlfriend a quick kiss on the lips.

Marie smiled, "Yeah, she's pretty dope, Nevaeh."

"Yeah, she is." Nevaeh paused. "I see the gears turning in there. What's going on with you, Marie?" Marie gazed into Nevaeh's eyes. "Is this, my current and my ex becoming friends thing, about to backfire on me? I need to know because I'm not sure I can handle this. I was just trying to be a decent human being," Nevaeh admitted.

"Nevaeh, you know I love you," Marie replied.

"Oh fuck. Here we go." Nevaeh's back slammed into the booth.

"No, it's nothing like that, baby," Marie reassured. "You know I love you, but there is something I want to talk to you about."

Nevaeh perked up. "Marie, spare me the pause for dramatic effect, what are you talking about?"

"You remember when I told you that I'm poly?"

"Of course. How could I forget?"

Marie sighed. "Hear me out. I don't know how much thought you've put into that, but would you ever consider bringing someone else into our relationship?"

"Like a threesome?"

"Not just sexually. I'm talking about mind, body, and soul, bring someone else into this relationship."

"Like who?" It was like a lightbulb went off in Nevaeh's head. "Oh shit. You mean…" she paused, "…you mean Saria, don't you?"

"Yeah, Saria."

"What in the fuck is going on with the world right now?" Nevaeh asked, confused. "So that time when I met up with Saria and she kissed me, why did you flip out?"

"I flipped out because it wasn't something we had discussed beforehand. And it was before I got to know Saria. If I'm being honest, I was intimidated. If you're not comfortable with it, baby, forget that I asked."

"Forget that you asked? Marie, I can't just forget that you asked something like this." Nevaeh paused. "Have you spoken to Saria about this already?" she worried.

"Of course not. Not before talking to you first. You know what, don't worry about it."

"Well, hold on now." Nevaeh held up her hand. "I never said I didn't want to, just give me a minute to wrap my mind around this. It's a lot to process. I never thought I would be in a polyamorous relationship. Especially because lesbians tend to be monogamous creatures. Let me think about it. Not going to lie, I'm kind of intrigued, but here comes Saria. Can we keep this between us for now?"

"Without a doubt," Marie promised.

"Here you go, ladies." Saria set the drinks down on the table as she sat down. "So what'd I miss?"

* * *

"I'm going to miss you so much when you leave," Deja confessed.

"Is that right?" Cassidy asked.

"Yeah. These past several months have been amazing with you. I'm glad that I went to that party that night with Marie because I wasn't going to go at first."

"Really? I didn't know that."

"Yeah. I wasn't in the partying mood, but Marie told me she was going to meet up with Nevaeh and she needed us to go with her. So, I decided to go. Good thing," Deja smiled.

"Yeah. Good thing," Cassidy returned the smile.

"Do you think she'll say something?" Tiara asked nervously.

"I'm not really worried about it, to be honest with you," Imani defeatedly admitted.

"Well, I'm worried about it," Tiara snapped back.

Cassidy gazed softly at Deja. "Deja, we've been friends with benefits for a while now."

"Yes, we have and it has been great," Deja agreed.

"Well…" Cassidy cleared her throat. "Well, what would you think about making it official?" she asked nervously.

"If I'm being honest with you T, I don't want to keep us a secret anymore. I want everyone to know that I want to make you mine and I am willing to do what it takes to do so."

"Imani, if I'm being honest with you, I still don't trust you."

"Still? I haven't been fuckin with anyone else," Imani exhaled. "Then why are we even doing what we're doing to begin with?" she demanded.

* * *

"Official like in a relationship?" Deja asked.

"Yeah, like in a relationship."

"Wow, I didn't know you felt that way."

"I do."

"I'd love to, Cass." Deja smiled and kissed Cassidy. "Maybe I can come visit you in Korea!" She was ecstatic.

"I'd really like that," Cassidy smiled.

* * *

Imani and Tiara glared at one another. "You know what? Fuck this." Imani broke the silence and stood up. "Excuse me!" she shouted.

Tiara sprang up and grabbed Imani's arm. "Imani, what the fuck are you doing?"

Imani looked down at Tiara's tightly clutched hand around her arm. "Something I should've done a long time ago, Tiara. I'm so sorry that I have not."

"Excuse me!" Imani shouted again, this time climbing on the table. "Turn the fucking music off, I have an announcement to make!" The music shut off.

"Hey Imani, Imma let you finish, but get the fuck off my girlfriend's table, bruh." Nevaeh stood up.

"Oh shit, you right, my bad, Marie." Imani apologized to Marie and climbed off the bar table.

Nevaeh sat back down. "Thank you, baby." Marie smiled and kissed her on the cheek. Saria gazed at the two with a slight smile.

"I'm sick of holding this in!" Imani continued. "I should've said something a long time ago, but I have been too much of a coward to even admit it to myself!" She glanced back at Tiara, then back to the crowd. Tiara unleashed the death grip she had on Imani's arm. "Tiara and I have been hooking up for a while now and I am in love with her."

"I fucking knew it!" Nevaeh shouted.

Everyone looked at one another in shock as Tiara buried her face in her hands. "Oh god," she groaned.

"Yeah, that's right! And I want to do whatever I have to, to prove that I can be the one that T needs. So as of now consider all my hos cut the fuck off, I'm a one-woman kind of lady now!" Imani chuckled to herself and glanced back at Tiara. "In all seriousness, Tiara doesn't trust me, as she has every right not to. So, I'm confessing in front of almost everyone I know and love how I feel so she can hopefully one day see how serious I am." Imani cleared her throat. "Thank you all for listening. Let's keep this party going!" The music turned back on.

"I caught them about to fuck in the bathroom tonight," Cassidy whispered to Deja.

"What?" Deja exclaimed. "Why didn't you tell anybody?"

"Because they seemed mortified that I walked in on them. If I told one person, the entire crew would know about it in a matter of minutes. I figured they would come out and say it in their own time, and I was right." Cassidy smiled. "Didn't realize it would be so soon, though. Good for them." She took a sip of her drink.

"Gross. It makes me sick how mature you can be sometimes." Deja rolled her eyes.

Cassidy grinned. "On that note, I think I would like to make a toast." Cassidy stood up. "Excuse me, everyone!" Cassidy shouted over the music. "I would like to call for a toast!" The music was shut off again. "Thanks to whoever keeps shutting the music off."

"You're welcome," some random voice shouted.

She cleared her throat. "First off, I'd like to thank all of you for coming out tonight. This has been an amazing night so far. Thank you, Marie, for allowing us to have a private event at your bar. This is the place where I was warmly welcomed into this family to begin with." Cassidy continued, "To my new girlfriend, Deja."

"Girlfriend?" Nevaeh shouted. "What the hell is going on tonight?" she said aloud to herself.

"Yeah, girlfriend," Cassidy continued. "To my girls Tiara, Imani, Nevaeh, Eliana, Jasmine, and Anita. What can I say to you all? Y'all make life so much more interesting. I never know what's going to happen next with you guys. I love it and I love you for loving me through it all. So, cheers to the past, if it weren't for it, we wouldn't be who we are today. Cheers to the present because spending my present days with you ladies is truly a gift, and cheers to the future. May we all grow old and raise our children together. Cheers!" Cassidy held her glass in the air.

Everyone smiled. "Cheers!" They shouted in unison.

"Hey ladies, y'all get together and I'll take a group picture for you," Marie suggested.

"Great idea! Thanks!" Cassidy responded. "C'mon ladies! Come take a picture with your favorite white girl," she smiled.

The crew all made their way to Cassidy and posed for the group picture.

"Say cheese!" Marie shouted.

"Cheese!" they said.

"Aw! Group hug?" Nevaeh stood in front of the group with her arms wide open.

"You and these damn group hugs," Tiara responded.

"Group hug!" Imani shouted.

"Feel the love, Tiara!" Nevaeh shouted.

They all gathered around and hugged.

"All right, enough of this gay shit, let's keep the party going!" Cassidy shouted. The girls laughed, the music was turned back on. They all laughed and partied the night away for their last Friends' Friday as a group.

THIRTY-THREE

It was the night before Cassidy flew out. The going-away party was not enough for the girls, so they all crammed into Cassidy's two-bedroom apartment. They slept wherever there was room but deemed Cassidy's bedroom off limits so she and Deja could have some alone time. They wanted to have one last family dinner before she flew out.

"Man, Cass, Deja sure did help you spruce up the place, didn't she?" Eliana asked as she was mixing the salad.

"You like it?"

"Girl, what? I love it. Your shit was bare minimum, bone dry for the longest time, and you refused to allow any of us to help you."

"Yeah, I know." Cassidy chuckled to herself. "I guess all I needed was a lady interest in my life to put a little pep in my step."

"I guess so." Eliana continued, "So how is she treating you, Cass? You all right?"

"All right? I'm more than all right. I really like this one, Ellie. "

"Okay."

"Why?"

"Nothing. Sometimes you have the tendency of falling into that lesbian stereotype."

"How do I fall into the lesbian stereotype, when I don't identify as a lesbian? And what are these stereotypes you speak of?"

"First date U-haul, second date pet adoption, third date marriage."

Nevaeh came into the kitchen. She grabbed a tomato out of the salad and popped it into her mouth. Eliana playfully slapped her hand. "What are you bozos talking about?" she asked Eliana and Cassidy.

"We are having a conversation on taking it slow."

"What do you mean?" Nevaeh asked.

"Do I have a tendency to fall into the lesbian stereotypes when it comes to relationship speeds?"

"Girl, what? You fall hard, fast," Nevaeh inputted.

"No, I don't." Cassidy paused. "Do I?" A lightbulb turned on. "Oh shit, I do."

"I just want you to take it slow and be careful. You know we all love you and don't want to see you get hurt," Eliana admitted.

Nevaeh nodded her head.

"I know, girl, and I appreciate it. I feel like I'm taking it slow."

"Cass." Eliana gave her the get real look. "You just asked this girl to be your girlfriend, right before you move to Korea. Korea, as in a country that is not the United States, hell, not even in North America. Then you said you're not even sure where you're ending up after that. In what world is that taking it slow? You think going from friends with benefits to a very-long-distance relationship is taking it slow?"

"I don't see the problem." Cassidy grabbed the chicken out of the oven and set it on a towel she laid on the counter. She blatantly ignored what she knew was true. "Food is done!"

Nevaeh laughed to herself. Eliana shook her head.

"Hey, before we eat, let's say grace," Anita suggested.

"Great idea," Cassidy agreed.

Everyone stood in a circle and joined hands.

"Bow your heads, I'll say it," Imani instructed. Everyone obeyed. "Dear Lord, appreciate you. Amen," she said and opened her eyes.

The girls looked around the living room at one another for someone else to take the initiative. "All right, well, I guess I'll say it," Anita suggested.

Everyone nodded, "Yeah." Imani cleared her throat. "That's probably best."

"Dear Heavenly Father." Everyone bowed their head and closed their eyes. "We come to you today to give thanks. Thanks for allowing us all to be here before Cassidy's departure. Thanks for this wonderful framily," Jasmine's head popped up and she had a big smile on her face. She quickly closed her eyes and bowed her head again. "Without them, I'm not sure where I would be. We also come to you to ask you to watch over Cassidy's spirit as she leaves us tomorrow. I pray for her safe travels and her peace of mind to get her through whatever may be thrown her way. I pray that she knows even though we may not be there in person, we are there in spirit and we love her. We would also like to thank you for this delicious meal that has been prepared for us. Allow us to keep all that is good for us and pass all that is not. In the name of the Father, the Son, and the Holy Spirit, Amen."

"Amen!" everyone shouted.

"Now let's eat!" Cassidy said enthusiastically.

"Yes, I'm so hungry," Tiara mentioned. Everyone fixed their plates.

They all sat around in the living room. They reminisced and made new memories. At one point Cassidy stopped to observe the situation around her. She was going to miss this. She was going to miss the Friends' Fridays and catching up on whatever gossip there was to tell. She was going to miss watching Anita and Jasmine fall deeper in love in their relationship every day. She was going to miss watching Eliana grow as an individual now that she got rid of toxic Trisha. She was going to miss witnessing Tiara and Imani unfold. She was going to miss Nevaeh and how it was going to play out with Saria being back in her life. She was going to miss being able to run to one of her girls when she needed a shoulder to cry on or just someone to hang and do random stuff with. She was going to miss it all. Her girls. Her framily.

As they ate Eliana asked, "Hey, so are we going to make a plan to take a family vacation so we can meet up with Cassidy?"

"I thought we were going to go to Korea?" Nevaeh asked.

"As much as I would love for you guys to meet me there, I'd rather go somewhere on my vacation where I'm not living."

"Makes sense," Nevaeh agreed. "All I know is wherever we go, Marie is not going to let me go alone. She cool, but she ain't that cool."

"Let's go skiing!" Cassidy suggested excitedly.

Everyone looked around in disgust.

Anita said, "Cassidy, sweetie, read the room."

"Oh, so y'all want to go somewhere warm, huh?"

"Uh, yeah," Tiara responded. "I'm not trying to vacation in the snow," she added.

They laughed. They sat around and tossed out ideas as they ate. Once everyone finished eating, they all pitched in to help clean.

The next morning there was a somber cloud that hovered over the girls. They helped Cassidy pack up her belongings in her car and caravanned to the airport. They all stood around and hugged as they waited for the last possible minute for her to walk through the security gate.

"Okay, I have to go," Cassidy sniffled. She turned and hugged everyone individually. "I'm going to miss you guys so much."

"Group hug?" Nevaeh extended her arms.

"Group hug," Tiara sniffled. They gathered in a huddle. They stepped away to give her and Deja a little alone time.

"So this sucks," Deja admitted.

"Yes. Yes, it does."

"I'm going to miss you," Deja said as her voice cracked.

"I'm going to miss you too." Cassidy leaned in for a kiss and gave her a bear hug. "Bye, guys."

"Bye, Cass," Anita said.

"We love you!" Jasmine shouted. Cassidy started to walk toward the security gate. She turned around to the sight of her girls tearing up as they all stood there. She waved bye and crossed over into the security gate. Cassidy looked down at her phone. Her lock screen was the picture she and the girls had taken at her going-away at No Man's Land. Tears began to flow down her face.

"Well, fuck," Tiara stated. "This sucks."

"Yeah," Nevaeh said.

"Come on, guys let's go," Anita stated and the girls exited the airport.

THIRTY-FOUR

Marie and Nevaeh were cuddled on the couch as Saria lay on the love seat as they watched a movie. Once the movie ended, Marie sat up. She looked at Nevaeh for reassurance. Nevaeh nodded her head.

"Damn, that was a good movie," Saria said, oblivious. "What's next?"

"Saria, Nevaeh and I have something we would like to talk to you about." Marie turned the TV off.

Saria sat up. "Uh oh, this sounds serious."

"It kind of is," Marie assured.

"Um, okay." Saria was hesitant. "What is it?"

"So we, Nevaeh and I, have been talking," Marie continued. "I came out to her as poly." Saria sat in silence. "And I asked her how she would feel if we asked you to be with us." She chose her words carefully. "We, Nevaeh and I, both would really like that. If you want, of course."

Saria was shocked. "Be with you guys? Like a threesome?"

"I asked the same thing when she suggested it!" Nevaeh chuckled.

"No, be with us, as in date. All of us. Together."

"Oh shit. So you mean like together together?"

"Yeah, like together. Three people in a relationship. Also goes by the word throuple."

"Lesbians do that?" Saria asked.

Nevaeh threw her hands up. "Same page, you and I. Same page."

Marie snickered. "Yes, lesbians do that. Not as often talked about, but we do it."

"I mean I don't know what to say." Saria was flustered. "I mean I know we live in a modern world, but damn. And Malik. What about Malik? I can't introduce him to something like this if it isn't serious. And my parents?" She placed her hands on her face. "I'm shocked they accepted me being gay, but two girlfriends, oh my goodness, they might die."

"Woah woah woah." Marie sat next to Saria. "Calm down. Nothing is set in stone yet. We don't have to do anything you don't want to. If it's not something you want, we can move on." Marie hugged her.

Saria wrapped her arms around her. "You smell so good," she whispered. "Wait, no." She jumped up. "No, I can't."

"Okay. It's no problem," Marie assured.

"No, it's not that I don't want to, it's that I'm afraid to," Saria admitted. "I can't say that I would be ready to come out as a throuple. If I'm being honest with myself, I like both of you a lot. Probably more than I should. I mean I've fantasized about..." Saria stopped herself. Nevaeh perked up. "I don't know if I'm ready for something like this. I have to go." She abruptly gathered her things and went out the door.

"Well, shit." Marie said. "I hope we didn't just ruin that friendship."

"Yo, she fantasized about us, though," Nevaeh smiled.

"That's what the fuck you got from that conversation? Really, baby?"

"What?" Nevaeh genuinely asked. "Marie, I don't think we ruined that friendship. I think she just needs time to process things like I did. She already admitted that she wanted to, she just isn't ready. We can give her some time and approach it as friends like we would do with any other girl."

"I guess."

"You're the poly one and I'm giving you advice?"

"Yeah, but you're the lady's man," Marie teased and stuck her tongue out.

Saria's mind was racing as she drove home. "What? Is this real life?" she spoke aloud to herself. "Am I really about to have a second chance to get back with the love of my life? And then Marie? Psh! She's gorgeous! Am I really considering this right now? Who are you, Saria?" Before she knew it, she was in the driveway. She sat in the car blankly staring ahead. Her phone buzzed; it was a text from Noah,

You good? I see you sitting in your car like a creep.

I need to talk to you, she texted back. *I'm coming in the house now.*

Saria speed-walked into the house. "Where's Malik?" she asked breathlessly.

"He's sleeping in his room. You okay?" he asked, concerned.

"Oh my goodness. I don't know." She placed her hands on top of her head to make it easier for her to breathe.

"Saria. What the hell is going on?"

"You remember Nevaeh, right?" Noah just looked at her. "Right, of course you do. Well, she has a girlfriend. Her name is Marie."

"You're giving details that I already know."

"Right. We've discussed them. Well, tonight, as you know, I was hanging out with the two of them at Marie's apartment. We were watching movies, eating junk food, having a gay old time. Pun intended because we were watching lesbian movies. At the end of the last movie, Marie came out to me as polyamorous."

"Oh shit," Noah said.

"Yeah." Saria started to fan herself with her hands and paced back and forth. "Then she proceeded to ask me if I wanted to date the two of them. Not fuck like a normal couple, but date. As in the three of us. Together. In perfect fucking throuple harmony."

"Polyamory? I didn't know lesbians did that."

Saria threw her hands up.

"Okay, so what'd you say?"

"Naturally, I freaked out and left. I mean that's not me, right? Like I'm not polyamorous, am I? I feel like I'm coming out of the fucking closet again and I hate it." She flopped down on the couch.

"Well," Noah stated in a calm tone as he sat next to her. "Uh. I don't think you would be so worked up if it doesn't bother you, so there must be a reason it's bothering you. You did mention that you thought you were catching vibes from them. I guess you were right."

"But. Is it logical, though? I mean I have a child. I can't just introduce him to that, and it not be serious."

"How about let's not fill Malik in on what's going on for a while?" Noah suggested. "The best things in life aren't always logical. If you like both of them, I think it's something you should explore."

"You think so?"

"Why not?"

"Because it could turn into a fucking dumpster fire, that's why."

"But what if it turns into the fire that lights up your life?" he said in a cheesy tone as he placed his hand over his heart.

Saria giggled and nudged him with her shoulder. "You think I should give it a chance?"

"I think you should at least talk to them to let them know how you feel. Take it slow and see where it takes you. I support you whether you decide to pursue it or leave it alone."

"Thanks, big bro. That means a lot."

There was a pause. "Oh man, what if you do this and then you have to come out to Mom and Dad?"

"I know! It was hard enough with me coming out as a lesbian. Then to say I have two girlfriends, and we're all in a relationship together!?" She shoved her face in a throw pillow.

"Yeah, they'd probably have a heart attack."

"Ooohh." She groaned into the pillow.

"I'm kidding, I'm kidding. They'll be fine," he reassured. "If it comes to that point, I'll do some damage control before you tell them."

"Noah, what would I do without you?" He shrugged.

Saria barely slept that night. That morning she decided to send a text to Nevaeh and Marie.

Can we talk?

Of course. When and where? You name it and we'll be there, Marie responded.

We can meet at No Man's at 2 if that works for you guys.

I actually will be busy with work up until 3, Nevaeh chimed in.

Ok so 4? Saria suggested.

4 is good for me, Nevaeh agreed.

I'll already be at the bar, so it's good for me.

Cool. 4 it is.

* * *

Saria was distracted all day as she anticipated the meeting later that afternoon. Before she knew it, it was four o'clock and she was walking into No Man's Land.

"Hey Ken," she said as she walked up to the bar.

"Saria hey." He smiled. "Always refreshing to see your beautiful face around here," he complimented.

She smiled. "Is Marie around?"

"Yeah, she's in the back." He pointed behind him.

"Cool, thanks." As she walked away she turned to say, "By the way, it's always refreshing to see that beautiful face of yours too." She smiled, turned, and kept walking.

He blushed and continued to clean glasses. Saria knocked on Marie's door.

"Come in," she called out.

Saria peeked her head in the door. "Hey Marie."

Marie stood up. "Saria. Please come in." Saria walked in and sat down. "Nevaeh should be here any minute."

There was an awkward silence in the room. Suddenly Nevaeh knocked and walked in.

"Hey you guys, sorry I'm a little late."

"You're good, baby," Marie reassured. Nevaeh walked in and kissed Marie on the lips.

"Hey Saria," she said as she sat in the seat next to her.

"Hey."

"So what's on your mind?" Marie directed her question to Saria.

Saria cleared her throat. "Well, first off, I want to apologize for the way I reacted last night. I just didn't know how to process what had just happened."

"It's okay," Marie and Nevaeh responded.

"So if we're going to do this, I want to state my terms," she continued.

"I think that's fair," Marie stated.

Nevaeh nodded in agreement.

"First of all, this is all very new to me. I never imagined myself being in a throuple before, so I'm kind of still in shock. I don't want to announce our relationship to the masses until we're sure about this. I'm not ready to come out of that closet. As far as Malik goes, this changes the perspective on everything. I normally don't allow people I date to meet him so early into the relationship."

"Aw man," Nevaeh pouted.

"But you two are already a part of his life and it makes no sense to have you guys disappear so soon."

"Yes!" Nevaeh clapped.

"But do know that Malik is my heart and soul. I am a package deal. If you want me in your life, you have to have him in your life as well and he comes first."

"Of course," Marie agreed.

"Next, I don't know the rules of this three-way thing or how this would even function, so I'm going to need guidance and patience."

"I will help with that," Marie nodded.

"Also, if this is some kind of ruse to hurt me, I swear—"

"I'm going to stop you right there," Marie interrupted. "This is no ruse or scheme. I am very much serious about this. I can't speak for both of us, but I am genuinely interested in you. You are funny, smart, a great mom, and not to mention gorgeous. I think all three of us together will be a powerhouse in life and in the bedroom," Marie smirked.

"Saria, I'm not going to lie; a piece of me left with you that day you broke up with me," Nevaeh added. "And Marie has been the only person that was able to fill that void. I fell as deeply in love with her as I did with you, and that's rare for me. Then when I saw you, those feelings I had for you slowly began to come back. Your laugh, scent, eyes, even the way you sneeze. Everything about you drives me wild. I needed some time myself to think it over, and Marie gave me my space to do so. After I took the time I needed, I came to the conclusion that the three of us just feels so... right."

Saria took a deep breath. "Okay. So where do we go from here?" Her eyes darted between the two.

Marie looked at Nevaeh. Nevaeh gave her a single nod. Marie stood up and walked from behind her desk over to Saria. She took Saria's hand and stood her up, "Well, we can start here," she said as she went in for a kiss. Saria was hesitant at first. She glanced over at Nevaeh. Nevaeh gave her a single nod. Once she had the confirmation, Saria slowly licked her lips and accepted the kiss from Marie. It was sensual. Her body lit up. She had not felt that way in a long time. Marie pulled away from the kiss. "Now her." She tilted her head over to Nevaeh.

Nevaeh stood up. They both took a moment to look deeply into one another's eyes. Their eyes were filled with lust, fear, and uncertainty. Nevaeh stuck out her hand. Saria looked down at it, then back up to Nevaeh's eyes. Saria looked back down at Nevaeh's hand and she gently placed her hand into hers. Goosebumps rose on Saria's skin as their hands touched. She slowly walked over to Nevaeh. This time there was no hesitation. Once they were close enough, Saria went straight in for the kiss. They both moaned. The kiss was deep and heavy. It felt as if Saria's body had been shocked back to life. She grabbed onto Nevaeh's face. It brought on a sense of nostalgia for them both. Saria pulled away. She was short of breath. She looked between Nevaeh and Marie.

"Well, I guess that was a good place to start," she smiled.

Marie smirked, "That's not all." She picked up her car keys. "Let's go." Marie led the two out of her office. She stopped by the bar. "Hey Ken, I need to go handle something." Nevaeh and Saria continued to walk out the door. "I'll be gone for a couple of hours, but I'll be back. Sherry should be in, in about fifteen minutes. Are you going to be okay by yourself until then?"

"Everything okay?" Ken asked, concerned.

"Yeah, just need to help a friend through something she's struggling with."

"Oh okay, well, go handle your business, I'll be fine."

"Cool. Thanks Ken, you're a lifesaver."

She walked out the door. She hopped into the driver seat and started the ignition. Saria was in the front and Nevaeh in the back seat behind Saria. Marie looked into the rearview mirror and made eye contact with Nevaeh. Nevaeh had a lustful look and smiled. The car was deathly silent as they rode back to Marie's apartment. Once they arrived at the apartment, they sat in the parking space for a few seconds. Marie glanced at Saria and then at Nevaeh. She said nothing as she hopped out of the car and started to walk toward her apartment. Saria followed suit.

Nevaeh took a deep breath. *Here goes nothing* she said to herself as she jumped out of the back seat.

Marie opened the door to her apartment. The three ladies walked in. Marie closed and locked the door behind them. Marie grabbed Nevaeh and started to make out with her. Saria observed. She was immediately turned on by the sight of the two of them. She watched the two as their hands roamed. Their bodies were in tune with each other. The two stopped kissing and Marie led them to the bedroom. Saria had a flashback as she walked past the spot where she had masturbated to the pair as they had sex. She smirked to herself as she couldn't believe this was about to happen. When they got into the room, Marie started to kiss and undress Saria. Nevaeh watched and began to strip. Before they knew it, the three were naked. Nevaeh laid Saria down and they began to kiss. Marie lay down, face first, between Saria's legs. She teased her with light strokes with her finger across her clit. Saria wiggled. She let out a moan. She spread her legs wider. Marie smiled. She took that as an invitation and sucked on Saria's clit. Marie stuck a finger inside her and when she found her G spot, Saria gasped. Nevaeh saw Marie and moved to Saria's nipples. She sucked, licked, and teased. Saria had never been touched like this before. Her eyes opened. She caught a glimpse of the two beautiful women as they feasted upon her body. Suddenly, her eyes rolled back. Her body tensed up, back arched, toes curled. Her thighs clenched Marie's head and her arms grasped around Nevaeh.

"Oh my god!" she gasped. Her body entered a state of euphoria. She began to shake as she had one of the most intense orgasms she had ever experienced in her life. She was out of breath. Saria couldn't speak, but she managed to push Marie's head from between her legs. Saria lay there breathlessly. Marie sat up and wiped her mouth.

"Come here." Nevaeh motioned to Marie.

Nevaeh kissed Marie. She could taste Saria on Marie. Still out of breath, Saria leaned up on her elbows to get a better view.

"You taste so good," Nevaeh said to Saria then continued to kiss Marie. Saria never thought she would enjoy something like this as much as she did, but she was wrong. She was thoroughly enjoying herself. She watched Nevaeh and Marie as they kissed. She felt herself beginning to throb again. She licked her fingers and started to play with herself. Marie and Nevaeh began to caress each other. They enjoyed the sight of Saria touching herself to them.

"Hold on," Marie instructed. She went into her toybox. She grabbed a vibrator and some lube. "Here." She handed it to Saria. Saria smiled. She put a light coat of lube on it and turned it on. She teased herself. Her body jerked as she slid it inside her. Marie and Nevaeh watched Saria for a bit before they no longer could take it. They reached their hands down between one another's legs and passionately kissed. With the intensity of the situation, it didn't take long for the two of them to cum. Saria followed soon after. Nevaeh and Marie breathlessly collapsed on the bed on each side of Saria.

"I didn't know it was going to be like this," Saria said, out of breath.

"Neither did I," Nevaeh admitted.

"Yeah, that was great," Marie agreed.

"If this is what our sex life is going to be like, I'm here for it!" Saria joked. "Shit, I don't know why more lesbians aren't polyamorous."

"Hell, beats me," Marie stated.

There was a moment where nothing filled the air but the sounds of them breathing.

"So, what's next?" Nevaeh broke the silence.

"That's the million-dollar question," Saria exhaled.

"Well," Marie chimed in. "I have to get back to the bar here soon." She glanced at the time. "I don't want to leave my people hanging."

"You know, I think I could go for a few beers. What about you, Saria?" Nevaeh turned her head.

"Yeah, I could do that," Saria smiled. "Noah has Malik for the night. Actually, I told Noah about this too."

"Really?" Nevaeh was surprised. "What'd he say?"

"Well, it wasn't so much of a confession as it was a freak out," Saria snickered. "He was supportive. He actually encouraged me to speak with you two about it."

"Oh, we remember the freak out," Marie laughed.

"Yeah, my bad," Saria apologized.

"No need to apologize. It's overwhelming at first. That's awesome that he's so supportive. He seems like a really great guy," Marie comforted her.

"He truly is. A great role model for Malik."

"Well, I need to head out." Marie started to get dressed. "Are you ladies going to join me?"

"Yes. I'm down." Nevaeh started to put her clothes on as well.

"Sure. I have a babysitter for the night, I'm in."

The ladies got dressed. They all kissed again before they headed out the door.

THIRTY-FIVE

"What's going on, Deja? You sound distant," Cassidy asked with concern in her voice.

"Huh? Oh nothing, baby, I'm fine. Sorry about that."

"It's okay. I just want to make sure you're all right."

"Just missing you is all."

"Yeah, same here."

There was a pregnant pause. "Actually Cassidy, I need to talk to you about something."

"Oh no. What is it?"

Deja sighed, "I'm going to keep it real with you; I don't know if I can do this long-distance thing."

Cassidy went silent. "Are you saying you want to break up with me?"

"I don't know what I'm saying. I don't want to break up, I just don't know how I feel about you all the way over there in another country. It just has me in my head."

"Well, get out of there. What do you think? That I'm cheating on you?"

"It has crossed my mind from time to time."

"Well, I'm not."

"Yeah, but I have."

Cassidy fell silent again. "What are you saying, Deja?" she managed to speak after being taken aback.

"I'm saying that I tried to bury myself in my work. Tried not think about my girlfriend being so far away. It worked for a while, until it didn't. I would hang out with your friends but hanging with them constantly reminded me of you and it hurt too much, especially because I don't even know if you're getting stationed in a different country after Korea. So I started hanging with Deshawn and his friends. There was a girl that had been trying to get with me, but I kept blowing her off because of you. Eventually, I caved. And we hooked up."

Cassidy muted her phone so Deja couldn't hear her sniffling on the other end, "My intentions were never to hurt you, Cass, but I also don't want to lie to you either." Deja sighed, "And I honestly can't promise you that it won't happen again." Deja fell silent. "Cassidy, can you say something?"

Cassidy unmuted her end of the phone. "All this time, everything we've been through." She spoke in a broken voice. Cassidy paused to compose herself. "And you can't promise me that it won't happen again? You don't think I have girls out here chasing after me? I turn them down because I am, well at least I thought I was, in a happy relationship. The bad thing is, I would've been willing to forgive you until you said you can't promise me that it won't happen again. And the shitty part about all of this is I'm getting stationed there again after Korea. I was waiting to tell everyone when we met up on my mid-tour."

"Well, if you know for sure you're coming back, then-"

"Get fucked, Deja," Cassidy interrupted. "Whatever you have to say, I don't want to hear it. I don't deserve this shit." Cassidy's sadness rapidly became anger. "I've been nothing but good to you. If that other girl treats you better than I do, then go do your thing. I'm not going to sit here and beg you not to do it, and I damn sure don't want to be with someone who doesn't want to be with me. I guess Margaret was right, but you won't have to worry about me calling you. Just don't come crawling back to me once you realize how much you've just royally fucked up. Have a nice life." Cassidy hung up the phone.

Cassidy didn't know how to feel. She was shocked, sad, angry, horny, and disappointed. She didn't know whether she wanted to fight, fuck, or cry. So, she called two of the most levelheaded people she knew, Anita and Jasmine.

"Hey Cass! What do I owe the pleasure?" Anita answered the phone cheerfully.

"Did you guys know Deja cheated on me?" Cassidy cut straight to the subject at hand.

"What!" Anita screamed into the phone. "Fuck no, we didn't know Deja cheated on you!"

"Deja cheated on Cass?" Cassidy heard Jasmine scream from the background. "That cunt!" Anita looked at Jasmine in shock because she rarely used that word. That's how she knew Jasmine was pissed.

"Well, she did. She stopped hanging out with you guys?" Cassidy asked.

"Yeah, but we didn't think too much of it, she has her own group of friends outside of Marie. We just figured she was kickin it with them."

"Yeah, she was. Got caught up in the single life and ended up cheating on me. Then she said she couldn't promise me that it wouldn't happen again. What kind of shit is that?"

"What the fuck. I'm so sorry. She's trash. Look. If you want me to, I can ask some of my cop friends to scare the shit out of her. I know she's probably doing something illegal."

"As funny as that would be, no thank you. I'm not trying to be vindictive like that. I'm going to get back at her by living my best life with a mean come up."

"That a girl," Anita encouraged. "Real shit though, I'm sorry that this has happened to you, Cass. I know you really liked her, but you're a strong, beautiful, intelligent woman and you deserve somebody who matches your awesome."

"Thanks, Nita. I am pretty awesome, aren't I?" Cassidy joked. "No, but really I wanted to ask you for some advice."

"Go for it."

"A while back Deja's ex, Margaret, ended up being our Uber driver. She told me to watch out for Deja because she'll break my heart. I thought it was random and was naïve to think Deja wouldn't do that to me. Maybe there was a reason why Margaret was there to give me, at the time I thought was random, a piece of advice. So, my question to you is, do you think I should link up with Margaret? Ask her what happened between her and Deja?"

"I mean it could help you find some answers that you won't get from Deja, if that's what you're searching for. But if you just want to know to start drama, then stay away."

"Well, I'm definitely not looking for drama. I legitimately want to know what happened and I definitely don't want to talk to Deja about it."

"I mean ultimately that's up to you, but I don't know if that's such a great idea. You might go sniffing around and it turns into a drama-filled debacle that you weren't expecting," Anita advised.

Cassidy chuckled. "Yeah, I guess that makes sense. This is why I called you first, so I wouldn't make rash emotional decisions. Also, I know you're wondering. You can tell the girls about Deja's dumbass."

"Oh." Anita sounded guilty.

"You were group texting them while we were talking, weren't you?"

"Yeah," Anita admitted in a childlike tone.

Cassidy snickered, "It's all good. Man, I love you guys."

"We love you too and miss you so so much!"

"We love you, Cass!" Jasmine shouted from the background.

"We can't wait to see you when we go on our family trip," Anita added.

"Framily!" Jasmine shouted from the background. Anita rolled her eyes.

"Neither can I, but I'm going to go ahead and hang up. I need to wrap my mind around some stuff."

"Okay love, take care."

"Bye, Nita."

Cassidy hung up the phone. She sat there in silence for a moment as she thought about her next move. She looked down at her phone. She went through her messages and landed on one of the girls who had been trying to get with her. As she stared at the blinking cursor in the empty reply box, she contemplated on what to write or if she should even respond. She was hurting and wanted some comfort. She knew deep down inside that she would message that girl for all the wrong reasons. She didn't want to become the girl that goes around using others for her own selfish gains. She decided against messaging her.

She then started to look up Margaret, but her gut feeling was telling her not to do it. She needed a clean break from Deja and discussing her with Margaret wouldn't help the situation. Cassidy put on some heartbreak R&B music, muted her phone, turned off all the lights, and wrapped herself up in her covers in her bed. She decided to cry it out.

THIRTY-SIX

Imani was bored one Tuesday afternoon after work. She decided to take some solo time and go to a bar on the beach she had been scoping out online. She texted Nevaeh to let her know so she wouldn't be waiting up for her. She was ready for a nice quiet Tuesday afternoon, to have a few beers, and chill. Imani was minding her own business when a girl walked up to her. Imani turned around.

"Natasha? What are you doing here?" she asked.

"I come here every now and then. I like the atmosphere."

"Yeah, it is nice. So what's up?"

"I miss you."

"You're drunk."

"No I'm not."

"Tasha, you have Whittaker eye." Imani was unamused.

"So? Just because I'm drunk doesn't mean I can't miss you."

"You don't even know me well enough to miss me. We hooked up a few times, that was it. No more, no less."

"Well, that's what I mean by I miss you. I miss those few times we hooked up. It was good."

"Well, what do you want from me?"

"I want you."

"I have a girl."

"Is your girl here now?" Natasha already knew the answer to that question.

"Nah, but Jiminy Cricket is." Imani was getting irritated. "Look, can you get the fuck out of my face with that temptress shit? Please?" she commanded.

"Fine, your loss."

"What I got is better, plus it's not my loss if I've already had it," Imani snapped.

Natasha sucked her teeth. "Bitch," she said as she stormed off.

"You brought that snarky response on yourself!" Imani shouted at the back of Natasha's head. "Should've stopped when I said no the first fucking time!" Imani shook her head. "Bitches can be so triflin sometimes," she said to herself. "I will never understand why straight women say they're turning lesbian because men can't be trusted. Women are just as bad, if not worse."

"Preach," the bartender said. Just then Tiara called.

"Hey T. I was hoping you would call."

"Yeah? Why is that?"

"I was hoping you could come meet me at this bar on the beach I found. It's relaxing and has games that we can play."

"Why didn't you just text me and ask me that?" Tiara wondered.

"Because I don't want to move too fast. I told you that I would allow you to take the reins, and that's what I'm doing. I'm giving you space to come to me."

"Well, I appreciate that."

"So what's up? Why'd you call?"

"I was just calling to see what you were doing."

"Well, now that you know, do you want to join me?"

"Yeah. Actually, that sounds nice. I would like to come spend some one-on-one time with you."

Imani smiled, "Great, I'll send an Uber to come get you."

"Oh yeah? So much for letting me take the reins."

Imani chuckled. "I can only let go so much or else we wouldn't get anywhere. I'll give you ten minutes to get ready, and then I'm ordering you one. So hurry up and get dressed."

"Ten minutes isn't enough time for me to get ready, Imani," Tiara complained.

"There aren't that many people here, and it's just us having a couple of drinks and kickin it. Just throw on some sweats and a tee."

"Yes ma'am," Tiara obeyed.

"Thank you. See you in a few."

∗ ∗ ∗

Tiara walked into the bar roughly thirty minutes after they hung up the phone.

"Hey T." Imani stood up and kissed her on the cheek.

"Hey. Wow, this place is pretty chill. How have we not been here before?"

"Because this isn't a gay bar," Imani joked. "I'm down to keep it our little secret for now."

Tiara smiled. Imani smiled back and they stared into one another's eyes. Tiara cleared her throat. "So I'm going to order a drink."

"Yeah, of course, that's why you came, right?"

"Hey, can I get a Corona with no lime, please?" Tiara asked the bartender.

"Coming right up," she responded. The bartender set the beer in front of her. "You want to start a tab?"

"You can put her drinks on my tab," Imani butted in.

"No. I will pay for my own drinks."

"Tiara." Imani looked at her, then turned back to look at the bartender. "Can you please put her drinks on my tab?" she directed.

"All right, will do."

"Thanks." Tiara was appreciative.

"You never had an issue with me paying for your drinks before," Imani joked.

"Yeah, well it's different now that..." Tiara stopped. She took a swig of her beer.

"Now that what?" Imani pried.

"You know, now that we're doing this." She motioned between the two of them.

"And what is this?" Imani mimicked her motion.

"I don't know yet, still trying to figure that part out."

"Fair enough." Imani looked around. "Hey, come on, let's go play Connect Four," she suggested.

"Oh, you're on!"

They walked over and sat at the table. They were playing for about ten minutes when Tiara said, "That girl keeps fucking looking over here like she got a problem."

Imani peeked over her shoulder to a side-eying Natasha and groaned, "Yeah, my bad."

"What? Who is she?" Tiara demanded an answer.

"Just some girl I used to fuck with."

"Ah shit, here we go." Tiara crossed her arms. "See this is what I didn't want, Imani. You come with a trail of girls. I know that you're usually pretty good with keeping the drama at a minimum, but it's bound to happen eventually. I don't want to live my life constantly looking over my shoulder for bitches coming at me with some kind of vendetta."

"Nobody is coming at you with no damn vendetta. She stepped to me, I told her I had a girl now, she tried again, I squashed it. End of fucking story."

"Oh, she stepped to you after you told her you had a girl? That bitch." Tiara started to get up out of her chair.

"T." Imani grabbed her, armed with a grin on her face. "It's cool. It's squashed. Plus, I think I hurt her feelings pretty bad. She won't want to have anything to do with me anymore."

"That's what I'm talking about." Tiara smiled and lifted her beer. They tapped their bottles together. "Now, where were we?"

"I was just about to mention, for somebody who doesn't want drama, you were quick to jump up and start something."

"I wasn't going to start shit. I was going to finish it. That shit is mad disrespectful, and I would defend you regardless if I were your girl or not. You should know that."

"I know you would."

"That wench almost had me going back to my childhood days. Don't let this money fool you. I'll fight a bitch."

"Don't I know it. Come on, let's keep playing," Imani smiled.

Tiara timidly started to place a checker in the Connect Four slot. "So we're not going to discuss the fact that you told her you got a girl?"

"I was wondering if you caught that," Imani admitted.

"Come on, Imani. You know damn well I caught that," Tiara laughed. "I've known you since our college days, you can't pull that fuckboy shit with me and think I won't catch on."

"What fuckboy shit?" Imani laughed.

"The coward approach of officially asking me if I want to be your girl. Try to work it into a conversation hoping I'd fall for it. Nah, fuck that. I want you to grab your lady balls and ask me straight up."

"Straight up?"

"Yup."

"Hm." Imani kept playing.

"Sooooo, do you have something to ask me?"

"No," Imani replied nonchalantly.

"I ain't got time for these games, Imani."

"What? You don't want to play Connect Four anymore?"

"Stop playing dumb. Why'd you tell that bitch you had a girl, if you don't have anything to ask me?"

"Because I don't have anything to ask you. I told her that to get her the fuck off my back. I didn't want to risk screwing up what I have with you."

"And what is that?"

"I don't know. You're the one still trying to figure it out," Imani teased.

Tiara smiled, "Well played." She peeked out the window, then looked down at her watch. "Oh man, the sun is about to set, it's getting late. Maybe we should head out. I have to meet up with a client in the morning."

"Let's go watch the sunset," Imani suggested.

"That sounds cute." She pondered for a few seconds. "Okay, okay, I'm in," she said as she smiled and nodded.

"Cool." Imani closed her tab and walked out of the bar. "Oh wait, look, there's a little shop. Let's stop there and get a towel so we can sit on it."

"Good idea," Tiara agreed.

They went in, purchased a towel, and wandered hand in hand out to the beach. Imani laid the towel down. Tiara sat down first, and Imani sat down behind her. She placed her legs on both sides of Tiara and wrapped her arms around her. Tiara grinned and leaned back into Imani. They sat there cuddled on the beach. They laughed, talked about subjects they never touched when they were just friends, and shared intimate details about themselves. As the sun began to set, they both fell silent. They allowed the sounds of the waves crashing and the beautiful sky to engulf them. Tiara closed her eyes as a slight breeze swept across her face. She took a deep breath.

"This is nice," she exhaled.

Imani looked down at Tiara. She was taken aback by how beautiful she was in that moment. She always knew Tiara was beautiful, but how the sunset's natural light hit her mocha skin perfectly, accentuated her beauty. Imani couldn't contain herself. She leaned down and kissed Tiara on the lips. As Imani pulled away, Tiara opened her eyes.

"What was that?" Tiara asked softly.

"Something I've wanted to do for a very long time," Imani whispered back.

"We've kissed before."

"Yeah, but not like that."

"Right." Tiara smiled. It was timid. She turned her head back to the ocean.

They sat in silence for ten minutes. By this time the sun had gone down completely, and they were the only ones on the beach. Imani's hands started to roam. She stroked Tiara's nipple over her shirt.

"What are you doing?" Tiara asked but didn't stop her.

"I'm trying to see something," Imani replied. She stopped. "If that's all right."

"Yeah, it's cool."

"Okay." Imani slipped her hand under Tiara's shirt. She started to play with Tiara's nipples. Tiara closed her eyes. She was entranced by the waves as they crashed, the moonlight, and Imani playing with her. She let out a slight moan. Imani placed her other hand at the waistband of Tiara's sweatpants.

"Oh, you really trying to see something," Tiara joked.

"Shhh," Imani instructed seductively.

Tiara didn't say another word. Imani slipped her hand onto Tiara's clit as the other hand played with her nipples. She went in slow circular motions, just like Tiara liked. Tiara squirmed. Imani breathed into Tiara's ear letting her know that she was enjoying it too. That turned Tiara on even more. She spread her legs to allow Imani to have better access. Imani knew what that meant, so she quickened her circles. Tiara's breathing became irregular. Imani knew she was close. She kept the steady quick pace. Tiara clutched onto Imani's leg and moaned louder.

"Shit," she whispered. Tiara stopped breathing as she came. Her body shook. Imani didn't want to stop, but she did.

Once Tiara was able to catch her breath she said, "Wow. That was, uh, different."

"Yeah," Imani agreed. "I liked it."

"I did too."

"I can tell," Imani teased.

Tiara playfully punched her in the arm. "It is late though. We should probably head out." Tiara adjusted her clothes.

"Yeah, you're right." Imani stood up. She stuck her hand out and pulled Tiara up. Imani was about to pick up the towel.

"Wait," Tiara instructed. She pulled Imani into her. She returned that slow passionate kiss Imani was previously looking for. It was deeper than any kiss they had ever shared before. Tiara pulled away.

"Okay. Now we can go," she smiled.

"All right," Imani grinned.

THIRTY-SEVEN

"We have begun to descend into Phuket. We will be landing in approximately twenty minutes. Thank you for flying with us. We hope you've enjoyed your flight and look forward to seeing you again," the captain said over the intercom.

"I can't believe we're in fucking Thailand," Saria said excitedly. She was mesmerized by the bright blue water as she gazed out the window.

"I know, I'm geekin like a motherfucker right now," Nevaeh agreed.

After the women deplaned and passed through Customs, they headed to Baggage Claim. When they came out the doors, there was an excitedly waiting Cassidy holding six flowers.

"Ah!" they all screamed in unison as they bum-rushed her. Marie and Saria stood off to the side to let the girls have their moment.

"I'm so happy to see you guys! I've been empty inside without you all," Cassidy said as she wiped tears of joy from her eyes. "Here, I got each of my ladies a single rose." She handed out the roses.

"Damn, Cass, you left us and turned into Lady Love and shit," Tiara teased.

"Yeah well, when Deja and I broke up I had to step up my game. I told y'all, man, she'll rue the day she cheated on me. I'm on my upgrade shit."

"Yas, queen," Tiara snapped. "If she ain't know, she better ask somebody."

"Hey Marie and Saria." Cassidy gave them each a hug individually. "You two are still looking radiant as always."

"Hey Cassidy." They both smiled. "We've missed you. It's just not the same without you there," Marie admitted.

"Man, I've missed you guys too. I wish you all could be in Korea with me. You guys would have a blast," Cassidy smiled. "It's been work, eat, party, sleep on occasion, repeat, since I've been there," she encouraged.

"Yeah, that doesn't sound like anywhere Nevaeh needs to be," Marie commented.

Saria smirked. Nevaeh rolled her eyes.

Cassidy chuckled, "Come on, ladies, I have a van waiting out front for us."

They all gathered their bags and headed out of the airport. Once all of them were checked into their rooms and settled in, they decided to head out to the beach where their hotel was located.

They all grabbed drinks. They had found a spot on the beach that had a few unused umbrellas and decided to claim it.

"This water is gorgeous," Eliana observed once they were all situated.

They sat around for a few minutes to soak in the ambiance. To appreciate where they were in life. "I've missed us," Eliana broke the silence with a sigh. "All of us together."

"Same," Imani agreed.

"Hey Ellie, I saw your interview on Arlie's channel. You slayed it," Cassidy complimented. "How'd your art show with Scott go?"

"That went so well. A lot of people showed up. I really enjoyed myself. Can't wait to produce more content. I'm thinking about doing a piece on friendship and how important it is while we're out here, if that's cool with you guys."

"Yeah," they all agreed.

"That'd be pretty dope," Imani said.

"How are things with you and Arlie going?" Nevaeh asked. "You two have been extra cute lately."

"Yeah," Ellie chuckled. "It's actually been great."

"Why didn't she come?" Tiara inquired.

"We've decided to keep it casual for now. Take it slow. We both came into this knowing we weren't particularly looking for a relationship. It's been really nice. It's refreshing compared to toxic Trisha."

"So, do you guys date other people?" Tiara asked.

"We can. I'm not. I'm still enjoying finding myself. Plus, I don't want to deal with the chaos of dating more than one woman." Eliana shrugged.

"Yeah it can become a little hectic at times," Imani agreed. Tiara glared at her. "What?" Imani responded, "It can." She shrugged.

"What about you, Cassidy? You juggling women out there in Korea?" Eliana asked.

"I sure am," Cassidy proudly claimed. "That Deja shit hurt me pretty bad, so I've taken to the old Nevaeh and Imani ways. Just hit it and quit it."

"Oh, so Cass out there hittin chicks with the ol fuck and chuck," Nevaeh joked.

"She out there smangin," Imani joked back.

"Smashin and bangin," Cassidy chimed in.

"Ayyyye!" Cassidy, Imani, and Nevaeh said together as they dapped one another up.

"Sit y'all dumbasses down," Tiara instructed with an attitude.

Imani sucked her teeth. "Maaaaan." They all sat back down. Marie and Saria laughed.

"I actually hooked up with a dude too. Just one, though," Cassidy added.

"Ew. Why?" Tiara asked bluntly.

"Don't play like it's breaking news that I'm bisexual. We were attracted to one another. We vibed. Yeah, I prefer women, but I'm not going to deny myself the opportunity to be happy with someone just because that person comes in male form," Cassidy stated.

"Respect," Jasmine nodded.

"Well, we love your ol bisexual ass. Do what makes you happy, boo boo," Tiara added.

Cassidy smiled, "Thanks."

"So, we've got some news we'd like to tell you guys," Jasmine said.

"Yes! Give it to us," Tiara exclaimed.

Anita and Jasmine looked at one another. Jasmine continued, "We've decided to adopt—" Everyone's face lit up.

"Oh my god! Are we about to be parents!?" Tiara excitedly interrupted.

"A dog. We've decided to adopt a dog," Jasmine finished.

"Puppy parents!" Eliana exclaimed. "Still exciting either way! I'm happy for you guys."

"Honestly, I'm surprised you guys haven't done it sooner," Nevaeh stated. "Y'all been together for what, like fifty years now and you have no animals."

"Lies! We had a fish tank at one point," Anita proclaimed.

"Right. A fish tank," Tiara chimed in. "Irregardless y'all were supposed to adopt a cat or a dog on like your third date. It's in the lesbian handbook. Y'all have defied the lesbian laws."

"T, irregardless isn't a word," Jasmine informed her.

"Really, Jas? You are constantly making up words, now you want to correct me? Get the fuck out of here," she laughed.

Jasmine shrugged. "Nevaeh and Marie don't have a dog or a cat," she stated.

"Yeah, but we don't live together, so it doesn't count," Marie chimed in.

"See," Nevaeh said. "There's a science to this shit. Thank you, baby."

"You're welcome, baby."

"Cheers to defying lesbian stereotypes!" Imani held up her glass.

"I actually have some more news." Anita took a deep breath. "A while back, my sergeant told me that he thought I would make an excellent detective. I was terrified of the change and thought I would fail. But after some soul searching and encouragement from one of the best women I know—" she glanced at Jasmine and grabbed her hand, "I took the exam and I passed! I'm going to be a detective!"

"Yes! You boss ass bitch!" Tiara clapped between each word.

"Anita! That is amazing. Way to conquer your fears!" Eliana encouraged.

"To conquering our fears!" Cassidy held up her drink.

"Speaking of conquering fears," Tiara chimed in. "I decided to give this fool right here a real chance. Imani and I are officially together."

"That's sweet," Anita said. "So who asked who and how?"

"I asked her," Imani confessed.

"Yeah, one day Imani and I were hanging out and I told her if she wanted to be with me, she'd have to ask me straight up. Well, she took that literally," Tiara smiled. "We were in bed one morning and when I woke up Imani was staring at me like the fucking Burger King man. I may or may not have been slightly creeped out. Anyway, she told me to look straight up and there was a poster she put up there while I was sleeping that asked if I wanted to be her girl. It was cute." They smiled at each other. "So, I said yes."

"Aw! About damn time," Cassidy gushed. "I think we all knew that you would cave eventually. I'm happy for you two. You're both amazing women and deserve nothing short of that."

"Uh, speaking of being together," Nevaeh mentioned. She looked at Saria and Marie for reassurance. They both nodded. The throuple had agreed prior to the trip that Nevaeh could tell the girls, but to keep it within the group for now. Saria wasn't quite ready for the world to know. "So, at Cassidy's going-away party Marie came out to me as polyamorous. I would like to think that I'm a pretty open-minded person, but that shocked me to my core. I mean Marie? My Marie? Poly? Really?" Nevaeh continued, "Anyway as you guys know, Saria was my first love and Marie has been the light of my life for some time now." She slightly smiled at Marie and Saria before she turned back to her friends.

"Oh shit," Tiara whispered as she started to put the pieces together. She grabbed Imani's arm. Imani sat with a dropped jaw as she hung onto Nevaeh's every word.

"Well, after some serious discussion, Marie, Saria, and I have decided to be a couple, or throuple if you will, and have been for about four months now."

268

Everyone's jaw dropped. Nobody said anything for ten seconds as they passed looks among one another.

"We do have one request, though, if we could please keep this between us for now. Nobody knows about this except for you guys and Noah. I don't want Malik to somehow find out and it not be from me," Saria pleaded.

Jasmine cleared the shock from her throat. "Yeah. Of course."

"What!?" Eliana rang out.

"We know a real life throuple! How exciting!" Cassidy clapped.

"Holy shit," Anita stated.

"Lesbians do that?" Imani asked.

Marie, Saria, and Nevaeh looked at one another and laughed. "Nevaeh and I were just as confused in the beginning, Imani. Trust me. Marie has been great with being patient with us." All three smiled at one another.

"Damn, this is beautiful. Y'all are beautiful. This entire moment is beautiful," Eliana complimented the throuple. "I love all you beautiful bitches," she said to the group.

"Well, shit! I ain't even mad at it!" Tiara supported. "Hey y'all are all grown-ass consenting adults and make a bomb-ass couple throuple. Do your thing! And if anybody has an issue with it, you know we got your back. Cheers to loving who the fuck you love, ladies! We are all here for it!"

"Aye! Cheers!" the girls said in unison.

"Oh! One more thing I forgot to mention! I will be getting stationed back with you guys after Korea," Cassidy finally confessed.

"Yay! We'll have the group back together again!" Eliana rejoiced.

"Man, I think I'm going to cry for real, man," Imani seriously stated. "We have the best most supportive group of friends." Jasmine cleared her throat and shot a look at her. "Excuse me," Imani continued, "we have the best most supportive framily that any lesbian could ask for. I wish more lesbians, hell, people in general, had this kind of love and support in their lives. Maybe the world wouldn't be so shitty. I am so thankful. I really don't know what I would do without you guys. You know what? Cheers to Anita and Jasmine."

"To us? For what?" Jasmine asked.

"Well, if it weren't for you two being such an amazing couple, you never would've reached out to Nevaeh to plan your anniversary party and we wouldn't be sitting here today."

"Aw. That's sweet, Imani." Jasmine blushed.

"So, cheers to Jasmine and Anita." Imani lifted her glass.

"To Jasmine and Anita!" they all said in unison.

That was the vacation that the framily would never forget.

THE END

ABOUT THE AUTHOR

Alesha Nichole is an outgoing, down-to-earth resident of Hampton, Virginia. She lives with her loyal fur babies Tucker and Suave. She spent the first eight years of her adult life serving as a Weapons Troop in the United States Air Force. After she separated she became a mail carrier, and soon after that she began contracting in Iraq with Lockheed Martin. Alesha had always wanted to write a book. Every time she planned to sit down and do just that, life had other plans.

At the age of 20, Alesha came out as bisexual, then shortly after identified as a lesbian. Prior to coming out and the years that followed, she noticed a lot of the lesbian content tended to be tragic, sad endings, or hetero normative. She also realized a lot of the content portrayed the drama of a woman leaving her husband (or boyfriend) for a woman, or struggling with the idea of being with another woman. Those situations happen in real life and are very much so relatable, just not to her. She wanted more. She wanted to see more lesbians as main characters who were already comfortable with their sexual identity. She wanted to see more women of color. Instead of waiting on the world to create stories that she could directly relate to, she got inspired, created her own story, and self-published.

Alesha loves to travel. She has experienced things such as riding the fastest rollercoaster in the world in Abu Dhabi, eating chef-prepared tarantula in Cambodia, floating in the Dead Sea in Jordan, and feeding monkeys in Kenya. When she is not travelling, Alesha loves to spend quality time with her family, friends, and dogs. She enjoys discovering new lesbian content and discussing it with her friends. Laughter and good vibes are truly the medicines of her soul. Alesha hopes to publish more books in the future.

Made in the USA
Columbia, SC
01 February 2020

87410213R00169